Swipe up for Secrets

Brigitta Estelle Burguess

ISBN: 979-8-3938-6661-7

DEDICATION

For Roland and Walden

CONTENTS

BRIGITTA ESTELLE BURGUESS

ACKNOWLEDGEMENTS

I am grateful to my extraordinary cover artist, Zachary Jarvis. I am also eternally indebted to my editor, Emily Zick, who has been editing my writing since our college days. This book is ours.

CHAPTER ONE

"It's like the heavens are bestowing this school upon us," Layla's mother whispered.

"My eyes hurt," Layla replied, squinting up at the arch in front of them as the morning sun flooded the sky behind it.

Beyond the arch was a long courtyard which, with a three-tiered fountain at its center and a large lion statue on either side of it, looked more like a college campus quad than a high school front lawn. As Layla and her mother passed under the arch, the blinding sun fell behind it, but Layla found the pain in her eyes lingered.

This may have been because she had only slept about four hours the previous night, going over and over again in her mind all of the things she was to remember the following day. Her locker combination was 24-18-36, her first class was in Room 227 (which was on the right, not the left, of the stairwell on the second floor), the principal's name was something-or-other Straws. Mr. Jonathan Straws? Was that it? She had already forgotten.

Today was Layla's first day at Burroughs High School as a sophomore. She had transferred there from Quarton High, the public school in her hometown of Falmouth, Maine. Last fall she had achieved high rankings on the National Merit examinations in both math and English. Within hours of the scores arriving at the school, Ms. Bagley, the guidance counselor at Quarton, had called Layla into her office. Ms. Bagley was going on and on about Layla's future, repeating kind phrases like "special gifts," "peak performance," and "the success Layla deserved."

Layla hadn't been entirely sure how this meeting was going to end. Was Ms. Bagley going to give actual guidance, or would she give out some nephew's phone number so Layla could eventually marry into the family? As Layla soon found out, Ms. Bagley had recommended Layla for attendance at Burroughs Academy in Portland. She told Layla that finishing her next three years of high school at Burroughs would be a huge step closer to ensuring her a spot at an Ivy League.

Today, as students in uniforms linked up in patches on the courtyard green before her, whizzing this way and that, Layla nearly lost her breath. She hugged her mother, then hugged her mother again. After this, she plugged her nose playfully and waved as she waded through the sea of plaid. Once she entered the large wooden doors of her new school, Layla reached out and grabbed onto the nearest long wooden bench as if it were a life preserver, unsure if she was kidding anymore.

Layla realized that she didn't know a single soul at this school. Every face was new to her. She felt the sting of no longer seeing the familiar faces she had grown to love at Quarton.

Mr. Murphy, Quarton's school secretary, always liked to guess what song Layla had playing in her headphones every morning. Somehow, after a whole year, he hadn't figured out that if he just guessed Springsteen every day he would have had at least a 75% chance of getting it right. Mrs. Gonzales, the cafeteria monitor, would always set the good salt and vinegar chips by the register just for Layla. Layla laughed now, remembering how you could always tell which room Mrs. Franklin was substituting in, because her service dog Gromit's long snout would poke out from under the closed door.

Layla felt a huge lump in her throat thinking that she had traded all of that for this real-time Catholic School Edition of *Vogue Magazine*. As the thought of the year ahead made her shake on the cold wood, Layla couldn't help but mutter some not-so-kind phrases directed at Ms. Bagley under her breath.

Groups of girls with shiny hair and too-short plaid skirts walked by, laughing at their own jokes. Groups of guys tossed around athletic balls where they probably shouldn't, forcing Layla to duck out of the way. Layla was amazed that these kinds of people actually existed, and, for a moment, grew terrified that she was going to become one of them. She looked down and saw the two distinctly different shades of red owned by her two very worn knee socks and followed them down to her mother's old dusty oxfords. She then realized that she really didn't need to worry about that at all.

It didn't help that today also happened to be Layla's sixteenth birthday. What a way to start the day: digging through her backpack for the important papers she was supposed to have on her at all times, and trying to think of excuses to hitch a ride back to Quarton. She found the pages in a ball underneath her calculus textbook. She unfolded one of them that read:

New to Burroughs? Come Join us for Our Fall Social in the Quad September 22nd! Games, Music, and Raffle prizes!

She crumpled that paper up again and moved her hand toward the garbage can to her right. She hesitated for a moment and then dropped the flyer inside, predicting she likely wouldn't need it. The next one looked promising, as it was yellow and not written in Comic Sans.

Information for New Students

Layla sighed. Last year, she would have squealed to see those words at the top of the page, welcoming her to one of the most prestigious high schools in the nation, and taking her out of a school where students hardly even showed up to class. She tried to remind herself how happy she was to be able to attend

Burroughs, to take advantage of this great opportunity, and to study under some of the best teachers in the country.

She took a deep breath and scanned the document.

Principal Strauss would like to meet with you at 8:00 am sharp on your first day. Room 107.

Strauss. Oh yes, Strauss. Like the composer, and the guy who made jeans. She could remember that. The time 8:00 had been added in the blank space in pen. She looked down at her watch and noted that it was 7:54. She had six remaining golden minutes to herself. What could she do with them? Of course, a good student would run ahead to find the room where the meeting would take place, take a seat quietly, and sharpen their pencil or something. But Layla was interested in something else. And from where she sat, she could faintly smell it.

She walked further into the lobby and scanned the hallways on its right and left sides. Down the left hallway she spotted two beautiful wooden doors under a golden sign which read *Cafeteria*.

"Coffee," she whispered. "It's somewhere."

She hustled to open the doors and found crowds of students sitting around at long brown tables under elaborate chandeliers. Behind them was a small glass counter with breakfast foods inside of it. She had heard that her new fancy school had a café in it, and while it was only about 10% of the reason she had decided to attend, it was climbing up to the 90th percentile at this very moment. How cool was it that students could go to the cafeteria any time they wanted and eat food and drink coffee? At Quarton, the cafeteria was closed outside of the two lunch periods, and all they had before and after was an old vending machine on the bottom floor with years-old snacks and Gatorades in it.

She ran up to the counter and asked the woman behind it for a small coffee.

"I'd love to give you a coffee, dear," the woman

responded, "but we close five minutes before the 8:00 bell. You'll just have to wait until lunch."

Layla almost wept. She looked down at her watch that now read 7:56.

"Oh, okay. Thank you, anyway," she said and slinked away.

They close?! How could they close? She had assumed this magical place would be open all day to students in need of caffeine. But the little sign on the glass read:

Hours:
7:30–7:55 am
12:15–1:55 pm
2:50–3:10 pm

"Great," she thought. Her coffee intake was actually restricted to three very arbitrary time periods during the day. She would just have to wake up earlier tomorrow.

Layla made her way to the door, but as she got closer, a tall brunette girl cut her off and pushed through it first.

"Oops, sorry!" the girl said in the least apologetic way possible. The girl turned around as she swung the door open to see who she had cut off. She then chuckled a little and raised one eyebrow at her.

"New kids…" the girl said and brushed her long, leave-in-conditioned locks out over her boney shoulder.

Layla sighed to herself and continued out the door and through the long hallway to the main office. She entered, found the door that matched the name on the page in her hand, and took a seat outside of the principal's office.

Layla opened up her laptop to the Blogiophile dashboard. Her thumbnail photo smiled back at her. Layla's mother had gifted her this laptop for her birthday, and she had placed it on her bed two days before with a note taped to the top that read:

My Darling,

For All of Life's Problems

—Soon to be Solutions.

Layla's mother was a math professor at the University of Maine. Head of the math department, actually, though she didn't like to brag about it. It was common for her to write these sorts of notes: encouragement with a bit of math terminology thrown in as her trademark.

Layla had grown up learning from her mother that all problems could be solved with a few variables, a reliance on logic, and a resounding statement of "QED." Whenever anyone asked Layla what her favorite subject was, she instinctively said math. She said it because in third grade she was the first person in her class to memorize her multiplication tables, and in seventh she was placed in the gifted class with only a few others from her original math class. It was her best subject, certainly, and she did enjoy it.

Truthfully, however, Layla liked writing more than math. She had always told her mother pretty much everything, but this was something she was a little afraid to break to her. When the subject of Layla's journaling on Word documents on the family computer came up, Layla always felt that a part of her mother, however small, still hoped she would become a mathematician like her.

This note with the gift of a new laptop gave Layla an enormous sense of hope. It showed a possibility that maybe her mother was easing into the idea of Layla being a writer as well as—or (gasp!) instead of—a mathematician. It meant that her mother supported this side of her just as much as the math side. It was an extremely special gift from an extremely special woman.

What Layla's mother didn't know was that Layla had moved on from Word documents.

Last year, Layla had started an anonymous Instagram account called Portland Posted. Here, she shared photos of

Portland's best coffee, food, baked goods, bookshops, museums, libraries, and anything else she fancied. All of it. She would take quick photos on her bike route to and from the library, and post them with quippy captions about the things she liked most about that particular Portland treasure. Other accounts would also share food, drink, or hipster hotspots with her in the DMs, and she would repost. Within the last month or so, Layla added another element to the Portland Posted account: a blog with the same name on Blogiophile. Occasionally, Layla would post a story to her Instagram with a swipe-up link to her blog.

Oh yeah, that's right, Portland Posted had enough followers for swipe-up links—a fact that Layla secretly prided herself on. She had stumbled into this rather large following over the past year. From the looks of her followers, it was mostly local businesses and students at the university nearby. They probably used the page to find local spots to hang out at. There were also a fair number of teens from Quarton who followed the page, likely in hopes of finding the best coffee and food in town. Truthfully, the best way she could explain it was that one day she woke up, looked at the Instagram page, and squinted to see the follower number was no longer 1200, but 12K, as if by magic.

Portland Posted being anonymous meant, by definition, that no one—not even Layla's mother, who knew *everything* about her—actually knew that Layla was the face behind the Instagram account and new blog. No one had any idea she was the one snapping pictures here and there around town and sharing cute hipster spots with the world. It even came up in conversation from time to time with friends and family, and Layla just nodded. "One of my students said she saw this latte on Portland Posted," her mother would say.

Layla loved writing. She wanted to be a writer like her dad when she grew up. Because she loved writing, Layla really enjoyed the blog aspect of Portland Posted most. She hoped to eventually make a name for herself with the Portland Posted blog. Layla would jot down musings as they came to her, compile them into a post every other week or so, and link it in her Insta story with a swipe-up link. It was still new, and so far wasn't getting much traction. Compared to the sea of Portland Posted Instagram followers, the blog stans would hardly fill her dog Bart's water bowl. But this was Layla's special spot to work on her craft. She actually liked that there weren't many readers, also, as it gave her a sense of freedom to write whatever it was that was on her mind these days. It wasn't much, but for some reason, having a blog made her feel like a real writer for the first time.

Layla clicked New Post. She leaned back on the bench and reminded herself that even if this school year didn't end up being everything she had hoped for, it would at least give her a lot to write about. She began thinking about what to write. She should definitely mention that Portland Posted was turning 16.

"Miss... Miss Whitaker?" A thin, middle-aged man interrupted her train of thought by opening the office door and stepping out into the clearing. He flicked his unkempt wavy brown hair wildly over his dark-rimmed glasses and looked over at Layla with big green eyes.

Principal Strauss was a tall man. Like, redwoods-tall. And his thin frame added to his tree-like impression. It took her what seemed like five minutes to lift her head from the brown leather shoes that now stood before her to the thick wavy hair on top of his head. She followed his crisp brown suit up to his square jaw and soft non-smile. Her eyes met his and she suddenly felt gentleness radiating towards her as she leaned back in the chair.

Layla closed her laptop suddenly. She wasn't sure exactly why she did this—it's not as if he knew what she was doing or could make out the website from his current place about seven feet to her right—but this had become something of a habit for her since she began blogging: always hide it, no matter the circumstances.

"Come on in." He motioned her toward the door.

"Oh, thank you," Layla returned, and took a seat in the dimly lit office across from his giant cherry desk. She then opened her laptop again and set up a new Google Doc for her notes. This way she would be ready to jot down anything important he might say, or equally ready to take pretend notes so as to look busy during awkward moments. This was another habit she hadn't really examined.

Mr. Strauss followed her in and took a seat in the tall wooden chair behind the desk. He straightened his tie and opened up the manila file that lay in front of him on the desk. He scanned the pages quietly as if he had forgotten that he was no longer alone in the office. Layla looked around the room a bit to pass the uncomfortably quiet moments.

Three giant cherry bookshelves filled the entire wall behind Principal Strauss's desk and made him look small and two-dimensional against a literary backdrop. Two more bookshelves lined the walls on either side of them, and a long fifth one spanned the wall behind Layla. From where she sat, Layla was able to make out some of the titles on the closest shelf. The books were arranged perfectly in what appeared to be alphabetical order by author's last name. Upon looking closer, Layla realized that they were actually ordered first by genre and then alphabetical by author's last name within each genre. Not only that, but the genres themselves were organized alphabetically from one wall to the other, with art and architecture in the bookshelf to the left of her and fiction on the wall directly behind Principal Strauss.

Impossible, she thought to herself. *No one has this kind of time to organize their personal book collections like this.*

This setup made it possible for her to, as she always did when she was at a library or bookstore, pinpoint exactly…

There! She stopped her eyes at the poetry section. And Principal Strauss's was quite the poetry section at that. Dickinson, Eliot, Frost, Plath, Shakespeare… the list went on and on. He even had not one, but three collections of poems by William Wordsworth, her father's favorite poet of all time.

Layla's father had been a poet, and to be in a room with other poets always made her feel, in some strange sense, completely at home. Suddenly, the person before her, bent over a large file filled with details about her entire academic career, was just a kind, middle-aged man who liked poetry and was weirdly anal about where his books were kept.

It wasn't just the books that were neatly organized and perfectly aligned in Principal Strauss's big office. In fact, everything in the office seemed to be organized: his coat hanging neatly on the coat hanger in the corner, his briefcase leaning against the side of the desk and somehow measuring its length exactly, one small wooden frame turned toward him at the upper left corner of his desk, and his writing utensils (one No. 2 pencil, two big black ball point pens, and one thin highlighter) lined up neatly at the top of his desk. Every single thing seemed to have its place. That is, everything except for a lone light-pink napkin which sat next to the spot where the file once lay on the desk before him. The napkin was slightly crumpled and cradled a few white crumbs in its folds. Layla was surprised by the little pink thing there on the desk. Obviously Principal Strauss wasn't that particular about his things if he had allowed garbage to sit in his periphery for even a moment longer than it needed to. Somehow, this little pink napkin made it possible that Principal Strauss was more like her than she had thought.

"Right then. Well, let's begin, shall we?" Principal Strauss looked up at her over his glasses and brought his hand up to his chin to rub it. "Good morning, Miss Whitaker. Let me just give you a copy of your schedule and go over the Burroughs Academy rulebook with you." He handed her a rather large stack of golden papers, the first of which read *Burroughs Academy Rulebook 2021*, and began to note key sections on its pages.

"Firstly, there's the matter of school performance. All courses are designed to challenge students, rewarding those who excel and punishing those who fall behind…"

Principal Strauss took a few sheets from the file and handed them to Layla without looking up from his handbook.

"You have been assigned to G Hall with others in your class. It's on the second floor, nearest to the north stairway. Uniforms are to be worn at all times except during physical education classes, when a separate uniform will be enforced…"

as Principal Strauss continued to recite the rules she would live by for the next three years, Layla couldn't help but wonder what in the world was going on inside of his head in that moment.

Did he blabber on and on about rules all day every day? Was this just second nature to him by now?

Suddenly, completely without warning, Layla grew cold all over and her heart began to race.

As she stared at the bookshelves behind Principal Strauss, they started to blur together, making the titles of the texts she had found so comforting moments before illegible. Her eyes squinted as she tried to hold the images before her still, forcing the doubles together to make singles again.

Layla suddenly noticed that Principal Strauss was quiet now. She snapped out of it and realized that he was looking directly at her. Without the slightest hesitation, Layla turned her eyes down to her laptop screen. She knew she needed to look busy, so she clicked to the Blogiophile tab, where she could write about how utterly absurd it was to spend so much time organizing your books. That would at least make it look like she was paying attention.

Layla gasped suddenly. What she saw before her was something completely astonishing. The new draft in her Blogiophile dashboard, which had been blank prior, was now written on. Not only that, but Layla's hands were tingling powerfully, something akin to when her limbs fell asleep but exponentially stronger. Strangely, the Blogiophile post was being added to—in this moment—with more words. And as her eyes moved down to the keyboard, Layla saw that somehow, without direction from her, her hands were doing the typing.

Layla tried desperately to stop typing, or at least to pull her hands off of the keyboard, but for the moment they could not be manipulated.

It was then that she remembered Principal Strauss, right in front of her and talking again. She forced her head up to look at him again and surrendered to her hands' sudden entropic episode. Then Layla remembered that she had just gasped audibly, which was probably strange to him.

"Ah, sorry! Just remembered I left my raincoat on the porch this morning. Oops! Haha…" Layla tapped her head like the comic relief character from a fifties sitcom, for some reason.

Meanwhile, she racked her brain for what could be causing this strange incident. What had she eaten and drank so far today? A bagel, an apple, two glasses of water… maybe just one glass of water? She wondered if perhaps she was dehydrated or having side effects from low blood sugar. Could it have been high blood sugar? Was it possible to have no blood sugar at all?

"Heh," Principal Strauss replied, awkwardly. "Well, on behalf of the faculty at Burroughs, I extend to you a very hearty welcome." His eyes returned to the packet below and he put it back into the manila folder beside it.

Thankfully, Layla could feel that her hands had stopped moving. They just lay there, spread out, as if exhausted by the work they had just done entirely on their own.

Layla was silent. Principal Strauss looked at her expectantly, as if watching a film he had already seen. It took a moment for this look to register in her brain, but as soon as it did she forced a reply.

"Great, thanks!" she said, shutting her laptop. She rose from her chair without thinking. "Happy to be here."

Principal Strauss stood up, stretched out his arm, and offered a firm handshake.

Layla responded in kind quickly, spun around, and hurried out the door as if late for first period. Was she late for first period? What time was it, even? She shook her head into attention and turned down the north hallway toward the stairs. When she reached the top, she turned immediately into the first restroom she could find. She ran up to the mirror eagerly. There she found her familiar old self, exactly as she had seen earlier this morning in her bedroom mirror. She was the same. Her hair was a little more tousled, perhaps, and her shirt more wrinkled, definitely. But she was absolutely the same old Layla.

Layla laid her books down on the restroom counter,

feeling like she wasn't really sure she wanted to be holding them anymore. She opened up her laptop and entered her password to unlock it. She then opened the Bibliophile tab once again, and her jaw dropped. On the page was a paragraph she had no memory of typing:

So many prolific writers talk about heartbreak lasting months, sometimes years. I wonder if they see it in me, still, almost twelve years later. Even now, I can hardly face yet another day without you. I love you so, Julia.

CHAPTER TWO

Layla ate her lunch on a bench in the courtyard, out of sight from most of the other students. She had been running this morning's events over in her head for the past three periods, and she didn't have the energy to try to make friends in the cafeteria. She would feel more like talking tomorrow.

Layla looked down at the document again and read the paragraph to herself in a whisper.

"Julia," she said. "Julia, Julia, Julia…" Layla tore her peanut butter sandwich into little pieces and ate the pieces somewhat frantically.

Layla was dumbfounded. She typed the name "Julia" again and again on the page, just to see if it looked familiar to her on the screen, to feel if the pattern of strokes felt familiar to her on the keyboard. Nothing. She didn't know of anyone named Julia. There was almost no way she had been the one typing that message. *But then, who had?*

Since starting the Portland Posted blog, Layla had only finished three blog posts. One was about new beginnings and going into a new school year, and the other two were just general musings about the end of summer in Maine. Since she still didn't have much of a following on the blog at all, Layla had a good deal of artistic freedom. But writing from some unknown person's perspective? Not exactly within her comfort zone. Should she just delete this paragraph? I mean, how could she really tie this into a local teen blog?

Layla sighed and clicked Save Draft. She would have time to think it over this week. She then looked at her schedule. Next was her fourth-period class—the class she was most looking forward to, and a huge part of the reason she had decided to go to Burroughs in the first place—Calculus 1 with a woman named Mrs. Chamberlain.

When Ms. Bagley had initially suggested the transfer to Burroughs last winter, Layla was unconvinced that she wouldn't be able to learn just as much at Quarton (while also having the added perk of not having to leave everyone she knew in the middle of her high school career). But when she and her mother got home from the meeting that day, they went to the Burroughs website—just to scope it out. The Whitaker women never made decisions without being fully aware of their options, after all.

There, on the front page of the website, was a photo of Mrs. Chamberlain. She was a beautiful, petite woman with gentle features and a confident but genuine smile. Something about her face was warm and comforting. Layla immediately knew she liked this woman.

Apparently, Mrs. Chamberlain was on the homepage because she had been named faculty member of the year last year. Next to her photo was a short bio about her interests, which included knitting, reading, and cooking. Layla assumed this was on the website as some ploy to make students feel more at-home when they were at school. It was sweet, in a way. Anyway, what stuck out most to Layla was that in her bio it said:

Mrs. Chamberlain longs to give all students the education they strive to receive, and thus permits entry into all of her mathematics courses, Algebra 1 up through Calculus 1 & 2, to any student who can test into them.

Layla had nearly yelped that day when she read that. If she transferred to Burroughs, she would be able to take calculus as a sophomore instead of going into pre-calc at Quarton. There, and

15

at most other schools in the area, you had to wait until you were a senior to take calculus, and most students opted instead to take pre-calculus as seniors. This happened because most colleges only expected you to take up to pre-calc if you were going into the maths and sciences.

Taking calculus now would put her on track to take AP math courses with all of the prerequisites for the heavy-duty math classes out of the way. Furthermore, there was a good chance that at Burroughs there would in fact be other sophomores in the class too. It sounded lame, and she definitely wasn't planning on sharing this with the JBC crew or her old friends from Quarton or anything, but she was excited to take calculus with other kids who actually wanted to be there. It also helped that that meant she might make it through the class without being made fun of by other kids. That was definitely a perk.

Layla's mother had nearly screamed. She'd been ecstatic and had started tutoring Layla on weekends so she was able to test into the course in April.

The bell rang to head to fourth period and Layla was very excited to hear it. She decided that, for the next hour at least, she would forget the who and why of this Julia person and focus on her math class. Which was a good decision, because when she got to Room 207 there was already an assignment written up on the board. She took a seat near the middle of the classroom and copied down the assignment as the other students filed in.

Mrs. Chamberlain took her place at the front of the class to welcome the students. She was as beautiful as Layla remembered from the photo, and even more so when she smiled. Mrs. Chamberlain was one of those naturally classy women. She wore fairly normal business clothing: a long, black cardigan atop a white oxford shirt, a black knit pencil skirt, and black Mary Janes. It was a simple outfit, but somehow, the way she wore it made it look like red carpet attire. No rumples, no folds, not a thing on her person out of place. And hints of simple beauty here and there, like the thin silver bangle on her wrist and the tiny light-pink tulip pin on her shirt collar.

Mrs. Chamberlain had perfect hair, too: the kind of hair that didn't hang, but rather lay exactly where it meant to, framing her face in delicate strawberry-blonde locks. It was nothing like Layla's hair because it actually did something, anything at all. Layla's hair refused to have an occupation, in spite of her many attempts to convince it with brushes, gels, and blow dryers. She could spend an hour fluffing and spraying it, but there it remained, flat like an oar. Flat like lots of other parts of her, too.

"I hope you all have enjoyed your first day back at Burroughs," Mrs. Chamberlain offered the smile again and folded her hands. She explained that they would begin by reviewing some problems from pre-calculus which she had put on the board.

As Layla began flipping through her textbook, she noticed that the girl in front of her had a black braid of hair that was so long it couldn't help but rest on her desk. It was thin and perfectly woven, with no wisps whatsoever.

Layla's father would call this a "plait," which was another word for a long braid. But he was English, so when he said the word plait it sounded like plat.

When Layla was a little girl she had longer blonde hair, which her father would braid for her every morning.

"And just like that, you have a plait!" he would say, spinning her around in front of the mirror so he could get a glimpse of the finished product.

She was only four or so at the time, but she remembered scenes like that one so well. Even now, she could still see her father's face. Behind it, she saw the sunlight falling in through the open bathroom window, then the plain white walls and black-and-white checkered tiles, and finally her own face in the mirror, with his face there above it, grinning widely. Her plaits were never as perfect as the one before her now—the wisps had formed colonies with other wisps—but her father had done his very best, and she'd always felt like a princess anyway.

"What do you say?" He would kneel down and spin her back around to face him. "Will it work?"

He would laugh and smile with his teeth clenched, as if nervous to hear the answer.

"It's perfect!" she would say, hugging him tightly.

"Plait" was one of those special words that—because of its English pronunciation and the fact that her father was the only person she'd ever known who was English—she could only hear in his voice. She repeated it over and over again in her head now: *plait, plait, plait*. For the first time in a long time, she felt him there with her.

"Strauss," Mrs. Chamberlain called, interrupting Layla's thoughts.

Her heart began to race. She had been startled by Mrs. Chamberlain's voice, but even more struck by the word it spoke.

"Strauss?" Mrs. Chamberlain repeated, scanning the room. Layla tried desperately to follow her eyes. Had Principal Strauss entered the room through the back door? Had he appeared on the television screen for some sort of announcement?

"H…Here," a voice from the other side of the room responded in a soft, low tone.

The boy sitting there whipped his long, dark hair out of his face and waved his finger casually. He gave what appeared to be a forced half-smile and a slow nod to Mrs. Chamberlain.

"Okay." Mrs. Chamberlain marked in her notebook.

"And… Whitaker."

Layla realized what was happening and straightened in her seat.

"Here!" she exclaimed.

"Right, then," Mrs. Chamberlain said. "I'll give everyone a few more minutes to finish up these problems. This should all be a review of last semester, so it will be a good stepping-off point for us to look them over together afterwards."

Mrs. Chamberlain moved back to her desk and everyone else turned their heads back down to theirs, as if on cue. Layla did the same.

"Strauss?" Layla whispered a few minutes later to herself, staring once again up at the boy.

The girl with the plait in front of her apparently heard this and whipped her head back to look. Layla's face reddened.

The girl had a gentle face that was expressionless for a moment until it smirked suddenly. She looked around from side to side quickly to see if anyone was paying attention and leaned in closer to Layla.

"The principal's son," the girl whispered.

"Oh, I—" Layla stammered. "I didn't know… he… had a son."

"Yeah… his name's Caleb," the girl continued. "You must be new."

There again was that word the girl in the cafeteria had used. Except this time it didn't sound condescending at all—just factual.

"Yeah," she said. "Wait, so, that's the son of Principal Strauss?"

She was processing this fact rather slowly and, as she spoke it she realized, also rather loudly.

"Whoa," the girl whispered a little louder, "Yes, that's him. That's Principal Strauss's son. His name is Caleb and he, like everyone else in this class"—her eyes grew a little wider and her whisper a little louder—"has ears!"

"Right. Sorry." Layla said, quieting and composing herself.

The girl smiled sweetly back at her and then turned back around.

What were the chances that, after Layla had just finally gotten the strange episode in Principal Strauss's office out of her head, she ended up being in a class with his son?

Caleb Strauss was tall like his father. He hardly fit in his desk, it seemed. And thin, with flowing black, Harry Styles hair. His hair covered almost all of his face from where Layla sat except when, every now and again, he pushed it back and combed his fingers through it as he worked in his notebook. He wore his required white button-up shirt rolled up to his elbows and untucked, with the collar popped proudly as if he were one of the Greasers from *The Outsiders* trapped in a Soc's body. His tie hung loosely and his buttons didn't quite reach to his neck like those of the other boys did. Instead of the frumpy brown trousers most boys wore as their uniform, Caleb wore tighter straight brown pants that actually looked somewhat fashionable. He looked sloppy, but not in an unkempt way. More like he just had other things to think about than how his shirt fell.

He sat surrounded by other guys in desks who would whisper and laugh to each other periodically. Suddenly one of them tapped on Caleb's shoulder and Caleb turned around.

Layla traded her breath for his eyes. This instant, somehow, was just long enough for her to really see them. They were massive, full, and bright blue, like the shallow part of a lake. But unlike that place, they weren't clear; you couldn't see through them, and no part of you reflected off of them. They just stood— stone cold, thick, and matte. Full of so much but closed off as to what it was. She caught herself and looked back down at her notebook.

She had given herself a moment to be distracted by Caleb, but now she knew she needed to get to work. *Strausses aside*, she thought to herself. *Strausses aside*.

CHAPTER THREE

The bus dropped Layla off a few blocks from her house at 3:17. She smiled as she opened the bright yellow door of her quaint, beautiful home.

"Haaaaaappy birrrrthday to you! Haaaaaaappy birrrrrthday to you!" Her mother's falsetto voice rose over the Belle and Sebastian that played from her headphones and she removed them. She bent over to hug Bart, their elderly black lab, and followed her mother's song into the kitchen, giggling.

"That's quite the greeting, there, Mom." She laughed and hugged her sweet mother tightly. "I thought you'd still be at work."

Layla took a seat at the kitchen table.

"Ahh, yes." Her mother sighed and then offered her wide golden smile. "But that was before you mentioned this morning's coffee conundrum. Oh, I know it's a sensitive subject for you, so we don't need to talk about it."

She sat down next to Layla and smirked. "But I just knew a few meetings with the faculty could wait. I thought we could have coffee on the porch together as step one of birthday fun. Step two may or may not involve… waffles!" Layla's mother stood up promptly and grabbed the plate she had set aside on the counter, filled with waffles and overflowing with strawberries and powdered sugar. The kitchen was a mess, with pots and pans filling the sink and powdered sugar all over the stove. Her mother was the greatest cook of all, and by far the messiest.

Layla's mother was, as most math professors tend to be, a left-brained, analytical, bookish woman. Unlike her contemporaries, however, she had another side—joyful, quirky, and exciting. She was gregarious beyond compare and genuine almost to a fault. When she listened, she listened as if for a pin dropping. In teaching, this meant getting to know who her students really were behind the homework assignments and test scores. It meant her mother tried desperately to make math fun and captivating—because to her it was. In her relationships outside of work, these qualities made her exceedingly lovable and easy to be around. She was beloved the whole town over.

Layla's mother hadn't always been this way, however. From her mother's stories, Layla knew that for about the first twenty-three years of her life, her mother hardly ever got her head out of her books. She saw little of the world around her and really didn't have any desire to see more. She was known as a mathematical genius, having gotten into Yale at sixteen. But she had trouble making friends, and her genius only made her feel more isolated. When Layla's mother met Mr. Whitaker at Oxford, he was even more isolated, focused intently on his poetry and hardly leaving the campus. He and his wife became an island together.

But on September 6, 2005, all of that had changed. For Layla's mother, at least. Layla's birth brought her mother a joy she had never known and instilled in her a desire to cherish every moment of their life together. As she would always tell Layla in her annual "My Beloved Daughter's Birthday" speech, Layla had sharpened her lens to the beauty in the world. And it hadn't blurred since.

"Oh my gosh, those look amazing!" Layla grabbed the plate from her mother and danced her way onto the porch. She put her books down next to her on the table and looked up over the railings. The sun shone bright over the garden of sunflowers in front and she felt the lingering moments of summer as she sipped her coffee.

"So other than the rough start, how did your first day go, sweetie?" Layla's mother walked onto the porch with her own coffee and a plate filled with more waffles for seconds.

"Oh, it wasn't bad," she said. "Classes were great, and I love my teachers. Mrs. Chamberlain is everything we thought, and more." She smiled at her mom across the table. She was really excited about Burroughs, even with today's strange events.

Layla knew her mom would want more details than that, so she played over the day again in her mind. She kept coming back to what happened in Principal Strauss's office. Layla wanted so badly to share the story with her mother, but she also worried that it might make her seem a little bit on the crazy side.

So what? she thought. *My mom is one of the wackiest people I know. I bet she would want to know that I had some weird episode and ended up thinking about a woman I've never met all day.*

Layla sighed softly and thought about how to word what she was about to explain.

"The principal is somewhat lacking in social graces, though…" she said, looking down at her coffee mug and fiddling with the handle. She hoped that perhaps the conversation would just direct itself to the mystery. But then she realized that conversations don't often direct themselves to strange meetings in which one person loses all control over their extremities. She opened up her laptop, planning to go over her homework list for the day.

"Yeah, I remember him being a little… nervous. But I'm sure the first few weeks are tough on principals," Layla's mother declared. She had met with Principal Strauss herself the week before to be briefed on all of the Burroughs goings-on.

Suddenly, as if reading her daughter's mind, Layla's mother spoke a word that had echoed through every inch of that mind all day.

"Julia?" she said.

Layla's eyes widened and she looked up at her mother

with intensity. *How had she known the name? How had she figured out what happened in Principal Strauss's office without Layla saying a thing? Did she know who Julia was?*

"Oh, you aren't already daydreaming about more sugar, are you?" Her mother broke the silence with a wild guffaw and motioned with her hand toward the Portland Posted draft on Layla's screen as she walked back inside through the front door. The blood returned to Layla's face. Her mother had simply spotted the name she had typed earlier over and over again on the screen.

"Well, it is your birthday after all," her mother continued, returning through the door. "But I thought we could at least get dinner first before diving into more sweets." She grinned widely. "We can go to the JBC tonight on our walk."

Her mother was referring to the adorable café downtown. Everyone called the spot "the JBC." Layla knew that this was shorthand, but because she so rarely used its real name, she had nearly forgotten it. The bakery was called Julia's Bakery and Café. After the woman who owned it, Layla had assumed. In this way, the very name she had typed on the screen hours before in Principal Strauss's office was somehow both unfamiliar yet completely familiar at once.

The JBC was a well-known stop for freshly brewed coffee and handmade baked goods. A stop which Layla and her mother frequented quite regularly. Very regularly, actually. In fact, Layla would go there almost daily to study, meet with friends, or have a muffin with her mother.

"Oh, that sounds fantastic," she replied.

"Whatever you wish, my dear!" Her mother stood up and slid across the porch, picking up the now-empty plates from the table and turning into the kitchen. Bart came running up behind her, ready to catch any scraps that might fall in the cleaning process.

Her mother giggled, twirling around so as to avoid tripping over the big lab.

"Bart's thinking he's going to get a jelly donut!" she called.

Layla chuckled to herself a moment, grabbing her books and preparing to move inside, but then froze in her tracks.

A jelly donut. The thought raced through her head as if trying to exit and land there on the document where all things mysterious to her now lived, greeting one another as if to say, "You must be another thing that's beyond Layla's comprehension. Come on in, stay a while!"

Layla sat back down on the porch and opened her laptop again. She moved her mouse over to the Blogiophile tab and began typing in the draft she had started for Portland Posted. She had thought earlier that day that she should just delete the words on the screen. Something about including them in a post felt like plagiarism or stealing, since she didn't really feel she had written them. But then she thought about her dad, and how he was always able to write from different perspectives.

Maybe keeping these words in her post was an homage to him. Of course, she hadn't yet figured out where the words had come from, or how to tie them in with her own writing. But if nothing else, closing this wild mosaic of an update on the topic of food would at least go with the Instagram page.

A jelly donut from the JBC. The small, round, delicate pastry. Not too fluffy but just fluffy enough, with an ever-exciting pool of thick, handmade fruit filling that oozes from its center immediately upon the first bite. Of course, like your average jelly donut, you get to choose the flavor of jelly inside it. So, in theory, you know what's coming. Like the first day of school—you can't say you didn't know it was coming.

But the jelly donuts from the JBC still take you by surprise, because you never quite know just how good that jelly center is going to be. Other jelly donuts offer a small break from the dough with a thin drizzle of syrupy goop, the kind you squirt onto a sundae or find fallen from a child's peanut butter and jelly sandwich into his lunch bag. But the JBC's jelly donuts let loose a deluge of real, handmade jam, making them a rather messy and adventurous dessert no matter which outer layer you choose to surround them with: plain or pow—

Powdered… powdered! POWDERED!

That thing that she had seen on Principal Strauss's desk eight painfully-long hours ago, the pale pink napkin covered in a layer of fresh powdered sugar: it was a remnant of a recently-enjoyed Julia's Bakery and Café jelly donut. The best in the tri-county area.

"What's the matter?"

The shadow of her mother now eclipsed Layla's own on the porch floor.

"Nothing!" Layla ejected, startled. "I, umm… need to go get started on calc homework."

Layla closed the laptop and headed inside and up the stairs. Bart followed her into her room. There, Layla pulled up Google in a new tab. She searched for Principal Strauss on the Burroughs faculty page and scanned the screen. There it was:

Principal Strauss loves spending time with his son Caleb and is dedicated to honoring the life of his late wife, Julia, who ran Julia's Bakery and Café in Falmouth.

Layla swallowed hard. It all made sense now. The words she'd written earlier had to be from Principal Strauss's mind. Somehow, the words had traveled through her and onto the screen. Layla sat for a moment, collecting herself.

Finally, she clicked over to her Blogiophile draft and finished crafting her post. As she brought the piece together, she changed the one word that had been playing in her mind all day, because it was someone's name. Names—real ones, at least—weren't allowed on the blog. She read the text over just to make sure there were no obvious hints at who she might have been talking about, or… writing for? She clicked Publish, then added a swipe-up link to her stories with a photo she had taken a few weeks ago of a JBC jelly donut.

Swipe up for a jelly donut exposition.

So Much Depends upon a Jelly Donut
September 6

Always make yourself coffee before you leave the house in the morning. I made the mistake not to this morning, and it has proven dire. But, on the plus side, I have already been snubbed by popular girls and sent to the principal's office, so at least I can say I faced more teenage nightmares before nine o'clock than most people do all day!

Yes, being an uncaffeinated teenager in this day and age can be a real struggle. Keeping up with the popular kids, going to seven classes a day, and having to do it all before 8 a.m. But I am working on appearing to have it all under control. Especially today. Oh yeah, because…

HAPPY BIRTHDAY TO ME! Portland Posted turns 16 today.

And what does Portland Posted want most for their birthday?

A jelly donut from the JBC. The small, round, delicate pastry. Not too fluffy but just fluffy enough, with an ever-exciting pool of thick, handmade fruit filling that oozes from its center immediately upon the first bite. Of course, like your average jelly donut, you get to choose the flavor of jelly inside it. So, in theory, you know what's coming. Like the first day of school—you can't say you didn't know it was coming.

But the jelly donuts from the JBC still take you by surprise, because you never quite know just how good that jelly center is going to be. Other jelly donuts offer a small break from the dough with a thin drizzle of syrupy goop, the kind you squirt onto a sundae or find fallen from a child's peanut butter and jelly sandwich into his lunch bag. But the JBC's jelly donuts let loose a deluge of real, homemade jam, making them a rather messy and adventurous dessert no matter which outer layer you choose to surround them with: plain or powdered.

I encountered a man today who was also eating—or had just finished eating—a powdered jelly donut. He was lost in thought about who knows what? Maybe he had lost love, long ago. Jenna was her name. And all he could think about was trying to face another day without her. In this moment, maybe he wondered if everyone could see the heartbreak in his face.

For my part, while I sat across from him, I pretended I couldn't. Because I am just like him, with my worries and my struggle to be composed through it all. Life is tough—a truth which we surely must have seen coming.

But I wonder for both of us what the jam will taste like when we get to it. Will

we have something unimaginably sweet ahead
of us?

I raise my jelly donut in the air as
a toast to us today, dear friend.

CHAPTER FOUR

The JBC was unlike most bakeries in that it was open from 7 am to 10 pm, serving as both a stop for morning coffee and donuts, and an after-dinner meeting place for old friends—in this case forever friends—to sit and chat. Layla took a seat with her mother at their usual table, the one in the front right window which stood foggy now from the opening and shutting of the door to the crisp night air.

Most of the kids who spent their time at the JBC were older than her; they were seniors or recent graduates from her old high school. Most of them had already been close friends when they started to come to the JBC, but a few new kids had been added to the crew over the time that she had known them. They weren't popular at school by most definitions, but they were cool in Layla's mind because they were fascinating people. They were sort of outcasts, but they held each other very close and had become a pack. They liked alternative rock, and they caused trouble from time to time. They were loud and gregarious. What Layla loved most about the JBC crew was that they were loyal. Even when the JBC had to shut down for months in the beginning of Covid, the crew hung out on the patio out front at all hours and were first in line for coffee at the makeshift take-out window.

When Layla first started coming to the JBC the summer before her freshman year, she desperately wanted to be noticed by the crew. She would say hi and join in the conversation for a bit, and somehow, somewhere along the way, it worked. Now they all considered her a fellow regular, or member of the usual crew of Quarton High misfits who frequented the spot. But she didn't come to the JBC for the purpose of socializing. She loved that she knew people there, that she had developed friendships with them, and that she could socialize with them; but she ultimately went to be alone in the crowd. She could sit across from someone like Emily or Megan, the two girls who were sort of the leaders of the crew, and hear about some concert they went to or the wild weekend of drinking they had. But she preferred to fill that seat with her writing, or her books, or her mother.

If she didn't know the other teenagers drinking coffee there, Layla always knew the baristas and the bakers. For the past few years, the same four people had worked behind the scenes at the JBC: Grace, Raina, Gavin, and Spencer.

Grace was the manager and was somehow there every time Layla was; whether it was morning or night, you could always see her thin, soft frame flowing from one spot in the café to another, setting out food, cleaning, and making coffee. Most people just assumed Grace had rented out a room in the back somewhere and that, after switching off the lights at 10:30, she just rolled out a cot and fell asleep. She was a busy, but very kind woman, with long, flowing blonde hair that she always had to force into a messy bun on top of her head. She would exchange pleasantries with anyone who walked through the door, and she was an incredible listener. She didn't speak of herself to most of the other regulars, however, so it seemed to Layla that she was one of the few who knew much about Grace's personal life. Grace was a huge Coldplay fan, she loved her golden retriever, Lila, more than most people, and she had a fellow named James who would come visit her often. She never called James her boyfriend or anything, but it was always obvious he was there to see her. James would arrive at about 7:30 every night and chat with her while she closed. Once a month or so, he'd bring some new type of plant which he would offer her with a grin. Grace would then set this plant up around the bakery somewhere, and eventually the room became filled with everything from ferns to succulents. Gavin told Layla that, supposedly, James did this because he thought that the act of giving a woman a flower was a selfish one, historically used to placate them and avoid conflict. So instead, it appeared that he was endeavoring to bring her everything that ever photosynthesized... *aside* from flowers.

Raina, a brilliant, reserved woman of about forty, was the head baker. She worked in the back, mostly, starting at 5 am and ending around 1 or 2 pm every day. She was a gentle, quiet woman who came and went as she pleased, coming back with heaps of new ingredients and always calculating and recalculating recipes in whispers to herself. Occasionally, Raina would stand at the counter and stare at the completed treats in the glass cases. Layla loved to watch Raina think and work in these small glimpses she was offered. It was a special gift to be able to watch an artist work. Especially since, in Raina's case, she would only be in public for a few minutes at a time before she would go back through that kitchen door into her own world again.

Under Raina was her assistant baker, Spencer, who was sort of the resident babe of the JBC. Spencer was in his mid-thirties, of average height, and exceedingly muscular, with more tattoos than canvas as skin. He was extremely handsome and resembled A$AP Rocky—except somehow even hotter. He rode a motorcycle to work every day and parked it in the back parking lot in a spot Grace had reserved for him. Layla thought Spencer hilariously unpredictable. When she first met him she thought he would be like any other macho biker dude. She assumed he was just working at a café to buy him time for other endeavors. But after a few months, Layla learned that he arrived every morning eager to follow the instructions of his female boss and bake elegant pastries, a task he knew was traditionally associated with women. He wore his apron with confidence and fancied himself a walking affront to the very idea of gender roles. This, of course, made him wildly popular with all of the female customers. His insanely beautiful body didn't hurt, either.

Then there was Gavin. Gavin Sherwood. A tall and thin character with longish blonde hair that was thin too and fell just above his shoulders. Layla had always been fascinated by Gavin. He wore these black-rimmed glasses like her own. He wore flannel button-ups, tall combat boots, and a soft smile that was nervous but pretended not to be. He had a pale face and green eyes, which Layla found she had to check twice to make sure they actually were green because sometimes his glasses fogged up a bit or smudged or he moved his gaze away when she looked back. But their color hardly mattered because they drew you in without asking permission, and certainly without allowing for categorization. Gavin was thin—it bears repeating—like a rail, but with a sign on the top that you were dying to read. His hands were thin, too, and long, like a pianist's, but he played the guitar instead—which doesn't require long fingers, but they do help. Layla played the guitar also, and there were times when she and Gavin had played a little together on her porch. Times past.

He was the barista or, as Layla often referred to him, "Sir Sherwood, Knight of the Round Mug," and the employee Layla knew best out of everyone at the JBC. He was nineteen years old and a Quarton graduate who had just finished in May. This meant Layla and Gavin had attended Quarton together, so occasionally she had seen him in front of his locker as she passed by. Truthfully, his locker was on her way to exactly none of her classes, but that didn't stop her from making excuses to pass by at least once a day. Now, Gavin lived in a house downtown with a few other Quarton grads and attended classes part-time at the local community college. He was beautiful to Layla in every way, and she felt a closeness to him that she didn't really talk about but never stopped thinking about.

Yes, Gavin and Layla were friends. Friends. It was a sentiment she had spent the entire summer trying to convince her mother and friends of. She had repeated it so many times she might as well have just gotten it tattooed on her arm and lifted up her sleeve whenever she entered the room.

For a few months last spring, however, Layla and Gavin

had been *something else*. Layla had not been sure what to call it so she called it nothing, and in fact rarely spoke about it at all. But Megan, Emily, Chase, Mark, and some others in the JBC crew often called it a "fling." Layla never ever referred to it in this way, because she couldn't think of a word she hated more than that one. The word had a tendency to sound lighthearted and fun—even, somehow, desirable. Layla learned that in reality, a "fling" was a complicated, frustrating, and in some ways debilitating agreement between two would-be friends to, instead of being friends, be romantic in a substantial but noncommittal way. For Lord knows how long and to what end.

Very little about what Gavin and Layla had had during that time, however, was fun. They had spent the months of January through April making each other mixed CDs, talking for hours in the back parking lot while he smoked Pall Malls, and going to his band's shows together (which wasn't really together at all, since Layla would spend her time in the audience with her friends while he was on stage). But they hadn't really dated, certainly, since they never actually, well, went on a date together. Instead, Layla spent those months growing closer and closer to Gavin, sharing more and more of herself with him, writing about him in the margins of class notes, and missing out on important things because she wanted to sit by the phone and wait for texts that never came.

On the seventh day of April, Layla had been in the middle of doing just that, waiting and waiting, when she realized that she had forgotten about her geometry exam on April 8th. Just completely forgotten; somehow the information had fallen right out of her head. She scrambled to study for the time she had left and managed to get a B, but she was still pained and disappointed. When she really thought about it, she realized that the information hadn't fallen out of her head after all; it had been replaced. Replaced by Radiohead songs and stale muffins. Replaced by Gavin's parting words from the night before, playing over and over again in her head.

Layla was furious with herself and decided then and there

that she would never let a boy come between her and her goals. She decided to end the fling on the afternoon of April 10th.

She thought that this lesson needed a ceremony, so while she waited for the bus that day, she dug through her purse and pulled out Bruce Springsteen tickets for the upcoming show in May. She dug further into the bag and pulled out a crumpled-up Nutri-Grain bar. After deliberation, she decided this would work for the moment. Then Layla laid the Springsteen tickets atop the Nutri-Grain bar so it looked like a thick, important book. "On these Springsteen tickets and this Nutri-Grain bar, I solemnly swear…" she began. The Nutri-Grain bar, apparently bordering on melted, bent down around her hand. She hurried up. "I promise not to let myself get distracted by boys ever again."

It was odd to feel that she had to break something off that had never even started. She knew it had to end and that he wasn't going to be the one to end it, so she decided to let Gavin in on a little secret she hadn't told anyone yet: the paperwork had come in two weeks prior, and next year she would be attending Burroughs Academy.

The conversation with Gavin actually went really well. She told him about Burroughs and he made a few cracks about how she was too good for Quarton and how all the geniuses he knew of ended up being manic-depressive. She told him that he needed to stop basing his entire life off of one midnight viewing of *Good Will Hunting*. They spent a bit of time talking about how Robin Williams should have won every award there ever was for anything, and then somehow got onto chatting about which Salinger short story was the best and why. It was a whirlwind, like most of the conversations they had. So much so that Layla started to forget how it had started in the first place. She suddenly grew panicked that she hadn't really done what she came there to do at all and was, against her better judgment, setting herself up to be walking home afterwards the same way she always did, with excitement in her smile and her hand on her cell phone, waiting for vibrations. So suddenly, as if it were someone else saying the words, she released: "I can't go to your shows anymore."

Gavin's hand paused on its way to grab his coffee cup for another sip and slowly met his chin instead, where it lay awkwardly for a moment, as if just looking to land somewhere—anywhere—but lost in transition.

"Oh," he replied.

Layla regained her train of thought and connected voice with body once again. "Yeah, I mean. You know... because Burroughs is a really intense school. And I have a lot of catching up to do to be ready for the fall and everything... I can't really go out as much, you know..."

"Um... yeah. Yeah, absolutely," he replied, nodding frantically as if he had just been told something he already knew like the back of his hand. He smiled at her knowingly and then looked back down at his coffee cup. His hand finally found its place back on the table. "I figured as much."

There it was—the thing Gavin often said to prove he was fine. Layla had overheard Gavin say it when Grace told him she wouldn't be able to give him the raise he had asked for at the beginning of the year. She had again heard him say it on the phone with his car repairman who told him it was going to cost much more than he had originally thought to fix his brakes. Gavin seemed to face unfortunate things with this phrase because it was what someone said when they couldn't be affected by bad news. It was wise and protective. It was confident and mature. Layla found it infuriating.

She packed up her bag, took the stale muffin off of the table, and walked toward the door, knowing they were done talking for now.

She opened the door to the balmy spring air and threw her backpack over her left shoulder.

"So, I'll see you around?"

She stopped in her tracks, shocked to hear him speak again. Her heart began to race and she grinned widely toward the street. She pushed the grin down into a half-smile as she turned back around to face him.

"You will," she said and walked out the door.

"You're sure you're ready for this?" Layla's mother put her hand on her daughter's arm, pulling her back into the present moment. Layla breathed deeply and nodded at her mother.

"Of course I am. Desserts before boys, right?" Layla smiled.

Her mother had taken to performing this small ritual whenever they went to the JBC since what happened in April. They had talked about everything when it happened, and her mother had always been on her side—and would have been whether she wanted to pursue things with Gavin or not. When Layla decided she didn't want to (or she had tried long enough, more accurately, and didn't want to *anymore*), her mother had sat her down at the kitchen table and declared: "We could never walk through those doors again. And it wouldn't matter to me in the slightest, darling. But those doors, the coffee, your friends: everything existed long before Gavin was even a second thought. And they remain yours to enjoy, to live, to experience! You have a right to be there and to feel what you feel every moment. Never forget that." Layla had been nervous to return to the café and see Gavin every day again, but she took her mother's advice because she knew that to leave would be to be weak. And she was not weak.

Of course knowing her mother would be there with her helped.

Layla and her mother walked inside and took a seat at *their* table. Layla already knew Gavin was there. Not only because she had memorized his schedule almost a year ago now, but also because her eyes had a team of peripheral-vision soldiers who had been trained specifically to spot him well before the first official viewing of him straight on at the register. "I saw you when I came in," as most people would say to one another.

Standard practice for this circumstance was for Layla and her mother to sit for a few minutes and talk about the day or what kind of pastry or coffee drink they were going to get until Layla was ready to go up and order the items they wanted. Meanwhile, Gavin would be *over there*, now having noticed Layla, pretending to be very busy cleaning, or preparing an order, or calculating something or other. It felt to Layla as if they both needed this time and, each knowing that, would give it dutifully to one another, no verbal or written agreement necessary. Though they had agreed to be friends, Layla knew that the end of the fling still needed to be handled delicately. And their relationship was past the point at which surprises from one another were pleasant ones.

After this five-minute routine, one of them could say hello to the other as if they had just noticed them, they could exchange pleasantries, and the desired food and drink could be administered. The system was foolproof.

"Hey," Layla said to him finally, approaching the counter.

"Oh, hey there," Gavin said, from a few feet away. He winked at her, acknowledging their little charade. Then he looked down again, shuffled some things around behind the coffee maker, and rinsed out the portafilter. He was obviously nervous to look at her for too long. After a few seconds, he looked back up, smiling with his eyes. He approached his side of the counter and gave all of his attention to her, which took her by surprise.

"I hardly recognized you now that you're so much older."

Of course. He knew it was her birthday.

"Oh, I know." Layla laughed and flipped her hair over her shoulder playfully. "I feel older."

He stared into her eyes intensely and held them there.

"Happy Birthday, Layla Jane Whitaker." He spoke quieter now, more seriously.

"Well, thank you," Layla replied. She held his gaze as long as she could, and then brought her eyes down to the counter. She was starting to feel more nervous than she expected, which made her feel like walking away. But then she remembered that she hadn't actually acquired any food or beverages yet.

Why was she feeling so overwhelmed? She and Gavin had given it a shot. A pretty good shot, anyway, at being more than friends. And it just didn't work. He didn't work, and she didn't work. It was no one's fault, really. The two of them just... weren't supposed to be together. So what? What she really wanted now was for things to go back to the way they had been before.

"How's it going?" he asked, awkwardly.

She thought for a moment, trying to grasp at something that would ease this painful tension.

"You know..." she looked back up at him now, a sly smile growing on her face. "It's going *really* well."

Gavin looked puzzled.

"Really, really well," Layla continued.

Gavin lifted his eyebrows suddenly.

"Oh yeah?" he replied. He grinned widely, understanding what was coming next.

"Ahem. Let's just say this is the world," Layla said, lifting up her hand and making a fist. "And this..." she lifted her other hand and stuck out her index and middle fingers and placed them on top of her fist. "This is me. Just..."

Gavin's smile filled his face.

"Just walking right on top of it?" he asked.

"Just walking right on top of it," she confirmed, nodding.

"That's what I like to hear," he said. They both laughed. This was the conversation they had had nearly every time she came into the JBC in the earlier days (pre-fling). It was what they had said, word for word, hundreds of times, before things had gotten too weird between them for them to say much of anything at all. It was their own little quiet tradition. Layla remembered that what she loved most about being friends with him back then were the quiet traditions. To be able to bring them back might erase the last eight months of emotional hacky sack.

"What can I get for you today?" Gavin asked, still smiling.

"We will have one blueberry muffin and one jelly donut," she said, feeling relieved and opening up her wallet.

"A jelly donut?" he asked, cocking his head to the side. "For your mom?"

"No, the muffin's for her. The jelly donut is for me," she

said, moving her hands fancifully to show excitement.

"Really? No way." Gavin laughed. "I thought you didn't believe in jelly donuts."

"What? I never said that," Layla exclaimed, laughing.

"No, you absolutely did," Gavin retorted. "What was it you said about them? Hmm… Oh right! You said that you should be able to tell exactly what you're going to get out of a baked good just by looking at it. That there needs to be an element of certainty to desserts."

"I really don't think I said—"

"Yes! That was it!" He nodded excitedly. "You said that the only people who enjoy jelly donuts are completely mad ones!"

"Well, then, what can I say?" Layla said. "It looks like today I've gone mad."

Gavin burst into his sweet, soft laugh. Warm and gentle, with eyes on the person who had created it, as if to say thank you. He got the muffin and the donut out of the display case and put them on plates. Layla thought back to her strange experience in Strauss's office and considered the possibility that her statement was truer than she ever would have thought.

"We all knew it was going to happen someday, Layla." Gavin put out two napkins for her, folded on the plate next to the muffin. He knew she liked them to be placed like this. Normally he put the napkin underneath the pastry, between the pastry and the plate. This was apparently more soothing to the eye for most people, but it didn't make any sense to Layla. If you wanted to actually use the napkin, you had to pick up the pastry first, and by then there was always a little sugar or chocolate on the napkin from where it touched the pastry. So that side of the napkin could hardly be used to remove food from the hands or face now that it already had food on it. The other common option was for the napkins to be placed on the counter next to the plates that had been put out. But she didn't like public surfaces very much because you could never really be sure how clean they were. Certainly the workers did clean the counters, but they remained, no matter how often they were cleaned, somewhat more precarious than a plate as far as germs went. Anyone could come up and lean on the counter or put their hands or their purse on it. The germs would build up every time someone entered the café. And of course she could still use the other side of the napkin, but where would her hand be when she wiped her face with the clean side of the napkin? That's right, it would be on the dirty side. Ergo, the beside-the-muffin napkin. Another system that was foolproof.

"On the house," Gavin said, sliding the plates across the counter.

"Thanks, Gav," Layla replied. "Hey, listen. Do you know anything about the woman who owns—or, owned—this place, Julia?"

Gavin paused for a moment.

"You know, I don't really," he replied. "I mean I've only worked here for two years now. And you know, I heard she died a long time ago, actually. I think it was ten or eleven years or so ago."

"Oh wow…" Layla said. "I—I didn't know that."

"Yeah…" Gavin said, seriously. "But man, she must have been an incredible baker. She was the real deal. Like a baking goddess, really. I mean, the only reason the muffins are stale is because you only ever get them after 8 pm, Layla." He laughed. "Have you ever heard of eating muffins, I don't know, for breakfast, like everybody else?"

"Ha! You know I don't believe in breakfast," she replied. "Coffee is breakfast. Everything else comes later."

"Yeah, I've heard," Gavin said, laughing.

"So you never met her, then?" Layla asked, returning to the topic she really wanted to talk about.

"Unfortunately, no," he replied. "But I can tell she was a really cool lady. I mean, did you know she made up every single recipe we have?"

"No way!"

"Yeah. And she wrote them all down by hand in this big notebook in the back." Gavin started to wipe down the glass on the display cases. "It's so amazing to see because she had this wild handwriting. Like desperate, almost. Everything is scribbled down on the page as if it's coming right out of her brain. And there are all these little notes in the margins, which makes it really tough to read the recipes. Raina actually told me she has to call the owner down here to have him decipher some of them from time to time. You'd think he would have transferred them to a Google Doc or something by now, but I guess he's sentimental about them being hard copies. And he can read his wife's handwriting really well."

Layla paused.

"Her husband?" she asked. "You know him?"

"Ahh, no. I never come in that early—you know how it is. The bakers get here before I even know what daytime is yet." He laughed. "I've heard he comes in from time to time, but I've never met the guy. Sorry. Why do you ask?"

"Oh, no reason," Layla said. She grabbed her treats and spun around, ready to return to her mother's side. But before she took off, she felt a sudden urge to get more information. She suddenly wanted to know as much as she could about Julia.

"Do you ever go back there and check out that recipe book?" Layla asked.

"Nah, Raina actually locks it up in the back room after she leaves."

"Oh," Layla said. "Okay. That makes sense."

"But I could," Gavin said.

"What?"

"I said, I could," Gavin said again. "I could try to get in there tomorrow and scope it out."

"Yeah?" she said. "I mean, if it's not too much trouble."

"Are you going to tell me why you want to know so much about this stuff?" he asked. There was that smirk again.

"I mean, I just wonder, you know? I eat these muffins almost every day, and I don't even know anything about the woman who invented them."

"Right…" Gavin said, still not convinced.

"Right," she said.

"I'll let you know," he said.

"That would be great," she said, buttoning up her jean jacket.

"Goodnight," she said.

"Goodnight."

When they got home, Layla went upstairs and took out her laptop. *There's so much happening that I can't seem to grasp*, she thought. *There must be something that I can know.*

She stared at the screen and then finally typed into her search bar: "Julia's Bakery and Café"

The JBC didn't seem to have a website, which made sense to her because it sort of existed outside of time. It didn't seem like the type of place that would flow with the tides of technology. Last year she had heard someone suggest to Grace that they post their weekly specials to their Facebook page, and Grace had guffawed in their face. Layla liked that about the JBC.

She scrolled through the results and stopped suddenly.

Before her was a photo from the *Portland Daily News*. There stood a woman, tall and slender, in the front of a small crowd. She had a gentle face behind thick glasses, and her brown hair was in a wild, messy bun on the top of her head. She looked young and happy, without a care in the world.

Next to the woman was a tall man with dark, flowing hair and a warm smile. Layla recognized him as being a younger Principal Strauss. Between them was a little boy, about five or six, with a wide, goofy grin on his face, missing a few teeth. He wore a baseball cap, striped overalls, and scuffed up tennis shoes. He had apparently squeezed himself between the man and the woman, wrapping one arm around the man's leg and one around the woman's.

Next to the photo stood the caption: *Julia Strauss at the ribbon cutting ceremony for new bakery, Julia's Bakery and Café, with husband Jonathan and son Caleb.* The article was from May of 2008. You could tell it was warm outside because Julia wore a ruffled pink dress with pink heels and Caleb and his father wore short-sleeved button-ups and shorts. Julia held flowers.

Layla went completely pale and slammed her laptop shut. She laid down in her bed slowly as the weight of the image she had just seen covered over her like a thick blanket. She stared up at the ceiling above her, which now served as a canvas for the three faces she had just seen.

The face on the bottom held her attention the most out of all three of them. The boy's face was bright and joyful, like that of children on Kodak commercials. Nothing about him was serious or stern. His eyes were quite different from those of the boy in her math class. They were full, just like the older Caleb's eyes—full to capacity and overflowing. But what they held wasn't pain and mystery. It was joy.

Layla sighed, knowing she wasn't going to come up with any answers tonight. She called Bart up onto her bed, and snuggled him to calm herself down. Then she hit the lights and fell asleep.

CHAPTER FIVE

As fourth period came to an end, Mrs. Chamberlain passed back the exam everyone had taken on Friday. It hadn't been super tough, since it was meant to be a pretest to gauge where everyone was at going into the course. Layla got hers back: her first A in math at Burroughs, and hopefully just the first of many. She was ecstatic and looking forward to telling her mother.

Layla opened up her Blogiophile dashboard in a new tab, just to see how many views her blog had gotten since last night. Her eyes traced the number 12. A whopping 12 views, and one comment from @tara_lane927 that read "we stan donut poetry" with four praise hands emojis after it. It was great news that Layla was excelling at math, because she wasn't exactly a famous writer yet.

Layla looked over at Caleb. She was thankful that there was both a clock and a window on the wall behind his desk. It was easy to pretend to be greatly invested in both time and weather so she could peek at him without drawing attention from his crew of bros.

It had been a week since she'd found out about Julia. She had used nearly every break from her studies to search the internet, old town publications, yearbooks, and any other documents she could get her hands on for more information about the Strausses, but she wasn't able to find much at all. Every search came up with the same thing, always landing on words like *mystery*, *unknown*, and *questionable*. For some reason, no one seemed to know what had happened to Julia Strauss. Or at least it wasn't in writing anywhere. The original news story from September 2009 referred to the "death of Julia Serene Strauss due to apparent carbon monoxide poisoning." But it went on to note that it happened during business hours, with no witnesses. Could there be more to the story?

When curiosity got the best of Layla over the weekend, she returned to the JBC to ask Gavin if he had learned anything about Julia since their chat on Monday. All he had to offer was an old business card he had found in the back of Julia's notebook. It had her photo on it and read "Julia Strauss, Baker" with some of her credentials underneath. Layla had pinned it on the bulletin board on her wall and would glance at it from time to time. Having it there made her feel more connected to Julia.

It was so strange to her that after two years of going to the JBC nearly every day she knew little more about the woman behind the entire company than what was on that business card. She hadn't known that one woman had created all of the recipes, cleaned all of the counters, and flipped the sign from *Open* to *Closed* almost every day twelve years ago. It was all the more strange that her principal would end up being that woman's husband. And the fact that a feeling had come over her in Principal Strauss's office that led her to type words about this woman on her blog—that was, well, definitely the strangest part of all this.

At times, this not knowing what happened to Julia frustrated Layla. At other times, she wished she hadn't been called to Principal Strauss's office last week at all; she wished that she had met with Vice Principal Marshall instead, or the office secretary, Mr. Johnson. She longed for a time when she didn't feel this overwhelming sense of uncertainty.

"You know he's a senior, right?"

Layla nearly jumped out of her seat at this question. The girl in front of her with the plait had spun that plait around and was looking at her with a massive grin on her face.

"Wha-what?" Layla replied, groggily.

"Caleb," she quipped. "The guy who you've been staring at all period."

Layla looked around, nervous that someone might hear them. Thankfully at this point the bell was ringing, and students were beginning to file out of the class.

"Heh," Layla ejected, rising from her desk. She was thrown off by the attention from this girl, but she also had to admit she was very happy to have it. It felt nice to have someone in the new school notice her (something that hadn't happened yet, really, save for the instance last week in the cafeteria with hair-flip girl). Layla wasn't the best at making friends, and she had actually been deliberating on how to get into another conversation with this girl since their last exchange.

"I wasn't staring the *whole* time," Layla said, as they walked out of the room together. "I'm Layla, by the way."

"Mia," the girl said in response. "So, where are you from?"

"I'm a transfer from Quarton. A sophomore. I live in Falmouth, but I come out here for school because—well, for a number of reasons, but mostly because the math program is advanced, and my old guidance counselor, Ms. Bagley, well… she sort of created this whole alternate future for me, and pitched it really, really well. Very Shark Tank situation. My mom and I ate it up, and here I am! Heh… Sorry, that was a lot."

Until just now, Layla had forgotten how much she rambled when she was nervous.

"Ha! You're weird," Mia replied, eyes wide. "I love that. So, is the business scalable?"

Layla realized Mia was making a follow-up Shark Tank reference and felt a deep sense of relief.

For some reason Layla hadn't really prepared a response for the question of "where are you from" yet. How far into it should she go, after all? Technically, she was born in the UK, but she moved to the States when she was four years old. She lived in Boston for a while while her mom was an adjunct professor at Harvard. Then her dad died when she was five. She and her mom moved to Falmouth so they could be with her mom's extended family. This way, her mother could take up her post as resident hippie math professor at the University of New England's Portland campus, and both of them could maybe not think quite so much about how devastating it was to be without Layla's father.

Alas, Layla opted to just stick with her original reply.

"What year are you?" Layla asked.

"I'm a sophomore, too," Mia said. There was silence. "There are only four of us in the class, you know," she said with another wide grin on her face.

"Really?" Layla asked. It made sense that most of the kids in the class would be older than her, but she hadn't really thought about it much. "That's cool."

"Yeah," said Mia. "It's you, me, Carson, and Jake. Well, Jake doesn't really count because he's an exchange student. Just here for the semester. So, I mean, he counts because he's a sophomore, but he's not really in our class. Like, he won't be valedictorian or anything…"

"Oh, sure," Layla smiled nervously. Mia knew quite a lot about the people in their class. And it was a little weird that she was already thinking about who was going to be valedictorian. They still had three years of classes left to decide that! Layla had noticed that Mia was an amazing student. She had peeked over once or twice and seen that Mia's notes were insanely detailed, filling the page even into the margins with graphs, bullets, and numbers.

"So, the exam." Mia smiled. "Did you do well?"

"I'm happy with my score," Layla said. "You?"

"Me too." Mia smiled back. Her brown doe eyes smiled enough for the rest of her face.

Layla was very happy to have met Mia, and she knew they

would get along very well. Plus, as an added bonus, they could study together when the next exam came along.

Layla realized that they were quickly approaching her locker. She remembered that she needed to grab her chemistry book and her notes for piano class too, just in case she didn't get a chance to come back to her locker in between the two classes. The music end of the building was on the first floor right next to the science wing. Both were on the opposite end of the school from her locker, so it really didn't make sense to come all the way back. She took a moment to map the school out in her brain and plot out her route.

"Well, I'll see you around," Mia said, probably noticing that Layla was spacing out.

Layla was startled back into communication. "Yes!" she said, excitedly. She opened her locker and smiled back at Mia. "Absolutely!"

Layla caught herself mid-panic. Here she was, doing exactly what her mother had told her not to do; getting so caught up in the little things that she was en route to missing out on the big ones. She liked Mia, and she didn't want Mia to think she wasn't interested in the prospect of being friends with her. While she was still daunted by pretty much every aspect of being the new kid at Burroughs, not to mention still out of sorts from her experience with Principal Strauss the week before, she had ten minutes here to get to class and she knew that realistically she didn't have to worry about being late. So she paused and thought of something she could say to get Mia, now walking away, to talk to her again.

"Hey," Layla called after her, smiling. Mia stopped and Layla motioned to her to come a little closer. "Just so you know, I don't have a thing for Caleb. And I wasn't really staring at him, it's just…"

Layla paused. She shouldn't say more. She knew that if she went into detail about why she wanted to know Caleb—Principal Strauss, Julia Strauss, the mystery of Julia's death, the tingling feeling in her hands… all of it—it would all be too complicated. It would sound too ridiculous. It would seem impossible. But it wasn't, really. Or was it…?

"No, it's fine, I get it," Mia replied. "I figured he wasn't really your type. Plus, he's still dating Amanda Jennings—who knows why. But he is objectively the cutest guy in school, so it wouldn't be crazy if you had been." Mia smiled.

"That's not false." Layla laughed. It clicked in her brain that she had seen Caleb walking with the girl who had performed the dramatic hair flip last week, and that this must have of course been his girlfriend. She repeated the name Amanda Jennings over and over again in her brain in a nasally voice for a minute. Then she remembered that life was happening.

"Actually, I go to the bakery his mom own…ed." She realized how strange that sounded. Some people didn't frequent establishments the way Layla and her mom did the JBC. Some people didn't view places of business as their second homes. It was possible Mia wouldn't really understand what Julia owning the JBC meant to her. It was possible Layla didn't fully understand what Julia owning the JBC meant to her. She looked up and saw that Mia had stopped in her tracks.

"Oh, I'm—I'm sorry!" Mia said, looking back at Layla with big, suddenly quite sad eyes. Her smile had disappeared and she looked uncomfortable now. "You must have known her. I had heard she was a baker but I didn't know where. Gosh, I feel terrible." Her voice was flustered and nervous.

"Oh, no, it's fine, really." Layla smiled, realizing she had made it seem like she'd actually known Julia. Which of course she hadn't. "I didn't really know her, just *of* her."

"Oh, well, I'm still sorry," she said. "It was so long ago, I had forgotten all about it."

"Did you know her?"

"No. But I remember hearing about it in elementary school. Caleb and I have been going to school together since Wilson. When his mom died, his dad pulled him out of school for the rest of the year…" Mia trailed off.

"How sad," Layla said. "That must have been so hard for

him."

"Absolutely. And with all of the questions and everything."

Layla looked quizzically at Mia.

"Questions?" Layla asked. "What do you mean?"

"Well, you know, it's a mystery, right?" Mia asked.

"I heard something to that end," Layla said calmly, as if she hadn't spent the past week looking for any information to any other end.

"Well, I guess…" Mia looked around to make sure no one was listening as kids whizzed by them through the halls. "I mean…" she looked down at her feet.

Layla looked on, entranced.

"There is a rumor that Caleb knows what happened to her," Mia said.

Layla's jaw dropped.

"What do you mean, he knows?" Layla pried.

"Well, supposedly he was there when it happened, but something happened to make him forget. Like he… suppressed the memory, or something. The whole school knew about it. His dad sent him to a million different therapists and doctors and all that. But word around the school was that Caleb just… just completely stopped talking. I remember for a few years everyone swore he didn't say a single word about the whole thing to anyone."

Layla was shocked. She stared back at her in a trance.

"And even now," Mia continued, eyes wide, "He never talks about his mom."

Layla didn't move. She couldn't move. All she could think about was that little boy in the photograph hanging on her bulletin board. She imagined his face must have turned suddenly from that wild grin to a cold terror; from eyes full of joy to eyes full of sadness.

She imagined Caleb again as he was today, as he sat at his desk in class, strong and quiet. Seemingly living the ideal high school experience: the principal's son, the popular boy, attractive and athletic. But still, he had lost his mother, and nothing could change that.

Mia suddenly looked down at her phone and jolted.

"Better get to class," she said, still solemn. "I'll see you later."

"Yeah," Layla said. She mustered up a smile and a nod, as Mia turned in the opposite direction. "See ya."

That night, Layla emptied her backpack onto the dining room table as her mother cleared it from dinner. She read over her assignments in her planner, and got organized for her psychology exam on Wednesday. She opened up her laptop to a Google Doc to take notes as she worked on her assignment.

Layla opened up her textbook to chapter four. Before her she saw a chart split into three colors: red, blue, and yellow. The sections were labeled *Id, Ego,* and *Superego,* and each contained the label's definition inside the box. The text on the page went on to detail Freud's theory of the unconscious mind.

That can't be right, Layla thought. She had already read this chapter over the weekend, and Ms. Glass had gone over these terms in class today. She realized she had been looking at the wrong date in her planner, and she turned the page to the correct one. While she looked through her notes, Layla pulled up the draft she had started last week on the Portland Posted blog. Maybe she would procrastinate a *little* and add some notes about her day.

Suddenly Layla felt a chill surge through her from her toes upward, extending across her arms and into her pale fingers. She could no longer make out her notes, to say nothing of the dates that ran down the side of them. The ink blurred across the page as her hands began to tingle feverishly. Her mother clanged the dishes as she cleaned them at the counter a few feet away.

Within seconds, a feeling of sickness fell over Layla. It wasn't nausea in the sense that she was en route, one-way ticket to Vomitville. It was more that pre-nausea that turns your whole body out of sorts and distracts you so much from the present moment that you wish it would just move into true nausea already, because then at least you would throw up and feel better afterwards. It would be a light at the end of an arduous tunnel. Until, of course, you're in the middle of true nausea, with your head practically in the toilet, and you regret ever wanting this at all.

She held this feeling for a few moments, and would have informed her mother that she thought herself sick if she hadn't suddenly recognized this exact series of feelings from last week in Principal Strauss's office. Instead, she slowly moved her gaze over to the new post page. As she predicted, it was no longer blank.

In real time, she watched her hand typing words on the screen, exactly as it would have had she been casually typing a draft to put up on the page herself. But the words she was writing now weren't first created in thoughts, repeated aloud through her own brain matter, ricocheted across lobes, and sailed along a familiar myelin sheath. No, these words were completely foreign to her, as if written by someone else entirely. As she read them back to herself, she became acutely aware that these words were in no way her own.

It's not as if I miss him more today than usual. Truly, I miss him every single day all the same. But today is harder than the others because twelve years ago now, it was the day of the fight. The first of many fights. The big one.

Oh, what I wouldn't give to go back to that day just for a moment to tap myself on the shoulder and whisper "Don't go." Just make myself stay and hear his point of view. I would make myself sit for a moment and consider why he really wanted to stay in Mansfield instead of coming with me to visit my parents in London.

Then I would tell myself not to say anything at all. Because in anger the words we say come out as daggers.

I told him I would leave without him that night, and that if he didn't allow me to be part of the world I would leave without him again. I would leave for good. And I know I had to get out; I had to see the world! But knowing what I know now—that we would spend our last few months together fighting—I can never forgive myself for those daggers.

So today I feel the pain of missing him as always; I feel the pain all the more because it rides along with its dear friend, regret.

"Woof, woof, woof!" Bart bounded into the room, startling Layla from thought. He took his usual seat next to Layla's mother, fur overflowing onto her socks, ready to catch anything that might fall in the cleanup process.

Layla took this moment to slam her laptop shut. Without thinking, she rose from her seat and pushed her chair away from the table.

Her mother turned around at the sounds, looking perplexed.

"You okay?" she asked.

Layla looked at her mother intensely. She wanted to tell her mother what had just happened. But she stopped herself, remembering how absolutely crazy it would sound.

"Fine," Layla muttered. "I was just heading… upstairs."

"Already?" Her mother asked, sweetly.

"Yes," she said. "So much psych homework." She grabbed her backpack and shuffled up the stairs.

When Layla got into her room, she sat on the bed and stared at the wall. Her body was still feeling warm and tingly. She opened up her laptop and read the text through again.

Layla tried to read the words to herself in a few different voices, as if trying on different people for them. But it was no use, because she knew the tone of the words she had written very well. The words were her mother's.

She had lived with her father and mother in their tiny home in Mansfield for four years. It was deep in the country, surrounded by farmland and hillsides. It was, from her memory, endlessly beautiful. She could almost smell the flowers in the yard.

Layla could remember her mother mentioning the trip to London. But she didn't know her mother had made that trip alone. Nor did she know that her mother was unhappy in Mansfield. This was all new information; the kind of new information that made your heart sink.

Had she been reading her mother's mind just then?

Almost as soon as Layla had that thought, she took it back. She hadn't been like one of those super heroes who stares deeply into the villain's eyes and hears their thoughts play out on a loudspeaker. It wasn't as if she had been desperately seeking this information and psychically surging into her mother's brain to retrieve it.

More accurately, Layla was leaving her body entirely for a moment. She was stepping outside of her brain and lending her hand to write for her mother's brain instead. She was writing her mother's journal entry instead of her own, just as she had written Principal Strauss's last week...

The only difference was that now she was learning things she wasn't sure she wanted to know. If it was true that these words on the screen were her mother's, then her mother and father had been fighting in their last months together. Layla's mother had never mentioned any fighting to her and Layla had certainly never suspected it. Layla knew that her mother loved her father with a desperate kind of love that only two soulmates could have for each other. Their love was not a want, but a need.

Layla was devastated to think that maybe the truth she had grown up knowing wasn't the truth after all.

CHAPTER SIX

Layla sat on the couch by the door the following morning, letting herself fall into the golden velvet material that always felt like home. She stared at the doorknob in a daze, giving in to her exhaustion. Normally, Layla sat at the kitchen table drinking her coffee slowly and finishing up homework or looking over assignments until the moment she had to leave, but today was different.

Last night's curiosity had gotten the best of Layla. After her writing incident, she had saved the draft she'd written for Portland Posted and tried to distract herself with calc homework. She'd then laid awake late into the night imagining various scenes between her mother and father, piecing together elements she remembered from life with them in the Mansfield house. Layla remembered little about her time there, so it was tough to place things.

On the couch now, Layla drifted back into those same scenes. She had one very vivid memory of her mother cooking on the stovetop, the smell of boxed macaroni and cheese wafting around the room. Not much more to it, but childhood memories are so often like that. Layla placed herself in that moment, left the kitchen, and walked up the wooden wraparound staircase and into her pink bedroom. Then she looked through the doorway and down between the staircase railing's bars to the hallway below. Her mother found her father there trying to fit three large books into his already too-full suitcase. They began to bicker back and forth about what types of things constituted necessary luggage and which things were completely unnecessary for their trip to London.

In another scene, Layla was outside on the porch steps studying the mud beneath a rock she had rolled over in search of rollie pollies. The sun poured onto her arms as she worked her hands through the dirt. Her mother and father sat on the porch chairs reading books. Suddenly, because of this recent revelation, the scene was expanding in her mind. Now, Layla could hear her mother whisper to her father. Her mother told her father that Grandma and Grandpa had planned a surprise party for Layla once they arrived to visit them the following day. Layla looked up to see that her father was flustered: he apparently had forgotten all about their trip to London. Layla's mother noticed this and grew upset. She stood up, walked a few feet, and turned around in front of Layla's father so as to block Layla from viewing the conversation. They quibbled softly.

In the final scene, Layla sat in the small guest room that her father called his office on the first floor of the Mansfield house. This room was almost completely bare, save for an old brown desk on the far wall next to the window. She sat on the carpeted floor with her hair up in a wild ponytail on the top of her head and a big white balloon in her hands. She was grinning madly.

Layla imagined her mother sitting across from her on the floor, playing with blocks. Her father was out in the living room, doing some writing. Layla's mother called to her father now, "Honey, don't forget that we're leaving to see my parents in an hour." Layla's father then grew frustrated by the work he had to do and the little time he had to do it in and groaned. Layla's mother heard this and went to the living room to chat with him. Layla couldn't make out what they were saying.

Each of these situations was possible, Layla reasoned. Each little moment would explain why Layla hadn't known of the potential fighting that had taken place between her parents in those days. She would permit them to be true if need be. But was it smart to grant them truth without being completely certain? Layla pondered this as she stared again at the doorknob, waiting to hear the footsteps of her mother coming down the stairs to her left.

She and her mother had just shared breakfast together. But they had done so to Bruce Springsteen's *Greatest Hits*, so there hadn't been much silence to fill with the questions she so desperately wanted to ask. She found herself happy to have missed that opportunity, though, because she was equal parts confused and terrified. She had decided to ask her mother in the best place there is to ask a mother anything at all: the car. Something about sitting in an enclosed space with someone else, knowing exactly how long you have to spend together, made talking to them about something important so much easier.

Finally, the footsteps came, and Layla was awoken from a second sleep. She looked over to see her mother, ready for the day, finishing the last wrap of her hair tie around the tight bun of hair that sat on the back of her head. Her mother continued toward the door to where three tote bags sat and grabbed them, one at a time, to slide them onto her arms. She looked up at Layla and smiled.

"Are you all set?" she asked, cheerily.

"Yeah," Layla replied, standing up.

She followed her mother out to the car. As they set out, Layla flipped through the radio stations, wondering if she would find something that might put this conversation off. After a few minutes, Layla decided to dive in.

"Hey Mom?" Layla started, taking her hand off the dial.

"Yeah?" her mother asked.

"Umm… how are you feeling?"

"Me? Oh, I'm great, why do you ask?"

Her mother navigated the road ahead, distractedly.

"I don't know…" Layla trailed off, nervously. Even though she and her mother were quite close, this conversation was new territory for her. What was she supposed to say? *Well, I read your mind—or, maybe wrote your mind—yesterday and it said you were having a hard time...* Layla shifted in her seat.

"You know, I met this girl in my chem class the other day, Rachel," Layla declared, after a while. She looked over at her mother who was still very focused on driving. "She's English."

Her mother turned suddenly and looked into her daughter's eyes. For a moment, she focused on them as if they were a crowded party she was trying to search through for the person she had come to see. She exhaled deeply.

"Wow," she said, looking back at the road again. "That's funny. Is she nice?"

"Yeah, yeah she is," Layla continued, feeling quite uncomfortable now. "We didn't talk much, really. She just asked me if she could borrow my notes one time and I noticed she had the accent. So I said 'Oh, what part of England are you from?' and she said 'London.'"

Layla could feel herself talking quickly now because of how nervous she was. Her mother didn't say anything.

"Yeah, so then I told her that you know, I was born in Mansfield and that we used to visit London and all that... And then she said 'Oh, did you stay there long?' and I said I really didn't remember much, honestly, because I was so young when we moved to the States and everything... And you know, she told me it probably hadn't changed much since I was there and asked if I thought the chocolate here was better... And of course I said 'No,' because, well, duh... And I felt confident saying that because, you know, even though we haven't been there since... well, in a long time... Papa and Nana send us that full assortment every Christmas so I still feel like, you know, I'm up on the latest chocolate... trends..."

Layla trailed off and glanced over at her mother. She was looking somewhat solemn and tired now.

"It was pretty funny," Layla concluded, trying to put an end to her rambling. She felt a little defeated, having taken a shot at bringing up the past only to meet such silence. But she desperately wanted to know more about what her mother had been thinking last night. She wanted to have a conversation, though it might be uncomfortable. But unfortunately it wasn't really up to her. Her eyes widened now as she waited to see if her mother would respond.

Moments later, her mother snapped out of her daze and forced a quiet laugh.

"You certainly are up on the chocolate trends," she said.

Layla let out a large exhale, relieved that her mother had thrown even the smallest of bones.

"And even when we were there, and you were so young," her mother continued, to Layla's surprise. Even more surprising was that when Layla looked up at her mother now, she was all smiles.

"There was one time when I had hidden two chocolate caramel bars in my purse as a special treat for us all to enjoy one day. Well, you somehow sniffed them out and stole them while I was making dinner. You completely polished them off! It was astounding because they were BIG bars, too... Quite the spectacle."

Layla was happy to hear her mother speaking fondly of the past like that. She always felt nervous bringing those memories up, but this one seemed a particularly fond one so she considered herself lucky.

"I must have gotten so sick!" Layla laughed, her mother's laughter joining hers.

Their laughter died off somewhat quickly.

"Man, it's been a while since I've thought about those days," Layla declared. She realized as quickly as she heard the words leave her mouth that they were a lie. "I mean, not those people, but those days."

Her mother smiled at her knowingly.

"Of course," she said.

A silence fell over them again. They were almost at Burroughs, so Layla bent over to make last-minute adjustments on her socks and shoes.

"You know, I was just thinking about the Mansfield house yesterday," her mother said.

Layla paused, shocked that her mother had anything more she wanted to say.

It wasn't rare for Layla and her mother to talk about their time in England and, in turn, Layla's father's life, but the conversations were always somewhat stilted. Normally they would chat about his crazy hair or his obsession with American singer-songwriters. Or Layla would be reading one of her father's published poetry books and have a question about something he mentioned. These conversations were short and casual. Layla would gather as many facts about her father as she could without causing that look of despair to pass over her mother's face, as it often did by the end.

"It's so funny that you would bring that up now, because I was just remembering that time," her mother continued. They had parked now, and her mother looked down at her hands on her lap. "I was just thinking about Dad and those quiet days we had there."

Layla suddenly felt a knot in her stomach, seeing her mother like this. She regretted bringing it up; she regretted saying these things that might be more upsetting than she could even begin to know. She wasn't exactly sure why, but in that moment she was sorry she had said anything at all. She swung her backpack over her shoulder and motioned toward the door.

"You know," her mother looked over at her and continued. Her head was sort of cocked at Layla as if she was perplexed by her. "Your father always did things like that..."

Layla looked back at her intensely.

"Things like what?" she asked.

"I don't know, just..." her mother said. "Just the way you brought up Mansfield like that, right after I had been thinking about it so intensely last night."

Layla stared back at her mother, frozen in anticipation about what she might say next.

"It's something your father used to do all the time," she

continued.

"Oh…" Layla said, softly and solemnly. Then she laughed a little to try to break the tension.

Her mother smiled and handed Layla her lunch bag from the back seat. She wrapped her arms around her daughter and squeezed tightly. Layla stepped out of the car.

"That keen sense of knowing what other people are thinking," Layla's mother continued, as her daughter stood outside the car before her. "It must be the writer in you too."

Her mother grinned, waving Layla off to class. Layla turned and stared blankly ahead, letting her mother's words settle.

At lunch that day, Layla told Mia she had some catch-up work to do for Mrs. Cooney's class. She sat in the courtyard by herself, replaying in her mind that morning's conversation in the car. Sure, Layla had known her father to be an especially intuitive person. But she always just assumed it was because he was a writer. As she understood it, writers were expert observers. They were supposed to know people in a different sort of way.

It struck her now that perhaps whatever had happened in Principal Strauss's office, and again in the kitchen with her mother, was something her father had experienced too. Was it possible he, too, had written the thoughts of others on paper, without even trying to? Could that be a secret they shared? It wasn't impossible. They shared the same hair, last name, and penchant for singer-songwriter ballads, after all.

Layla opened up her laptop. She clicked over to her Blogiophile draft with all of her mother's writings in it. She felt sick thinking of sharing such intimate writings about her family. But then she remembered that this was her gift. Layla felt that her ability to write for others was something special. A gift for writing was something she had always wanted to have, and maybe this would be what made her writing unique. Now that she found this gift, it only made sense to share it with the world. She thought it was what her father would have done, anyway.

She went through the draft and removed everything that seemed too specific, too close to home. She thought for a long time about how to preserve her mother's thoughts without exposing too much. Then she looked through her camera roll to see if anything from around town could relate.

Aha! she thought. *The new bookshop on Fourth!*

When she had visited last week, Layla had snapped a few photos of Frog & Toad Books, this adorable new bookshop named, of course, after the characters in the Frog and Toad children's book series. It was the perfect place to be alone and get a little bit lost. Layla and her mother had already gotten lost three or four times there, and it had only been open for a few months. The picture she had taken showed a little round turquoise table in the back of the shop. It was the best place to be alone and be a part of it all at the same time.

She clicked Publish, then added a swipe-up link to her stories with her photo from the bookstore.

Ever find you want to be alone, but also want to be surrounded by others at the same time? Swipe up for thoughts on wanting both.

Wanting to be Alone in a Community
September 14

Frog & Toad Books on Fourth is the most adorable bookstore. It's packed to the brim with floor-to-ceiling shelves of books that weave along the walls and into one another like a maze. They bend and turn, holding a sea of books, with sliding ladders so you can achieve your Beauty and the Beast library dreams. The best part is that it smells like old books, which is one of the very best smells to ever exist. It's a reader's dream.

There's this table there that sits where two shelves meet in the far corner, almost behind another set of shelves. It's the perfect spot to dig into a story, because it sits at such an angle that it's not easily visible from the rest of the store. At the same time, it soaks up some of the light from the front windows. You can hear the hustle and bustle of people coming and going through the store doors and you can see out the front window to the street outside. It's the perfect spot to sit and read if you want to be alone, but also want to be a part of it all.

Lately, I'm coming to understand that desire more and more. Some people want to be a part of the world so desperately. They want to go out and see passersby, friends and neighbors, their families near and far.

Others want to be alone, quiet and content with their thoughts.

I have recently found that I'm the sort of person who wants both. I come from both types of people: the extroverted, wild communicators, and the introverted, quiet observers. I want to be a part of the chaos, but I can't help but turn inward in its midst.

I'm the little round table in the back, hoping you notice me. Sit, and stay a while.

CHAPTER SEVEN

Layla sat on the bench in the school lobby that she was beginning to establish as her own. Mostly because for the past two mornings, she had sat on it and tried to read *Moby Dick*. The only thing about *Moby Dick* was that some of it was this wild, intense story about Captain Ahab and his crew and revenge against the white whale. But a whole lot of it was just facts about whaling and whale parts and whales, whales, whales. So, of course, Layla often found herself thinking about other things during these parts. Those other things being her writing and her father. The possibility of her father and her sharing this unique skill was becoming more and more apparent to her.

Her phone lit up with a Blogiophile notification. Her recent post had amassed 17 total views and 5 likes. She hadn't expected for people to be reading her blogs much. It was nice to feel like her writing was getting some small recognition. It had to be more amusing than whale content, at the very least.

Someone tapped her shoulder and stirred her out of whales and fathers for a moment. There was Mia, smiling broadly beneath her thick black glasses. She held *two* cafeteria coffees in her hand.

"Bless your soul." Layla smiled, bright eyed.

"It's Thursday, after all," Mia said.

Mia had told Layla the other week on their way out of

fourth period about a new theory she was developing. Mia believed that, contrary to popular belief, Thursdays were actually the hardest days of the week to get through. Mondays, though admittedly difficult, had over time gained recognition as such, and thus everyone was more understanding of one another on Mondays. More patient. She said that Wednesdays had a similar reputation. They were often referred to as "hump days," making them an even more painful day of work or school because they dangled the carrot of Friday, while still demanding much by way of getting there soon. Mia found that oftentimes people felt they could be lazier on Wednesdays because of the understood difficulty associated with getting over the hump. Layla agreed with this, and realized during Mia's diatribe that day that she, too, had a strange, subconscious feeling about Wednesdays.

When Layla pictured the week, it was a bar graph with seven bars on it. Saturday and Sunday were similar in height: both mid-sized. Then Monday was a bit shorter, matching Friday in size. Tuesday and Thursday also matched, but were a bit taller. And, in the middle of the school week, Wednesday stood as the tallest bar. Wednesday was taller than all the others. She wasn't sure why she pictured it this way. It was similar to the way she always imagined the number five being red and male, while the number two was yellow and female. Brains are silly, fascinating things, she thought.

Fridays, Mia said, were exhausting but quick days. At Burroughs, math teachers tended to test on Fridays. But by the time Friday came around, people were only talking about the weekend ahead. Fridays were easy to get through because you almost never had to really look them in the eye.

Thursdays were the real deal, she said. No one was going to be tossing any bones on a Thursday. Thursdays were the days that you were nearly completely drained of all energy, yet still expected to perform at your best because the day offered no excuse for error. Mia had thought a lot about this, and Layla wasn't about to question it. Plus, for the past three Thursdays, this had meant that they drank coffee together on the long benches in the lobby between second period and third period. Layla really liked this new tradition.

Since becoming "friends" (were they officially friends now?) in calculus, Layla and Mia had realized that they also shared their third period film studies class with Mrs. Cooney. The two girls walked to class together to find the projector set up in the center of the room. Layla remembered that Mrs. Cooney had said the day before that they would be watching and discussing the Hal Ashby film *Harold and Maude* over the next two class periods. This meant that they might be able to get away with passing a few notes back and forth during class, since Mia now sat directly in front of Layla in this class as well.

Layla was getting into the movie. This guy was obsessed with death in a very peculiar way; it made her feel uncomfortable. But Maude, the woman in the movie, was the exact opposite. She was ecstatic about life and sensationalized every moment. She probably could have spent hours talking about how pretty a leaf was! This lady was something else.

Pretty quickly, as Layla predicted, Mia reached her hands back as if to tidy up her signature black plait and dropped a small folded piece of paper on Layla's desk.

Psst. I heard something altogether fascinating yesterday. It has to do with John Francis.

John Francis was the nickname that Mia and Layla had established for Caleb. It made no sense at all, but they couldn't just go around talking or writing about Caleb using his given name, so Mia came up with this alternative. Layla got great joy out of the whole thing. She had put Caleb mostly out of her mind over the past two weeks or so, and so too his family history. Gavin hadn't had any more details to give Layla about Julia. She was glad he hadn't, because her mind had been on other things (her father, namely). Furthermore, it always complicated things to have Gavin talking to her consistently, so it was okay that he wasn't. She took her pen out and wrote in her smallest writing so she wouldn't fill the remaining space underneath Mia's sentence.

Fascinate me.

She placed it on the top of her desk and, with the same motion, tapped Mia gently. Five minutes or so later, when Mrs. Cooney looked sufficiently preoccupied, a response was returned to her.

Krista told me she heard Mrs. Chamberlain is "suggesting" to the crew's parents that the whole crew get tutors for the midterm.

Layla knew Krista was good for this kind of information. She was a good friend of Mia's (Mia seemed to have many good friends in various different social groups, which, truthfully, sort of made Layla a little bit jealous) and seemed to always know what was going on in everyone's lives. Layla knew that this "crew" was Caleb's group of bros who all sat together in calc and seemed to float together through the hallways to all of their classes and everywhere else. She almost never saw Caleb without several of these boys hanging around him. Layla replied:

That's good. It doesn't seem like they're doing that well in the class.

This note had a faster turnaround since Mrs. Cooney was now fully into the television screen.

So are you going to take the ring to Mordor? Or do you not know the way?

Layla grinned. Mia was always making *Lord of the Rings* references, which was hilarious in a totally nerdy, private-school sort of way. This was Mia's way of asking if Layla was going to volunteer herself for the tutoring position. Which of course was absolutely absurd, given that Layla had never even spoken to Caleb. And that she couldn't even think of a situation in which they *would* ever speak to one another. And that Layla had only recently really gotten a handle on her own calculus work and therefore definitely wouldn't be the best candidate for a calc tutor. And on and on. She took her pen to the page again.

I can't carry the ring to Mordor, but I can carry you.

It came back.

I have a lot of money on Chamberlain asking you to do it since you have the best grade in the class, I'm sure of it. Just be ready, is all I'm saying.

Layla's heart jumped a little to read this. She had worked hard and it was possible that she had one of the top grades in calc, but certainly not the best. It couldn't be, could it? She was working hard... She felt like she was swamped most nights, working out on her porch while her mother did lesson plans until 9 or 10 every night. And still she never quite felt comfortable in class. But, she supposed, she had gotten 9's and 10's on every homework assignment and even an 11 one time for solving an extra credit problem that had taken up much of her Sunday. She felt proud to know her hard work was paying off.

When Layla arrived to Mrs. Chamberlain's class, she was called up to the front of the room.

"Ms. Whitaker," the teacher began. "I wanted to congratulate you on your performance in my course so far."

"Oh, thank you." Layla reddened and stared down at the top of Mrs. Chamberlain's desk as if fixated on the wood grain.

"Certainly the course will grow more difficult as time goes on," Mrs. Chamberlain continued. "But I predict you will be able to stand up to the challenge."

Layla offered a small smile and brushed her hair behind her ear. Her eyes darted to Mia, who looked on intensely from the back of the room.

"And so I wanted to ask if you would be interested in tutoring a few of your classmates in the math center on Fridays

70

after school."

Mia's prediction was coming true.

Layla felt an ache in her stomach suddenly. She wanted to tutor, and she knew it would look great on college applications, but since she knew exactly which students required a tutor she was nervous and panicked.

She had stopped in the math center once on her first day as part of her tour with Ms. Galston, so she knew the basic setup. There was a big main area with desks for students to study independently or work on projects in groups. Along the back wall, there were desks where the tutors sat. On the desks, the tutors had their class proficiency written on a card in front of them. This way, you knew who to go to for which subjects. Students could approach the tutors with questions that would then be discussed one-on-one. If one tutor didn't feel they had the experience to solve a problem, they'd pass that student along to a higher-level tutor. The process was rather efficient—and actually wildly exciting in Layla's mind. She would have loved to participate in such a joyful afternoon. That is, before she knew that Caleb would be there and that she would likely have to actually speak to him. Though she was desperate to talk to him, she was nowhere near ready to. Like Emily Dickinson, Layla dwelled in possibility. She was just now realizing how far in possibility.

And now, with the chance to make that possibility into a reality, she was struck still and growing cold. Because this reality was so far outside of her comfort zone that she felt herself looking back at it as she waved goodbye.

What was there to be afraid of, though, really? Layla had guy friends. Even with the awkwardness of their fling, Layla could talk to Gavin for hours about anything at all these days. But Caleb was a different type of character.

She stood there, staring at Mrs. Chamberlain for what she now noticed was far too long. She knew she had to say yes to this—it was too good an opportunity to pass up.

Layla straightened her oxford shirt, plastered a smile

across her face, said "I would be honored to, thank you for the recommendation," grabbed the packet that Mrs. Chamberlain extended to her, and spun around.

Layla felt Mia's grin follow her back to her seat.

CHAPTER EIGHT

Layla opened the door to the JBC to hear Radiohead's "Reckoner" flowing through the chatter and movement. She knew that meant Gavin was at the helm of both sound and beverages for the evening.

"Hello, dear friend!" she called to him, waving, as she passed the counter to meet her mom at their usual table.

Gavin grinned and saluted her while bopping his head to the music.

Layla took a seat, removing her mother's head from a very concentrated typing of lesson plans.

"Hello there, darling," she said, smiling. "How was your day?"

"Great," Layla replied.

"Shall we head home?" her mother asked.

"Sure," Layla responded. "Could I grab a coffee first?"

"Certainly!" Layla's mother grabbed a few dollars from her purse and passed them across the table.

Layla approached the counter and asked Gavin for a small coffee.

"And could you make it quick?" She laughed a little. "Because you know I can't get through 'Videotape' without crying."

Last winter Gavin had played the Radiohead album *In Rainbows* for her in full through shared earbuds on the walk from the JBC to her house one night. It was the first time she had ever heard the album. When the last song, "Videotape," ended, she burst into tears and determined it was the most perfect song that had ever been written. She meant this, and maintained this claim to this day. It was *the* song. But she hardly ever listened to it around anyone else because it made her very emotional.

"I remember." He smiled. He closed the lid on her coffee cup, popped it into a sleeve, and passed it across the counter.

Layla nodded, pleased to hear that he remembered that night as well. The part she remembered most about that night was what had happened next: when Gavin had caught Layla's tears with a firm kiss. The first kiss they ever shared, and, it should be noted, the first kiss Layla had ever shared with anyone. It was funny how time had transformed all that into a memory.

Layla followed her mother out into the late-afternoon light.

"I thought about what you said about Dad this morning," Layla said suddenly, surprising herself with her own boldness on the subject. "I mean about Dad knowing so much about people, as if he seemed to know what they were thinking."

"Yes," her mother replied. She, too, seemed more comfortable with the conversation now than she had been this morning. "It's true: you both have this grasp of people... I can't quite put my finger on it."

"Well, I wanted to ask you..." Layla continued. "Did you ever notice that type of thing in his writing? I mean, did he ever write things about you that you hadn't ever told him before?"

Layla's mother's eyes widened at the question.

"He did," she said in a quieter voice now, nodding. "Anything he wrote about anyone was like that. It was completely brilliant."

Layla watched her shoes crunch the leaves under her feet, hoping her mother would expand on this.

"I know we've read so many of his poems together," her mother continued after a while. "But I suppose I didn't always think you were old enough to understand how much truth there was in them. Most of his writing, in fact… his characters… they were mostly based on real people."

Layla sipped slowly as she walked. She had always assumed that most of the people in her father's poems were made up, or altered in some way. Her mother always told Layla that the family didn't go out into town much—or really see people outside of the family at all. So it didn't make sense that the characters could be based on real people.

"But I don't understand," Layla said, looking over at her mother. "You said that you and Dad hardly spent time with anyone outside of family."

Layla's mother looked down and began shaking her head.

"No, that was after everything…" her mother muttered.

She stopped herself. Then she caught Layla's expectant gaze and exhaled deeply.

"It was different in the later years," Layla's mother continued.

Layla noted a stark difference in her mother's tone. This was upsetting her.

"I'm sorry," Layla said, suddenly. "I shouldn't have asked about all this."

"No, no," her mother replied. "I shouldn't have not told you about all this."

Her mother stared into her eyes intensely for a moment. A silence fell over the pair as they continued walking.

After a few minutes, Layla noticed that her mother's face was no longer pale and still. There was a warm glow rising in her eyes. She finally said something Layla truly hadn't seen coming.

"Let's read them."

Her mother's face filled with joy, as if she was about to take her daughter home to a surprise birthday party.

"Absolutely!" Layla responded with equal excitement, hurrying them along down the street toward home.

Her father's study—or, as she occasionally referred to it when she feared someone might follow up with perplexed looks or nagging questions about dead fathers, "the study"—was a warm room with golden light that floated through it and onto its four walls of tall bookcases filled with books. On top of the bookcases, her father's collection of records wrapped around the room similarly. In the space between the two bookcases on the far wall was a large window with a built-in window seat and gold cushion inside. Above the white trim around the top of the window, Layla's mother had hung a frame in which she had written a quote from her late husband's favorite poet, William Wordsworth, in beautiful calligraphy: *Poetry is the spontaneous overflow of powerful feelings: it takes its origin from emotion recollected in tranquility.* It was the perfect space for Layla and her mother to sit and read her father's books.

In the middle of the room was the long pine desk that her father used to write at, just as he had left it: with nothing on it and a white antique Windsor dining chair pushed into it. Layla couldn't recall a time when her father had had books or papers on his desk aside from the ones he was working with in that moment. He was a minimalist in life—always focused on one task at a time instead of dabbling in many interests at once—and the state of that desk mirrored this.

The study was, of course, not truly her father's study, because her father had died while they were still living in Mansfield many years ago. But she and her mother had worked to set this room up as an exact replica of his old study, and both felt it achieved the essence of the original quite well. The only difference was that this new study had an additional white antique Windsor dining chair pushed under the opposite side of the pine desk. This was so that Layla and her mother could occasionally sit there together.

Layla's mother hopped over to the shelf on the far-right corner of the room. This shelf was packed with the forty-two books of poetry Layla's father had published in his lifetime. They were alphabetized by title with varying heights, widths, and binding colors. They were a perfect meadow of different flowers, all of which Layla had picked and smelled before. But Layla knew that books of poetry—especially those written by her father, in her opinion anyway—held a new gift each time they were read. A poem could be read at any time and be found to hold a unique meaning for someone, or to fill a unique spot in their heart. So although she had read each book several times, she was always interested to read them again.

In a way, reading her father's books felt to Layla like having an ongoing conversation with the man himself. She would sit down with a book of her father's whenever she needed some time to think, to calm down, or to collect herself. It was what she imagined most of her friends and classmates were able to do on a daily basis with their living fathers. But for her, it felt all the more magical.

"A-ha!" her mother yelped and pulled a book from the shelf. She brought it over to the desk, where Layla sat now, excited as ever.

Layla watched her mother lay the book *Where Shadows Climb Trees I Take Shelter* down on her father's desk and open it up before them. Her mother skimmed the pages before her intensely, her eyes growing wider and wider.

"This. This is the one," her mother said. "I know something in here came to mind the other day when we talked. Hmm…."

After a while, Layla's mother stopped on a page and grinned wildly. She spun the book around on the desk so that Layla could see it.

Layla looked down at the poem on the page. The poem was short and only took up a single page. She recognized the title and knew she had read it before, though the only detail she could remember at the moment was that it took place in a dusty old café much like the JBC. She stared at it for a moment and then began to read the poem aloud, filling the room with her father's words.

The Truth Writer

There were days, when young, I thought
A special gift of mine, just that
- Golden twine tied 'round
Blue-and-white wrapping -
To be torn open with glee.

The way friends of mine played piano
Or did multiplication tables by memory,
Or jumped fences without bruising their ankles,
I would write words on a page about other people
As if I'd stolen them without asking.

I grew old and sat in dusty cafés and knew
Everything someone there needed to say, but couldn't,
Everything their life needed to write, but didn't
Dancing here on a blank page.

When my hands tingled in your presence,
Warm all-over I would write it for you.

They called me Truth Writer.
A name that made me sigh
When your truth became mine.
I would cover my hands in gloves
And slam the book shut

Instead dark the dawn of responsibility fell
Because truth is responsibility.
Truth is a burden I could not bear.

Layla swallowed hard. She thought about all the times she
had read this particular poem. Certainly it had to be about five
times at least. But up until now, Layla hadn't realized that this

poem was about more than just meeting new people at a café. It also hadn't occurred to her that this poem might be more than a metaphor for the writing process. Now, it seemed like this poem was about the speaker's unique ability to write *for other people*. Not only that, but the words used to describe it all—the warm feeling, the hands tingling—perfectly matched the feelings she had had when she was typing the thoughts of Principal Strauss and her mother. Everything she had been replaying over and over again in her mind had happened exactly the way her father had described in his poem.

Layla looked up to see her mother sitting at the desk in her signature deep-thought stance: one arm bent on the table and the other on top of the first with her hand holding her chin up between her finger and thumb. She was staring at the far corner of the room behind Layla, as if completely lost in the poem she had just heard.

"Wow," she said a few minutes later, moving her hand down from her face and widening her eyes to their widest and then some. She nodded slowly.

"I mean, I don't know if it *is* him, necessarily. No one called him 'Truth Writer,' certainly. But the idea of him being able to write in that way—to so perfectly speak for his characters and be keyed into the intricacies of their thoughts and feelings—that was him, Layla. That was exactly who he was."

Layla nodded.

"I see what you mean," she muttered. In a way she already knew this, but in a way she had just learned all of it at the same time. She wanted to read this poem again, and a few of the others, to see if there might be more similarities between what she had been experiencing lately and her father's words on the page.

Her mother stood up suddenly, as if jolted by her own thoughts.

"There is something that I haven't ever shown you!" she exclaimed. "Well, many things."

Layla's eyes widened. She had read all of her father's poetry before, listened to his records, and read his personal favorite literary books. She had basically known her father through these things for years. What more could there be that she didn't know about?

"What do you mean?" she asked, intensely interested.

Her mother left the room quickly and Layla raced out behind her. She followed her mother to her mother's bedroom and watched her kneel down next to her bed and open the top drawer of her bedside table.

In the drawer were a few of her mother's lesson plan notebooks from this year and past years, stacked one on top of the other with a few pens laying on either side. She removed these notebooks quickly. Underneath them sat three or four other small black Moleskine notebooks without labels. Layla had never seen these notebooks and they didn't look at all familiar to her.

"I never told you about this," her mother began. "Because I didn't think it was imperative and I felt they were your father's private things. But since we were talking about your father's—and your own—unique ability to read people, I think it's time to show you these."

Layla's heart nearly stopped beating as her mother passed these four notebooks into her daughter's hands.

Layla opened the top one up to find page after page filled completely, from top to bottom, with writing. Some pages were filled with well-written sentences, placed neatly on the page in perfect handwriting. Other pages were scribbled on erratically, with words floating over the lines or cutting across them altogether in a drunken mess. Even the handwriting on these pages varied, as if the books had been written in by four or five different people over time.

The sentiments on each page were mostly garbled and incomprehensible, sometimes completely lacking a subject.

My mother is never home, and my big brother can't afford to get lunch most days, read a line on one of the pages. *I'm not the best doctor in the world, but I sure did cut into the woman and remove the baby when it was time to do so*, read another.

One page simply read in big, capital letters, *MY DREAM*

IS TO FLY.

"What... are these?" Layla ejected. She was so confused, because her father didn't have a big brother, nor was he a doctor, nor was he dying to learn how to fly. At least she didn't think so. She was completely thrown off by what she was holding. She took a seat on the bed as if to settle into this new mystery.

Her mother took the seat next to her quickly, and looked on as Layla flipped through the pages. The two took in one fascinating blurb of text after another.

"I know..." her mother began. "It's hard to explain. And sometimes I can't really understand, myself. These poems, if you can call them that, are almost like gibberish."

"But did he really write this? All of it? It's all different, from one page to the next. It doesn't make any—"

"He really did. He took these notebooks when he went out writing during the day, and at the end of the night, he would put them back in our nightstand. He kept them all here because he wanted them to be safe."

"I can't believe..." Layla trailed off, confused by all of this.

Her mother stayed quiet a moment and then sighed deeply, seemingly sensing her daughter's concern.

"I should have told you, Layla. I should have shown them to you. But..."

Layla stood up suddenly, staring down at her mother now and turning a deep red. She didn't like when her mother kept things from her, because it messed with the entire foundation of their arrangement of being both mother-and-daughter and best friends.

"But what?! What reason do you have for withholding any part of my father from me?" Layla shouted.

Her mother stood up next to her and grabbed Layla's hand.

"Layla, I'm so sorry!" she pleaded. "I know it's your right to know your father and I shouldn't have kept these writings from you. But honestly, the reason I didn't show them to you, is because"—Layla's mother trailed off for a moment, and sat back down on the bed. She looked down at the notebooks and traced the golden stitching on one of them as she continued— "Is because I don't think he wanted anyone, even me, to read them."

Layla sat back down on the bed and sighed deeply. She leaned her head on her mother's shoulder apologetically.

"He never showed these particular notebooks to anyone. I knew these were the notebooks he took out to do his thinking and writing at the café or the library—in the beginning, at least—so I always wanted to see what he came back with, but he wouldn't have it. There were a few times when I would come in and peek over his shoulder as he wrote in one of them, like I did with drafts of his poems or letters. But before I had the chance to read any of it, he would slam it shut. I almost never saw these notebooks open, to be honest. I always thought it might be because he didn't want me to see his process, and maybe that's what it was… But it felt strange to show them to you when I didn't even feel comfortable reading them myself."

"I'm sorry, Mom," Layla whispered. "I'm sure there was a reason he kept this from you."

"It's fine, my sweet," her mother replied. "But I want you to know about it now. I want you to see how your father could write as if he were writing *for* other people, and not himself. But I also want you to see that this… all of this, the way your father wrote these amazing, intuitive things... the way he knew what other people were thinking, in a way…"

Her mother trailed off.

"Yes?" Layla asked, expectantly.

"It wasn't exactly good for him," her mother said, solemnly.

Layla froze. She turned to look her mother in the eye now. Her mother was in tears.

"What do you mean?" Layla asked.

"Well, there came a time… when he stopped taking them out of the nightstand. He stopped going to cafés and libraries and park benches. He stopped wanting to see other people altogether.

He was overwhelmed and terrified to be in crowded places, and he never brought his notebooks with him anymore to observe. Instead, he tapped his foot impatiently anytime we had to enter a public place. He begged to skip family parties over the holidays. The only people he really ever wanted to be around were you and me.

"He loved us so much, Layla," her mother continued, in a whisper. "But the notebooks... and his almost... *fear* of people... it was hard on him. And it was hard on our marriage."

Layla nodded silently, remembering the words she had typed for her mother the other day. She and her mother sat on the bed silently for what felt like ages. Finally, her mother stood up, returned the notebooks to their drawer, and closed the drawer quietly. She picked up *Where Shadows Climb Trees I Take Shelter* and held it close to her chest. Then she grabbed her daughter's hand and helped her up, and the two of them went down the stairs for dinner.

Layla returned to her room after dinner and set out her homework on her desk. She had brought the book of poems back up with her, though she wasn't exactly sure why. Layla grabbed it from where it lay on the stool next to her bed and opened it up to the poem she had read earlier that evening, *The Truth Writer*. She took out a pen and began to copy it down word-for-word onto a piece of copy paper from her printer, paying special attention to punctuation and line breaks.

As she wrote, Layla recalled the garbled notes her father had scribbled in his secret notebooks. Those writings had to be a result of the same magic she had experienced in Principal Strauss's office, and again in her kitchen the other night. More than that, it had to be the very same truth-writing her father spoke of in this poem. She felt a little safer knowing that it wasn't just her, and powerful knowing she was linked to her beloved father in such a profound way.

But before she reached the end of the poem, she remembered her mother's pained, glazed eyes when she told Layla that her husband had kept these things a secret from her.

Why had her father chosen to do all of this writing alone? And why had he closed his notebooks anytime his wife had entered the room?

Layla finished copying down the poem and added it to her bulletin board, next to the picture of the Strauss family. She leaned back in her chair, folded her hands, and rested them on the desk.

Somehow, *The Truth Writer* meant the world to her. And before this evening, she felt almost nothing about the poem. It was funny how words on a page could transform your life in an instant.

CHAPTER NINE

Layla sat on what had now become unofficially *her* bench in the Burroughs front lobby the next morning, drinking her coffee slowly and thoughtfully. She was still shaken by the events of the night before.

The change in Layla's perspective on her blogging was a significant one. Learning that her father had the same magical writing powers as she did—or at least as she had experienced twice before—made her feel a profound connection to him. Initially, sitting down to write and having other people's thoughts and feelings pour onto the screen had been terrifying. But knowing now that her father had been there, too, made it feel safe. Furthermore, Layla felt a sense of honor in that she had inherited this special gift. It was almost like a legacy she never knew she was a part of. That's why, for the first time, Layla found herself wishing she could truth-write again.

Layla opened her laptop and pulled up her Blogiophile dashboard. She sat for a moment, staring straight ahead as students passed by on the way to their lockers.

After a few minutes, Layla looked back at the screen again. Nothing.

Layla exhaled heavily and resituated herself on the bench. She took a few sips of coffee, centered herself, and then put her fingers to the keyboard again.

A few minutes went by. She looked around the lobby and watched a few members of the dance team practice a portion of their choreography together. Then she looked back at the screen. Again, nothing.

Maybe if I focus really hard on one thing, she thought.

Layla looked across the lobby and spotted Amanda Jennings sitting between her two best friends, Nadine and Lindsey, on the long step next to the window. The three girls didn't appear to be looking at each other or communicating at all. Instead, Nadine looked down at her phone, Lindsey scribbled in her notebook as if frantically finishing an assignment, and Amanda just sort of watched the world pass before her eyes. Her face was stern, obviously judging everyone who wasn't in her group of friends.

Layla would have loved to be able to write what Amanda was thinking in this moment. What did the matriarch of Burroughs think about all of her classmates? What nasty details did she know about their personal lives? Or maybe, she would have something to say about her bae, Caleb Strauss.

Layla stared intensely at every detail of Amanda's face, as if preparing to paint it. She traced the follicles of Amanda's perfectly microbladed brows and admired the exquisite wingtips of her eyeliner. Her gorgeous cheekbones shimmered in the light that fell through the window next to her. She was sipping from her glass water bottle. Her soft pink lips were small but plump and powerful on her face. Layla stared so hard, hoping so desperately that she might feel the familiar tingle in her arms that she almost put it there herself. *Come on, come on.*

"Come on!" she uttered audibly, startling herself out of her gaze suddenly.

She looked around to make sure that no one had heard her and noticed a shadow on her arm. She turned around to see the figure of her mother standing behind her.

"Wha…?" Layla stammered.

"Um, are you okay?" her mother asked. She had obviously been standing behind Layla long enough to notice her daughter's sudden outburst.

"Uhhh," Layla muttered and faked a smile. "I was just, uh… getting frustrated with this math problem." She looked down at her laptop now, and quickly switched to another tab filled with Google search results about sine and cosine.

Layla's mother smiled and shifted her eyes for a moment. Her face scrunched up, somewhat perplexed.

"Okay…" she said, and took a seat next to her daughter on the bench. "Whatever you say…"

Layla's mother smiled again, and wrapped her arm around her daughter.

"You forgot your lunch!" she said, holding up a little cloth tote that she often packed Layla's lunch in. It was cream-colored, and somewhat tattered by years of use as a school lunch carrier, but it was adorned with a few little pink flowers that her mother had embroidered by hand.

"Wow, thanks, Mom," Layla said, smiling. She took her lunch out of her mother's hand and tried to compose herself. Or at least to appear composed. Maybe her mother hadn't noticed Layla watching Amanda from afar. But who cares if she had? Layla could have just been observing the way writers so often do. Her mother knew that Layla had a major girl crush on Saoirse Ronan, so maybe this was just another girl Layla was into at the moment. Sexuality is so fluid—it's 2021, for goodness' sake.

Layla tucked her stack of books under her arm and stood up now, pulling her hair over her right shoulder casually.

"I should get to class," she said, looking down at the time on her phone. "Something about birds and worms, I don't know." Layla laughed nervously.

Her mother grinned. "I'll see you at the JBC after tutoring?"

"Yep. I'll be there," Layla responded. As she turned around and walked down the opposite hallway to her locker, her smile slipped and she gritted her teeth. She was terrified that her mother would wonder what had just happened and would have more questions later.

Layla wasn't ready to tell her mother about truth-writing. She couldn't think of anything she hadn't been able to tell her mother over the years, but this particular thing was... complicated. Layla tried to imagine how that conversation would go, and when she got to first period she jotted out a potential script as other students wandered in.

L: Hey, so, you know how Dad wrote all those poems that were so amazingly accurate about so many different people?

M: Yeah.

L: And you know how he kept those other notebooks with detailed notes about people which read almost like those people had written them themselves?

M: Yes.

L: So yeah, that's a thing called truth-writing, and it's actually a special power he had.

M: No way!

L: Yes way! Oh, and by the way, I have that power too. Though I don't quite know how, why, or when it happens. Or how to make it happen. Or how to make it stop happening, for that matter.

M: Nice! [high fives Layla]

END SCENE

Layla laughed to herself. Nothing about this imaginary scene seemed probable, but it was nice to see it written out on the page. Words on the page seemed easier than real life these days.

The Burroughs High math center was a dismal place. Its vacancy at 3:27 caused Layla to recheck the sign on the door as she entered to be sure it opened at 3:30. One of the seven long desks in the back of the room had a name plate on it that read:

Layla Whitaker
Sophomore
Geo, Alg, Pre-Calc, Calc

She took a seat at that desk and hoped desperately that someone else would come in soon. Sure enough, a few minutes later, two students skulked in through the door and took the first two desks in the main area. They put their backpacks on their desks, unzipped them, and removed their necessary books, notebooks, and folders unbearably slowly. It was like watching honey drip off the side of a kitchen table.

The room was dimly lit and somehow took on every single shade of blue at once. The desks, the carpet, the curtains, and the walls all held different aspects of the hue, together making a full Pantone color palette.

Layla really didn't like the color blue, honestly. Blue was the kind of color that was easy to love. So often, if you asked someone their favorite color, they would say "blue" and smile at you, because no one could ever be offended by the color blue. Blue was, by degrees, the safest choice of all the colors. Conversationally, it was a gateway drug to other extremely safe topics, like the weather, college plans, or—heaven forbid—exchanged wishes to "have a great summer."

Furthermore, blue was the color with the most distinct shades: from navy blue, to baby blue, to teal, to royal blue, to powder blue, to dark blue, to sapphire, and on and on. In this someone's head, they could be picturing any of these species of blue when they said "blue" aloud to you. But to say only the genus was to lay the first of likely many bricks of the wall that would stand around them and require your best militia to break down. "Blue" was what you said when you didn't want someone to really know you at all.

Fifteen minutes or so passed with a few more students filing in, some sitting in the tutors section and some in the main area. No one approached Layla during these minutes, but she did recognize one girl who entered shortly after. Kelly Battins was a shorter girl with dark hair and a sort of sad face. She took out her calculus book and flipped through it on the desk, so Layla knew this would likely be her first customer.

Kelly took a seat across from Layla around 4:15, at which point Layla had already made quite a dent in her chemistry homework.

"Hey," Kelly said, catching Layla's eye and smiling.

"Hey," Layla replied, pushing her books aside.

"You're in my class, right?" Kelly asked.

"Yeah," said Layla.

"So you must be pretty smart then," said Kelly.

Layla laughed nervously.

"No," she said, "I just did pretty well on the last exam and Mrs. Chamberlain said I could help out here if I wanted to. Just figured I'd get my homework out of the way and use it on college apps."

Layla hadn't thought until this very moment how strange it might be to be tutoring her own classmates. She suddenly felt very aware of how arrogant it must seem to her friends that she took the tutoring position in the first place. To sit before your fellow classmates and inadvertently brag about how you know the material better than them... yeesh! Layla suddenly really wanted to go home, and would maybe have up and left if Kelly hadn't still been sitting right in front of her. She shrugged that self-deprecating shrug that she had performed time and time again.

"Oh, sure," said Kelly. "I get that."

"Yeah," Layla continued. "It's really no big deal."

"So I was just wondering..." Kelly swung her book

around so Layla could see the problem she was working on. "How do we know this one is $y' = 3x^2 + 4x + 4$?"

Layla looked down at the page. The problem was one she had seen before, where they gave you a y-function and then you had to find the derivative at a specific point of x=2. She noticed that Kelly had gotten stumped on the first part of the problem, which was finding the derivative itself.

"Yeah, that's a tough one," Layla said. "Can I see your work for this one so far?"

Kelly passed her notebook over to Layla, who matched up the problem number from the book to the notebook page. Kelly had derived most of the function correctly, but had messed up the derivative of x^3.

"Well, it looks like you've got everything right except for this x cubed," Layla began. "So in order to derive x cubed, we just bring the 3 down to the front and subtract 1 from the exponential value."

"Ohhhh," Kelly said. She leaned over her notebook and did what Layla said. "Okay. Is this right?"

Layla looked over to see that Kelly now had before her a correctly derived function.

"Perfect," she said, smiling. "Now you just have to do the second part of the problem."

"Oh," Kelly said, sadly. "I didn't know there was more."

Kelly read the problem again and started working on it again.

Layla smiled to herself, pleased by how smoothly things had gone so far. Of course, she had only really had to help one person with one problem. But still, it felt like a huge victory. She felt more confident now about being there in the first place. That is, until she saw the tall and lean figure of the most beautiful boy in the universe out of the corner of her eye.

Caleb Strauss walked in alone, which was the first time he had ever been that way in her sight. He had always been with his crew, so it was strange to see him by himself. Layla knew it would be noticeable if she were to look directly at him, but she desperately wanted to.

As Kelly packed up her things and got up to leave, Layla pleaded with her periphery to gather as many details as humanly possible about Caleb. *Focus, focus, focus…*

At the very least, Layla was able to track Caleb's location, which meant that, as he approached her desk, she felt him like the humidity before a rainstorm. But if that rainstorm were the only water she had seen in weeks.

"Your parents Clapton fans?" he asked, standing before her now. What a storm it was: his voice was dense and cold. Every drop of sound from him stung her as it landed on her skin. It all sent chills, like water on the scalp where your hair parts.

"I… ummm… I…" she ejected, nervously. "My dad… he loves Clapton. I mean… loved. He loved Clapton. Clapton was actually his favorite American artist… He was English. English, as in, from England. He was from England and now he is… passed. But he was really into… Clapton. Eric… Clapton."

Caleb held her gaze now, taking her breath away for a moment. She forced herself to calm down and focus on her job.

"I'm sorry to hear about your dad," Caleb cocked his head and replied now, never once looking away. Layla realized then that she had sort of made the conversation awkward by bringing up her dad being dead, which she really hadn't intended to do. She felt embarrassed and looked down at her books.

"Thanks," she said, flipping through the pages as if she were looking for something specific. *Focus, focus, focus.* "Did you have a question about the exam?"

Caleb took the empty seat across from Layla, and she tried not to panic.

"How much time do you have?" he said, chuckling slightly.

Layla had only heard him say a handful of words before, and usually it was just a *hey* or *what up* in passing to one of his friends. Overall, this probably totaled about eight words over the past two months of them being in the same class. And here he had just beat that record for her in two minutes.

It wasn't just the quantity of words that shocked her; the manner in which he spoke was completely astonishing. He was gentle and kind and clever and thoughtful. He was speaking to her and about her and listening to the words she said back to him. This was not at all the way she thought a conversation with Caleb Strauss would go, and she was pleasantly surprised by it.

Layla had heard people use an expression before, *hanging on your every word*. She had never understood what that meant because, of course, words were just entry points to conversation. She felt words were segues into something bigger: the communication of the topic at hand. For Layla, it was more about the ideas behind the words.

But in this moment, though, his words were overwhelming and new to her, and she felt the urge to keep every one of them. It was as if she were reaching out to grab them. She could almost feel herself holding them still so they wouldn't be gone too soon.

"Well, there's this one portion in particular," Caleb began again. He was scouring over the paper on the desk now. "Do you think you could help me with it?"

Caleb's eyes rose to meet hers now. They were unbelievably blue and stunningly beautiful. She almost choked as she tried to get out a response.

"It would be my great pleasure," Layla replied, smiling slightly as she tried not to look too deeply into his eyes. As quickly as she let the words out, she realized just how strange they sounded and wished she had choked after all.

"Did you just say it would be your great pleasure?" Caleb asked, chucking a little and cocking his head to the side again. Layla was mortified. What century was that response even from? Was this Shakespeare?

"I mean..." Layla started, stammering a little. She tried to act normal, and forced herself to shrug off the Shakespearean dialect she had just used for some odd reason. "I can help, sure."

Layla motioned toward the test in Caleb's hands. He tossed it over to her, leaning back in his chair as the paper fluttered down on Layla's side of the desk.

Caleb had gotten a C+ on the test, which explained his overall disappointment. Layla was sure that having a father who was the principal did not make coming home with C+'s a positive experience.

Oddly, though, the exam wasn't covered in red ink as she would have expected. She flipped through the pages to find that Caleb had answered almost every single question on the exam. Not only that, but these answers were partly-right, mostly-right, or very close to perfect. They were often just missing a term or a variable, or the answer was right but Caleb hadn't finished the problem by plugging in the value that the problem had indicated.

What was interesting about Caleb's test was that, for so many of the problems, Mrs. Chamberlain had circled the answers. Next to these circles, she had written in her signature all-caps writing, "HOW?"

"I don't understand," Layla whispered, perplexed.

"I guess I'm really behind with this stuff," Caleb replied, shrugging.

"No, I don't think that's what it is," said Layla, continuing to pour over the test. As she looked closely at the problems, she realized that, for every single one that he had gotten wrong in some—usually quite minor—way, he had shown almost no work. Caleb had written the problem out, and then he had written the answer he had come up with. But there were no steps between problem and answer. He had gotten everything right to some degree, but he had shown almost no work at all in getting there.

Layla looked up at Caleb, who was staring right at her. This shocked her at first, because his huge blue eyes were piercing. They were deep and full, painfully potent.

"What do you think it is?" Caleb asked, fixing his eyes somehow more closely onto her.

Layla stared back into them, letting them envelop her.

"I think you're just..." Layla tilted her head sideways. "You're just missing some steps."

"Alas, a lack," Caleb replied, smiling with his eyes. He

leaned back in his chair, wrapped his arms behind his head, and cradled it there.

"No, I just meant that you seem to have gotten the right answers—or very, very close to them—but Mrs. Chamberlain took off points because you didn't show your work."

"Yeah, I usually have an okay time getting an answer," Caleb said. "But I don't always know how to show how I got it."

"I mean, I'm not really sure I can help you much," said Layla. "Because it seems like all of the information you need is in your head, but it's just difficult for you to focus on putting it on the page."

"Well, I think you're right," he replied.

"Do you know how to do this one, for instance?" Layla turned the page before her around so Caleb could see it. There was a story problem on it that had three parts: the first involving writing out an equation, the second involving deriving it, and the final step being putting the numbers back into the equation.

"I thought I got that one," Caleb said. He put his finger on the page where he had written *(5,10)*. Isn't that right?"

"Yes," Layla said, looking up at him excitedly. "It's perfect! That's absolutely a point on the tangent line. But I don't understand how you got that."

"Well, I guess I just..." Caleb said, staring intently at the page. "I just took the derivative of the original equation to find the slope of the tangent line at that point. Then I used that and the point itself to make the new equation. And then I found another point on that same line."

"Absolutely!" she exclaimed. She caught herself, realizing how strange it would come off if she got too excited. "I mean, that's exactly it. But you didn't get points for all of those in-between steps you just described, because... Well, they're not there."

Caleb stared at her again for a moment, and then stared off at the back wall. He seemed distracted, and like he wasn't following. It was as if he had something else on his mind. He was so smart, but if he didn't do the work the proper way then there was no way Chamberlain was going to give him the A he deserved.

"I see what you mean," he said after a moment, nodding. "I'll try harder."

Layla felt that comment like a brick, and regretted what she had said to warrant it. She hadn't meant to make him feel bad.

"No, no!" she declared. "I wasn't trying to—"

"Don't worry about it. I'm used to hearing that. Explaining myself has always been a struggle of mine."

Caleb stood up and swung his backpack over his shoulder.

"Thank you, Layla," Caleb said, heading off toward the door.

As he walked away, Layla found herself wanting to call after him to say something. What, exactly, she didn't really know. She coughed faintly to herself, as if choking on whatever words wanted to come up. She pursed her lips together to seal them in even tighter and looked back down at her Chemistry homework.

She slumped in her chair a little, feeling a hint of sadness at Caleb's absence. Layla played his words over and over again in her head, trying to remember exactly what he had said and how he had said it. But so much of it was lost now, in the space between two blue chairs in a blue room.

Now Layla found herself wishing that those people who spoke of hanging on words had mentioned the part that comes next. That moment when those words could no longer hold your weight, and you fell.

CHAPTER TEN

Layla fell onto her bed that night—in prime dramatic-teen fashion—and swung her legs up after her. Her pillow felt softer than usual, more ready to catch her head. She scanned the wall to see her father's poem on the bulletin board. She read through it again, and she found she knew it better than she thought. For the last stanza, especially, she barely had to look at the page. It was funny to her how quickly a person's relationship with a text could turn on its axis. Just days ago, Layla had only read this poem in passing and thought almost nothing of it. There were so many other poems that had meant much, much more to her. But now, this poem was beginning to etch itself onto her heart.

As her eyes floated over the words, she started to feel sleepy. Her eyes blinked and fought to hold the words there.

Then her eyes lit up. They forced her head up off the pillow. She sat upright now on the bed, eyes piercing the page on the wall like knives.

Her eyes had landed on a line she had never really focused on before.

Warm all-over I would write it for you with blank page waiting.

She had thought this section of the poem spoke to the nature of truth-writing: the fact that the truth-writer did the writing for other people. But she had never noticed the second part of this line, *with blank page waiting.*

Layla thought back to the times she had done truth-writing before. In Principal Strauss's office, she had typed the words into a new post on Blogiophile. Her laptop had been lying open on her lap because she'd been about to write some of the details of her first day. But she hadn't typed anything yet.

The truth-writing about her mother happened in almost the same way. She had gone to start a new post on Blogiophile but had been hopping back and forth between tabs, so she hadn't actually started typing anything in the post yet.

Both posts had been blank.

"That's it!" she said, grabbing a notebook and jotting this down. She didn't want to jinx it, but it seemed like she had just discovered one of the rules of truth-writing, and she couldn't wait to go out and truth-write again! She looked down at her phone and saw that it was 9:48 pm.

Layla sighed a heavy sigh that woke Bart from his sleep on her bed. Layla's mother would already be getting ready for bed, and the JBC closed down in just 12 short minutes—less time than it would take her to walk there. So she couldn't find someone to write about tonight.

Layla settled herself back into her bed and smiled, knowing that she had so much to look forward to now. This was turning out to be a perfectly perfect day, and it did that thing that perfectly perfect days do best: it gave her hope for an even better tomorrow.

Layla had spent the weekend pondering who she wanted to write for next. First, she thought of her mother, of course. But after reflecting on all of the new information she had gleaned from her mother last week and how overwhelming it had been for both of them, she decided not to try that. Then she thought about Gavin. That would be an easy way to experiment with truth-writing. But unfortunately, Gavin was up north with his family for the weekend to visit his grandma.

As Layla moved through her Monday, things kept piling up with her school work. Mr. Fox had planned to have a period entirely on the last four chapters of Moby Dick, but he'd forgotten that the following Monday was records day. So instead, he rushed through the last four chapters and started introducing Hemingway's short stories. Then Mr. Morrisson had a fit about everyone falling behind on their chemistry homework. Finally, Ms. Krempa had just announced a piano recital in October, and Layla couldn't grasp the bass clef to save her life. Layla was exhausted by the time she fell into her seat in calculus class. She had forgotten altogether about truth-writing.

Layla felt someone come up beside her as she loaded up her backpack after class. Assuming it was Mia waiting for her so they could walk out together, Layla said "hey" and lifted her head casually. It was not Mia.

Caleb Strauss looked down at her with his massive blue eyes and his curtain of dark hair. Layla froze.

She brushed her hair behind her ears and forced an "Oh, hi."

"Layla," Caleb began, a chorus of angels seemingly following close behind. "I'm sorry to bother you."

"No," Layla replied. "I'm just… getting some things organized."

"Well, I realized I kind of hopped out of tutoring early on Friday, and it was my last chance to get help before the exam this Friday."

Students filed out around them as Layla stared up at him and focused on forming a smile.

"And I have so many problems with this… Well, this entire page." Caleb showed her his book, already opened to the section on the chain rule.

SWIPE UP FOR SECRETS

Layla was overwhelmed. She looked down at the page.

"O...okay," she spoke, composing herself more and more every minute. "I just…"

She noticed Mia, staring back at her, wide-eyed as she walked out the door. Mia mouthed "Oh my god."

"I was thinking, if you have a second after school, maybe I could…" Caleb's eyes softened and his head bent to the side. "I'm sure you're super busy, but I could really use someone to just check this over and make sure I did it right."

He unfolded a pile of loose-leaf paper with his homework assignment on it.

"Yeah, definitely," Layla said. "I mean, I have to wait for my ride anyway. I can just meet you in the library if you want."

"Great," Caleb said and offered the only full-length grin she had ever seen on him. It was bright and warm. It was strong and bold. It was altogether remarkable.

Layla walked out of the room to find Mia waiting, still picking her jaw up off the floor.

"Oh. My. God." Mia ran up to Layla and immediately hugged her.

Layla realized that Mia had never hugged her before, and this made her very happy. *This must be one of those very special bonding moments*, she thought, archiving it quickly before it ended.

"What did he say to you? Tell me everything!" Mia practically squealed.

"He asked me to tutor him—or I guess help him—after school. Today!"

The girls smiled at each other, eyes wide.

"I cannot even believe that. That is unbelievable. Ineffable!" Mia pivoted and the two girls walked back to their lockers.

"You left out terrifying," Layla retorted.

"I did," Mia said. "On purpose! Because it isn't."

"I mean, yeah, it's really not a big deal…" Layla trailed off. "Like I said, I don't even like him like that."

Layla swung her bag over her shoulder and pretended to

search for something in it.

"OH." Mia laughed unnecessarily loudly. "You are *such* a liar."

Layla turned to look at Mia, and her new friend's massive grin made her feel pretty silly in that moment. She couldn't help but laugh unnecessarily loudly right back.

"Ughhh, you're right," Layla said, walking over to the nearby bench and sliding down onto it. "He's incomparable, Mia. He's unreal. He exists solely in my imagination. My whole body feels warm when he so much as walks by me."

Mia took a seat next to Layla, put her hand on Layla's shoulder, and nodded professionally, as a therapist serving her patient would.

"Well, okay. I wasn't ready for *that*, exactly. But okay."

Mia caught Layla's eyes with a stern expression and pointed a finger directly at her.

"Layla Whitaker," she started. "I know you work well under pressure. So I say this as a friend. This is your shot." Mia took Layla's shoulders now and stared into her eyes with intensity. "Today. After school. This is it."

"I am ready as I ever shall be," Layla replied firmly, but with a slight grin on her face.

"Once more unto the breach, dear friends!" Layla said, standing up to say goodbye to Mia. Layla straightened up and saluted. Mia stood, saluted back, and started to march off down the opposite hallway.

Little did Mia know that today was an important day for a few reasons. Not only was Layla going to spend time with Caleb, but she was also planning to figure out truth-writing once and for all. And she would use Caleb as her subject.

CHAPTER ELEVEN

Layla found Caleb sitting at a table on the far end of the library. He was leaned over his books, but he looked up when she walked in—as if he had been looking up periodically every so often, waiting for her. She casually smiled and nodded in his direction. He nodded sweetly back.

"Thanks for coming," he said when she arrived at his table.

"No problem," Layla responded. She took the seat across from him and busied herself with unpacking her books to avoid his gaze until she was ready to meet it.

Moments later she looked up and there it was. He looked at her expectantly, as if she were going to tell him something. But she had nothing to respond to yet, so she felt as if she were floundering like an actor on stage, searching for her next line.

"So the chain rule," she said finally.

"Yes," he replied. His eyes held hers for too long until they finally fell to his book on the desk. "It's debilitating."

Layla laughed.

The two went over their notes together for a while. Every so often they would run into a problem they had worked through in class that Caleb didn't follow. So Layla would write it out for him and they would work through it together.

All the while, Layla had her Blogiophile dashboard open

on her laptop to the right of her. The new post screen sat there, just waiting to be filled with words. Periodically, Layla would put her fingers to the keyboard, pretending to check their virtual textbook for more info. But mostly she was just waiting for the tingling feeling to come again.

As time ticked on, Layla began to grow more worried that she wouldn't be able to use her magic today. There was still no tingly feeling, and she was being picked up in ten minutes. Across from her, Caleb worked through one of the problems she had written for him. She looked around the room for an explanation—some reason the truth-writing wouldn't come. There were a few other groups of students studying at the tables, and a librarian walked here and there putting away books and closing down the TVs, computers, and copy machines. There were only a few more minutes left before after-school hours ended and everyone went home.

Is it too bright in here? Too dim? Too quiet? Too loud? Too cold? Too hot? Layla ran over reason after potential reason in her head for this truth-writing thing not working out, but she couldn't figure it out. What was she missing?

Suddenly Layla noticed out of the corner of her eye that Caleb was looking up at her. She was nervous and swallowed hard. She looked down and moved her eyes over to her laptop screen. It was still blank. She immediately felt a pain in her stomach.

When her eyes landed on his paper, Layla saw that he had done the problem perfectly, save for one step that was missing. Layla had been dealing with this overall trend in Caleb's work, by adding stars in the margins next to where he could have added more detail but hadn't. In this problem she only added one star and then grinned up at him.

"How'd I do?" he asked quietly, flipping his hair back.

"This is awesome," she said. "You're only missing one part. Can you tell what goes here?"

"Oh, yeesh. Yes. I see it," Caleb said, scratching a note down next to the star on the page. "Well, I was close."

"Mere centimeters!"

The librarian was now walking from table to table, telling the stragglers to head home.

Layla suspected Caleb would start packing his books up like everyone else. Instead, he leaned back in his chair and put his hands behind his head with his elbows bent out to the sides. His white button-up was folded so the sleeves were at his elbows and his forearms were completely exposed. Layla could trace her eyes over the muscles, if she wanted to. It wasn't the end of the world if she did. Just for a second.

But he was staring at her, hard and intense across the table. And for how much she longed to see his every muscle, she wanted tenfold to hold his eyes. Caleb Strauss's gaze somehow had become her sun: the thing she needed most of all to feel, and which, when it hit her, would charge her up for the winter ahead.

"Can I be real with you, Layla?" he asked.

"Goodness, I hope so," she replied, chuckling. "If you can't be real with your math tutor, who can you trust these days?"

"I'm terrified," he said.

Layla paused. She stared back at him, even though she could feel his eyes making her nervous now. She could feel herself losing control.

Layla looked down suddenly and grabbed her books. She packed them away in her backpack.

"You shouldn't be," she muttered, glancing back up at him. "You're too smart to be terrified by anything…"

He squinted back at her. She froze.

"Are you always so nice to your students?" he asked, grabbing his sweatshirt and wrapping it around his neck.

Layla shut her laptop, knowing that no truth-writing was going to happen in the one minute she had left with Caleb. She decided, rather in-the-moment, to make a move. She was feeling particularly bold today, and she wasn't going to miss this chance to make some sort of magic—especially if magic wasn't going to happen on Blogiophile today.

Layla licked her lips gently and brushed her golden hair

over her right shoulder. Then she leaned her chest over the laptop so that her face was about two feet from Caleb's. Layla locked eyes with him and inhaled deeply. Caleb seemed thrown off by this and froze in his seat, mouth hanging loosely open. Even Layla was surprised at herself for how much of a power move this was, without actually being overtly a move at all.

"You're smarter than most of my students," Layla replied.

Caleb broke the tension with a half-grin.

Layla felt emboldened by her exchange with Caleb. She always forgot that talking to guys was something she was actually quite good at. She had her guy friends all through middle and high school to thank for that, Gavin included. The thought of Gavin reminded her that she had some chem homework to do. It would be nice to sit in the JBC for a bit by herself to get it done. So instead of heading home, she had her mom drop her off at the JBC.

The bell on the door jingled its familiar cadence, and Layla made her way to the counter slowly. Gavin stopped her with a wild wave from behind the espresso machine, and she removed her headphones and smiled back at him. Only then did she realize that, other than the two of them, the café was completely empty. Normally, she would have a minute to herself to collect her thoughts while Gavin made something for another customer or finished another task. But no one was in front of her today. She looked up at the clock on the wall. It was 4:07. Layla was quite a bit later than usual today because of tutoring, so the rush from Quarton probably had already died down.

"Hey," Gavin said. "Been a minute!"

"Hello, friend," she replied, lifting her eyes to him while her head was down, unpacking her wallet from her backpack. She brushed her hair behind her ears and looked through the glass for a blueberry muffin.

"How goes it?" Gavin asked, following her motions with intense eyes.

"This week has been pure, unadulterated chaos," Layla declared, sliding three dollars across the table.

Gavin passed a coffee and muffin over the counter to her. Her usual.

"Oh yeah? Is it your Virgo rising catapulting through the ether and destroying your Gemini moon, or something?" Gavin said, laughing.

"My god, you're an astrological genius, Sir Greenwood. They should be studying you at Yale."

"I know, I know," Gavin replied. "My flaws are few, my skills are plenty!"

He then winked at her, breathed heavily onto the inside of a metal spoon, and then balanced it on the tip of his nose.

"Absolutely magnificent," Layla replied, grabbing her goods and finding a seat at her usual table. Layla opened up her chemistry book. She had an assignment still to do, but it would be a quick one. If she did it first, she'd have the rest of the night left to review for the math test. She opened her laptop to get to her chemistry assignment. There was the blank Blogiophile screen open to remind her that she hadn't blogged in over a week.

Layla sighed. She opened her backpack and took out her planner. Just as she grabbed a pen and was about to write "BLOG this week!" a familiar tingling came over her fingers. She looked down and watched her hands intensely. The tingling went through each finger, from the pinky to the thumb and back again. It then surged up her arms to her shoulders, then her head, and the blurriness came back into her eyes. All of a sudden she felt her heart flow into a race. It was happening.

She looked around to see if anyone else had come in, but no one was there. Through the window into the back kitchen, Layla could just make out the side of Spencer's face, with one Tom Waits-tattooed arm rolling dough for the next morning's breads. She wondered if she would start typing his thoughts.

Words started to fill the screen, and she vaguely felt herself typing them quickly. Every aspect of it was so disconnected from her mind, it was almost dizzying. She tried to read the words as she typed them, but her eyes wouldn't cooperate.

After five minutes or so, Layla could feel her hands pull to a halt. She slowly regained control of them and placed them delicately in her lap. *Typing other people's stories is exhausting,* she thought to herself.

Before she read the text, she made a quiet wish that the words would be Spencer's. She had nothing more than a surface-level connection with Spencer, so telling his story would be easy. More than that, Layla just hoped beyond hope that the words wouldn't be Gavin's. She was not ready for that.

There's nothing I can do. She's way out of my league. I wish I could just be normal with her. Why do I have to make it so weird between us? Why do I have to make her feel uncomfortable every time?

Layla forced herself to stop reading. She looked over to see Gavin standing where he always stood, behind the counter at the workstation. He finished filling the creamer pitcher and started wiping down the coffee machine. She had seen him do this—all of it—hundreds of times before. But in this moment he was like a flame, and she couldn't look away even if she tried.

She was struck by him now. The way he leaned over his task, his hair falling in his face and shutting everything around him out, captivated her. The simple act of filling a pitcher became his entire world for a moment.

Layla watched his hands closely, as they moved on to unscrew the sugar dispenser and bend around the fold of the sugar bag. When the task was complete, Gavin's thin fingers nimbly flicked through the pages of product inventory on the back shelf. They stroked his scruffy chin as he read. Then, for a moment, Layla couldn't help but remember how those same fingers felt laced between her own.

She could remember Gavin's fingers so vividly, and how they would rub her hand gently as he drove her home last year. He would park on the corner most times, just before her house.

There, he would look into her eyes, and his fingers would rub her hands harder, more intentionally. Soon, Gavin would slowly expand his massaging path to her thigh. And she couldn't help but start kissing him. It always ended on her thigh, and she respected him for that. But all she wanted then and there was for the path of his fingers to graze delicately between her legs. And then not so delicately.

Layla swallowed hard.

No, no, no. She couldn't. She didn't want to. She didn't have the right to. But just as quickly as she thought these thoughts, she knew she had already done it. The words on the page, when she looked at them, would continue to be Gavin's. She would be reading Gavin's deepest thoughts as if he had written them. She stared at the wall behind him now, in a daze.

Time went by. It felt like hours. Finally, Layla moved her eyes to the page and picked up where she left off.

What is she up to? What kind of music is she listening to lately? What books is she reading? There isn't anything I don't want to know about her, and it can never be enough. I am desperate to be the one who she confides in. I want so desperately—

Abort, abort, abort! Just as she had expected, Gavin's writings were putting her in a panic.

She slammed her laptop shut, shoved it in her backpack, and slid her textbook in behind it. Without thinking, Layla ran out of the JBC, fumbling with her coat and hat. She could feel Gavin's eyes rise to watch her exit.

When she got outside, Layla ran down the block and then stopped to catch her breath. She turned her head down and closed her eyes as she breathed, reassuring herself that she was fine now; she was out of there and alone again.

When she had gathered herself, she set her backpack on the ground. She unzipped it and took the laptop out. She opened it up and skimmed the screen she had just been on, as it showed bright in a now-darkening evening sky.

When she read the ending of Gavin's post, excitement filled her. There, on the screen, was the Gavin she had always wanted to see but had never been allowed to meet—not fully. After all those months of him keeping his feelings in, everything was out for the taking here. After all those texts and calls with half-answered questions, she finally had full answers.

Layla tilted her head and a smile grew on her face. A big one. There he was, in the form of three words she had never heard, but always secretly hoped were true:

to be hers.

CHAPTER TWELVE

Layla slid down into the couch in her living room and stared blankly at the bookshelves in front of her.

"Layla?" Her mother called to her from the dining room. "You home?"

Her mother's footsteps grew closer down the hallway.

"I didn't even hear you—"

Her mother stopped in the doorway to the living room.

"Are you okay?" Her voice seemed to echo off every wall in the room and circle around Layla like water in a drain. Apparently, Layla was still feeling thrown off by today's truth-writing adventure.

She swung her head over to meet her mother's gaze.

"Yes," she exhaled with a grin. "I'm fine! Just been a weird, long day."

"Ah," her mother replied. "Well snap out of it and come eat. We're having lamb!"

Her mother's solution to everything lately had been to cook something extra special. And Layla didn't hate it. A nice dinner with her mom sounded like exactly what she needed. If only she could actually explain to her mother what had just happened at the JBC. But seeing her mother experience such sincere joy over something so simple was a gift in and of itself. It did help that she loved lamb, too.

Layla and her mother enjoyed their meal together by candlelight. As her mother rose to go get out the ice cream for dessert, Layla started to feel her heart race. She felt wild, like she desperately wanted to tell her mother that she knew Gavin still liked her.

What a feeling it would be to tell her that. Like opening up the back door and letting a thousand balloons into the kitchen.

"Weeee!" Layla would sing as she grabbed onto the lot of them and flew from room to room. She would hop and dance across the furniture. Her mother would laugh so hard she'd just about fall out of her chair. And on her next go-around, Layla would reach out and grab her mother by the hand. And off they'd both float through the bay windows in the living room and up over their little town. Feeling loved by someone you had liked for so long was a lot more like that Disney movie *Up* than she had imagined it would be.

She leaned her head into her hands and sighed gleefully.

"Sunshine?" Layla's mother's voice rose over her thoughts.

"Oh." Layla stirred. "I'm sorry! What did you say?"

"I just asked whether the sauce was better tonight than the last time." Her mother laughed. "But you seem to have something much more important on your mind." Layla's mother smiled knowingly.

Layla couldn't help but grin.

"So." Her mother leaned into her hands with her elbows on the table. "SPILL!"

Layla practically leapt out of her chair.

"Okay, so..." She brushed her hair behind her ear, ready to dig into today's events from start to finish. "So I was tutoring Caleb after school, and... Well, it went really well. He seems really ready for the exam tomorrow. And it helped me feel more confident, too."

Her mother smiled from ear to ear.

"But it was kind of..." Layla knew she couldn't tell her mom about everything. Truth-writing wasn't a topic she was ready to address tonight. But she could tell her some things. "It was kind of... weird. Like, he's just a really difficult person to get to know, you know? Like very... closed off."

Her mother nodded. "That makes sense," she said. "He doesn't know you very well yet, after all.

"Right, sure," Layla said. "But after that, I went to the JBC, just to chill for a second."

"Okay," her mother said.

"And Gavin was there."

"Ahh, here's the good stuff!" Her mother rubbed her hands together earnestly.

"And he... Well—"

"He tried something, didn't he? I knew that kid was no good at all, I just knew he was going to overstep—"

"No! Mom!" Layla stopped her. "It wasn't that. Really!"

Her mother settled down.

"We just... talked?" Layla said, knowing that this was where she was going to have difficulty with the explanation.

"Okay..." Her mother tried to follow.

"And I think, maybe... Well, maybe Gavin likes me. Again. Or... still? Maybe?"

"What?!" Layla's mother's mouth dropped open. "What did he say?"

"Well, so..." Layla began. "It wasn't so much what he said as... well, more what he... didn't say?"

Layla's mother cocked her head and nodded. "Okay, okay. That makes sense. So much of love is not spoken, my darling."

"But I'm very sure that's what he was... getting at," Layla concluded. "And I just don't know what to do!"

"Wow." Her mother's eyes were wide as she processed. "Yeah, I mean, I thought that was long over. And I know you have been talking an awful lot about one Caleb Strauss lately."

"Mom!" Layla rolled her eyes with a big grin.

"I mean, it's not often that I see my daughter volunteer at a tutoring center after school just for the fun of it," her mother ejected, chuckling to herself.

"Okay, I'll bite," Layla conceded. She grabbed her mom's hands. "I mean, Caleb is… he's *incredible*. There's so much to him, and I just want to know everything there is to know about him. He's next-level fascinating."

"That sounds amazing!" her mother replied.

"But then Gavin... I mean, there's so much history there. And I liked him SO MUCH last year. It definitely felt great to know that he liked me, I'll say that."

"Absolutely! It's great to finally have some understanding there," her mother said.

Layla nodded enthusiastically. Her brain was running wild in all directions at this point.

"Well, I can't make this kind of decision for you—of course you know that," her mother said.

Her mother leaned back in her chair and stared up at the rafters for a spell.

"But could it be...?" her mother began.

She paused and looked down at her plate for a moment, seemingly lost in thought.

"What is it?" Layla asked, trying to find her mother's eyes.

"I just wonder if..." her mother said, trailing off again.

Layla was starting to get a little frustrated by this.

"Yes?" Layla asked, expectantly. "What are you thinking?"

"Well, I'm just not so sure Gavin is the guy for you," her mother declared, finally making eye contact again.

"Well, you can't possibly know that, Mom," Layla said. "He's so great, and obviously there's a reason I've been thinking about him for almost a year now."

"Well, all I'm saying," Layla's mother began again. "Is that sometimes the man for you isn't the one who gives you what you always thought you wanted."

Layla put her face into her folded hands. She was processing her mother's words. She knew that her mother was letting her in on something very important.

"Sometimes," Layla's mother continued, leaning in closer to her daughter now. "Sometimes the man for you is the one who opens you up to a world of things you never even knew you wanted in the first place."

Layla laid in her bed later that night, staring at the Portland Posted draft.

She clicked Publish and added a swipe-up link to her stories with a picture she had taken at Chrome Café downtown the other week of a cappuccino with a heart drawn in the milk.

Swipe up for a few romantic leaf puns.

Leaves Weren't the Only Things that Fell

September 23

So, it happened, Posted fam. We all knew it would. Your humble narrator fell for a guy.

The only thing is that I fell for that guy a whole year ago. I'm a last-fall leaf, I swear!

So, I spent the last many months getting over this guy. Only to find out that he still has feelings... some kind of feelings, anyway, for me.

According to him, he wants to know what I'm up to. He wants to know what kind of music I'm listening to lately, and what books I'm reading.

But I can't quite understand why he wants to know all of these things about me now. Shouldn't sharing those very personal details with someone mean something? Shouldn't the exchange of personal details about one's life ultimately lead to something real, and true? What's the point in confiding in someone if it doesn't go anywhere?

And it didn't. I fell to the ground and then got covered. Other leaves, snow, dirt, all of it covered me. Then footsteps—I was trampled for months. It's long over. Or is it?

CHAPTER THIRTEEN

"I'm not saying that we solved world hunger or anything. I'm just saying that we worked hard and we deserve to take a night off."

Mia gestured wildly with her hands in between bites of an apple. Both girls had just finished their calculus exam and were feeling pretty great about how it went. On top of that, Mia had just informed Layla that she had tickets to see Harry Styles at the Palace next Saturday. And she was inviting Layla to go with her! Which officially made them real, honest-to-goodness friends. Layla was particularly enjoying having friends.

The only problem was that Mia's mom was kind of old-fashioned. The Harry Styles tickets were given to Mia by her cool aunt Jamie, who had gotten some kind of free package from work. Mia's mother was up in arms about how Mia was way too young to be "partying" at concerts, especially without an adult present. So at this point, there was almost no way the girls would actually be able to use the two crisp, beautiful tickets for anything other than bookmarks.

"I mean, it's a Saturday night, for goodness' sake!" she continued, as they took a seat on a wide wooden bench in front of the school to hang out for a minute before the buses took off for the afternoon. "And it's Harry Styles. I mean, Layla Whitaker, can you believe!"

"I hear you," Layla replied, digging into her backpack for a granola bar. "And I one hundred percent agree with you. But just because you and I both know how hard that exam was today, and how much we deserve one evening of respite and pure bliss at the Harry Styles concert next weekend as a result of completing it—and doubtless acing it—"

"And doubtless acing it!" Mia echoed.

"Does not mean that your mother is going to agree with us."

Mia rolled her eyes.

"Oh my god, she's Reverend Moore, isn't she?" Mia laughed and brushed the hair out of her face.

"Ha! As I live and breathe!" Layla shouted, almost keeling over with laughter. Mia was making reference to the movie they had watched in film class the last two days, *Footloose*.

Layla divided up a bag of pretzels and put half into Mia's outstretched hand. The two girls relaxed, feeling pleased with themselves. To be finished with an exam was an incomparable joy. Even if you thought you didn't do well, just to be done with it was a weight off your shoulders like nothing else. Layla and Mia were feeling good. They were feeling great.

Not only that, but this morning Layla had been pleasantly surprised to find that her Blogiophile views hit 92, with 37 likes and 7 comments. It seemed her audience was interested in a love story, even if the love story had ended well before it was written.

"Oh my god, I forgot," Mia exclaimed, nearly spitting out her drink. "I have even more good news for you."

"Honestly, how could this day get any better?" Layla asked, focused on the task at hand.

"I heard John Francis and Amanda broke up," Mia whispered into her ear.

Layla dropped the pretzel bag onto the floor. She covered her mouth so tightly her glasses started to fog up with breath.

Mia jokingly cowered and slid back on the bench slightly, apparently not quite ready for how big the reaction would be. "Hm, is that bigger than Harry? Should I have led with that?"

"Oh my god," Layla whispered. She swung her legs up onto the bench and put her face into her knees. "Oh my god!" she said again, this time a little louder.

"Yeah, I should have led with that..." Mia said, watching Layla sway back and forth in a ball.

Mia coached Layla off of the bench and walked her to her locker. It was almost time for Mia to leave and for Layla to head to the math center, so they needed to gather their things.

"Okay, Layla. You and I have to pack up and go home now," Mia said in a maternal voice. She started to put Layla's books into her backpack as Layla paced back and forth manically. Thankfully, most of the other students had already gone home, so there wasn't an audience for whatever was happening with Layla in this moment.

"I think we can talk about you and Caleb tomorrow," Mia continued. "Do you have to bring *Moby Dick*?"

"No, no. I don't want to talk about me and Caleb," Layla interjected. "There is nothing to talk about there. Nothing there. Not at all anything. There." Layla realized that she was sort of rambling whilst pacing back and forth, and that this was sort of peak *One Flew Over the Cuckoo's Nest* for her.

Mia couldn't help but burst out laughing.

"Oh, right. And you don't even like him. And you don't want to date him. And you haven't been stewing over the mystery of his mom's death for weeks."

Layla stopped pacing now. Mia demonstrated a dramatic deep breath for Layla, and Layla followed her coach's calming movements mockingly.

"I would not say *stewing*. *Stewing* is definitely not the word."

"Okay, what is the word, then? *Deliberating*? *Brooding*? *Ruminating*? Oh, I don't know, *obsessing*?"

"Listen, I'm pretty good at words. And I just know the words. Okay?" Layla swung her locker door shut and stumbled into Mia in a daze.

"Okay, I'm gonna be honest, I don't know what you just said," Mia said, catching her friend by the arm.

"I am not obsessing," Layla replied, composing herself. She patted down her rumpled sweater.

"Okay, I believe you," Mia said. She looked into Layla's eyes seriously now.

Layla exhaled loudly. Now that they were really friends, she couldn't keep hiding her feelings from her.

"Honestly, I know he and I have hung out a few times," Layla said, taking a more serious tone now. "And it's strange, because I actually think we could be good friends. But I've tried to… connect with him, in that way. And it hasn't really worked." Layla shifted her eyes to the football field out the window, absently. "It's just that it's very hard to get to know him."

Mia nodded. "I bet he's somewhat reserved. I mean, his mother disappeared and his father is the principal. So that makes sense."

"But I've seen you guys together, Layla," Mia continued. "And you guys are definitely friends. I think he probably needs people in his life who will be there for him, not just because they think he's hot or they want to get in good with the principal's kid or whatever. You talking to him about the mystery, if it will make you any less ob—"

"Mia, I'm not—"

"I mean, *preoccupied* about it… might end up helping both of you."

"I guess." Layla threw her backpack over her shoulder and leaned up against the lockers, thinking hard about what Mia was saying.

"But how do I talk to him about that? How would I even begin? It's like he's unreachable."

"Layla," Mia began in a whisper. She gestured for Layla to move in closer to her. "Have you tried just asking him?"

Layla exhaled, smiling widely now.

"You are a real piece of work, Mia Tanner. I hope you know that."

"Oh, I do, my friend. My mother is going to have me framed and put up on the mantel."

Layla laughed and pushed Mia playfully.

Mia nudged Layla and passed off a handful of Sour Patch Kids to her.

"Gotta go, have a good rest of the day," she said, starting down the hallway in the other direction. She turned back around and gave Layla two thumbs up. "Oh, and congratulations on being brilliant."

"Same to you! Good luck with Reverend Moore."

Layla sat at her post in the math center that day, finishing up her calculus homework. Only one student had come to her desk so far, so she had had a lot of time to work on her own studying. But that meant she also had a lot of time to think about what Mia had said to her earlier. Mia's advice had struck her, because her suggestion to try to grow closer to Caleb, especially right after his breakup with Amanda, was a little forward. But she really, *really* liked him.

For so long, Layla had been hung up on Gavin and stuck imagining the two of them together. And even if she was under no illusion that she and Gavin would be an item forever or get married or anything, it had left her somewhat out of the dating pool for a long time. It also didn't help that Layla was a writer. This meant her writing grades were fantastic, and her blogs were pretty good, too. But this also meant that Layla was, by nature, an observer. She watched and studied the lives of other people so deeply, she often forgot to live her own. Her father had been this way, too, but of course now she knew that that temperament wasn't always great for the family.

Layla sighed. She knew she wanted to try new things and get out there. It was a new year at a new school, so what better time to be bold? But when, exactly, would she have the opportunity to talk to Caleb in a deeper way? Or about what happened with Amanda? Or really, about anything but math? These things didn't just happen, she thought to herself. You had to wait for the right *time*.

A few minutes later, a shadow fell over Layla's chemistry book.

"Layla!" a voice said, and she knew whose voice it was before she even looked up.

To her surprise, Caleb's face was bright and full, like her mother's sunflowers in her bedroom window. Her own eyes jumped ship to trace the outline of his bicep where it slid delicately under the sleeve of his shirt, and followed the navy blue fabric up to the collar, which was off-kilter and disheveled, as if he had just been through the wind. Then came his strong neck, his chiseled jaw, clean-shaven. Then prominent, strong cheekbones. His tantalizing lips, always more to one side than the other when he smiled. An unintentional, sly half-smile. Then that gaze again, deep and sharp.

"Layla? Are you okay?"

The sweet sound of his voice shook her back into presence and she realized she was now squinting at him with her head obviously tilted, like a dog watching a rollie pollie on the sidewalk.

"Caleb! Hello!"

"Hey." He nodded.

"How's it going?" Layla forced.

"Great! What'd you think? How was the test?" His voice rose with excitement as he pulled a notebook out of his backpack and took the seat across from her.

"I think it went well," Layla said, brushing her hair behind her ears. "I mean, it was hard, absolutely. But I think it went well. What about you?"

Caleb grinned widely, and without any warning whatsoever grabbed her hands loosely, delicately with his own. Layla stopped in her tracks and could feel her entire face turning red. She had suddenly stopped functioning. The moment reminded her of a poem her father had loved and kept hanging up in his study for many years. It was called "The Love Song of J. Alfred Prufrock," by T. S. Eliot. A line in the poem kept running through her head now:

Should I, after tea and cakes and ices,
Have the strength to force the moment to its crisis?

Here it was: the moment, meeting its crisis. The only thing was that it had come on so suddenly, she hadn't really had any time to go looking for strength.

"I can't believe how confident I felt, Layla." Caleb was smiling so wide his dimples showed, and that was officially it for her ability to speak words.

Brain cells, signing off, Layla thought to herself. *No, wait! Stay with me.*

"That's so awesome. I'm really happy for you, pal," Layla replied. She couldn't handle the silence that followed, because there were those eyes again, and those dimples. She pulled her hand away because it felt like time to do that. Everything about this entire exchange was very uncomfortable for her.

"And it's all because of your help!" he said, still smiling. "So I just wanted to thank you. Again. It's the first time I'm at tutoring just to say I don't really need it today." Caleb laughed, showing those gorgeous teeth.

Her eyes landed on the floor, and suddenly, without really knowing what was happening, she asked, "Do you want to hang out? I don't know, maybe study together on Sunday?"

She swallowed hard after she heard the words escape her. The earth stopped spinning then, for a moment. Viewers rose from the comfort of their couches. Wires burst on amplifiers. Birds took off, sensing a storm.

Caleb's eyes fell and then traveled out the window nearby, where he looked with some urgency now. The serious look on his face made Layla immediately regret what she had just said.

"This Sunday?" Caleb asked, looking into her eyes again. He was quieter now, as if someone else were listening.

Why are you asking him to hang out right now? What's happening? Abort, abort!

Caleb was fiddling with his backpack and not saying anything, which made it extremely difficult to read him. Layla felt herself wanting to backtrack but not knowing exactly how to do so without making things even more awkward.

"I mean—"

"Davis Street Café?" he interrupted, before she could finish. Caleb was now smiling at her. Layla was highly confused.

She forced a smile.

"For sure," she said.

"I have a thing in the morning, is all," Caleb said, flicking his hair out of his face.

Layla now understood that maybe he had something very important going on that Sunday. So maybe the interaction's painful lull had nothing to do with her at all. Her smile grew wider.

"Can we do three-ish?" Caleb asked.

"Three-ish is the very best time I can think of," Layla replied.

CHAPTER FOURTEEN

"I am still wrapping my head around the fact that your dad is a Dylan fan and also my principal," Layla said, stirring cream into her coffee and leaning over Caleb's phone at a photo of him and Principal Strauss at a Bob Dylan concert in Boston. Layla made an exploding hand gesture around her head.

Caleb laughed and swiped through the photos.

"How did you ever get VIP tickets?" she asked.

"You know Mr. Schwartzman, the tech ed teacher? His son runs the venue," he replied. "It was just a stroke of luck that he was able to get us in, honestly. Not our usual concert-viewing MO."

"So you guys go to a lot of concerts, then?" Layla asked.

"Uh, yeah. That's kind of, like, our thing," he replied.

"Anyone else I'd know of?" Layla asked.

"Well, we've seen Elton, Seger, you know… Springsteen… Rolling Stones a few times."

"ROLLING STONES A FEW TIMES?! You have got to be kidding me."

"I mean, he loves the big guys, you know. He's all about the classics."

"Okay, I am never going to feel bad for you again," Layla said, slapping his bicep playfully.

"Oh yeah?" Caleb laughed.

Caleb put his phone away and opened his calc book back up again.

"Don't get me wrong, he's still a real hardass. He's the principal at home, too." He spun his pencil around each finger as he spoke.

He looked out the window now and watched the rain fall for a moment.

"But you guys seem to get along pretty well?" Layla asked, breaking eye contact and pretending to look through her notes for something.

"Maybe it's because we excel at sitting in silence next to each other," he added in a distinctly wistful tone.

Layla watched him. Just being near him put her stomach in knots.

This was the first time Layla had ever seen Caleb in something other than his Burroughs uniform. He wore light wash jeans with a forest-green plaid flannel and a Stooges t-shirt underneath. His dark bangs curtained his forehead and fell atop his dark, thick eyebrows. The rest of his hair was full and wild around his ears such that, when he concentrated on the page before him, it would occasionally fall too much in front of his eyes. When this happened, he would use his hand to toss the strands out of the way.

She caught his big blue eyes for a moment and, panicking, pretended to be very interested in the sign behind him about at-home guitar lessons offered by a woman named Sue Bachelder. *Smooth, Layla. Real, real smooth.*

The two sat at a big table in the café with their books spread out on top of it. She had had a plan that morning. She had texted him saying that she might get there a bit early and so she would bring some chem homework to do. He said that was fine and that he would bring some studying to do too.

It worked out nicely, because when Caleb showed up, Layla already had her chem notebook out. She also had her laptop open to an empty Blogiophile draft. She was there to talk with Caleb, not to truth-write. But of course she wouldn't be upset if it happened, either.

They chatted about their day, and just kept talking. But anytime there was even a hint of awkward silence, he got into his history book and she started typing some chem notes. Occasionally a barista would sneak by and ask if they needed anything, but mostly the staff was in and out of the back room, and no one else was around. Layla was elated to be alone with Caleb.

All things considered, Layla was having a surprisingly easy time talking to Caleb. She had been terrified that they would cover all the topics they usually covered in conversation (math assignments and how Mrs. Chamberlain's voice sounded when she got really serious with the class) and then twiddle their thumbs until one of them made an excuse to go home.

But it wasn't like that at all. The two quickly lost sight of history and chem homework, in fact. By 5:15, when a text came in from Layla's mom about dinner soon, Caleb had told her all about growing up in Burroughs Academy schools. He talked of the rich people parties and all the friends of friends who later became politicians, or celebrities, or even criminals. It was a hilarious gamut of clever anecdotes and she was roaring with laughter almost obnoxiously the whole time. Caleb could tell a story well without even trying. His tales very nearly distracted her from the familiar tingling that came over her as they wrapped things up.

When it was time for Caleb to go, Layla watched him walk out the café doors the way you watch a candle in a window from outside on a cold day. She then breathed deeply and looked down at her laptop to see the words in the Blogiophile window. Words she hadn't meant to type.

Layla stopped herself. She looked forward to reading what Caleb had written for her, but for now she wanted to wait. She would give herself time to collect herself. Time to feel everything to its fullest.

As she rode the Uber back home, she thought of what it would be like if she had him. If she, not Amanda, were the one who had dated him and spent all summer with him. If, more than that, he now walked her to class and held her hand and sent her goodnight texts every night. They would be inseparable. Not inseparable in an unhealthy way, like so many couples her age were. But inseparable in a way that made them a partnership; inseparable in a way that challenged them and made them grow. They would have it all figured out.

For now, she would settle for being his friend.

Before she knew what she was doing, she had dialed Mia's number and put the phone up to her ear.

"I've honestly been sitting by my phone for the past twenty minutes waiting for an update," Mia declared, jokingly stern with her.

"I'm sorry I'm late," Layla replied.

"How was it? Tell me everything!" Mia said, squealing so loud that Layla had to pull the phone away from her ear.

The Uber driver turned around, and Layla laughed nervously. She mouthed "sorry" to him and grinned apologetically. To her surprise, the driver just smiled wistfully, as if longing to be young again himself.

"Mia," she started, bringing it back to her ear and speaking quieter now. "Caleb is PER. FECT."

"Well, that's brand new information!" Mia replied, sarcastically.

"Right. Well, we did finish our assignments! And then we… talked. A lot."

Mia squealed again on the other end of the receiver.

"About what?!" Mia pleaded. "This is SO great."

"About so much! He told me all about growing up at Burroughs and all the rich kids everywhere. And how he has been in the same crew of friends since basically birth. We laughed a lot about how different our childhoods were. And oh my god, Mia, he likes Springsteen. And the Stones!"

"Okay, I'm crying. Brb while I go put my phone in rice because I'm crying all over it."

"He's amazing," Layla whispered.

The two sighed happily back and forth to each other.

"The only thing is…" Layla began again. "His life is so different from mine. I mean, he has a *lot*, a lot of money. His dad is highly influential, obviously. I mean, they live in West End! That's like the Beverly Hills of Maine. And what if he wants someone more…. More in his world? More like Amanda? What if he wants someone whose parents can host extravagant school fundraisers and bring tiramisu to bake sales? What if he wants someone who doesn't have to scoop ice cream all summer for concert tickets? What if he wants one of those… 'West End Girls'?" Layla tried to match the tone of the 80's synth-pop track as best she could.

"First of all, it does not take a Pet Shop Boys scholar like myself to know that they were talking about the West End of London, *not* West End of the second-most famous Portland in the U.S. Secondly, if he wanted that, Layla, I can tell you with 100% certainty, it would not be a struggle for him to get that. He has had Amanda before, mind you. And lots of beautiful, rich girls before that, too."

"Oh, gosh," Layla interjected, grumbling. "Not helping!"

"Thirdly," Mia interrupted, loudly. "No one spends three hours in a café talking about their childhood with someone they only consider their math tutor. It sounds to me like he likes *you*."

Layla straightened up in her seat now, really hearing the words as they escaped Mia's mouth.

"Caleb wants you because you are smart and funny. You're quirky, and totally weird, and annoyingly right about everything. You're kind, and generous, and honestly, dangerously clumsy—we should all be a little worried about you. Caleb wants you for you, Layla. I know that, your mom knows that, and I can't wait for you to finally see it. Gotta go, Mom takes my phone at 9. See you tomorrow."

Mia hung up and Layla kept the phone on her ear for a moment. Her heart was racing. She was overwhelmed by Mia's words of encouragement. She was also elated, equally by the thought of Caleb liking her back and by the thought of Mia thinking so highly of her. It was a great day.

"So, tell me how the study date went!" Layla's mother sang, gliding into the room after her daughter entered through the front door. She extended her arms like a ballerina and danced around her daughter wildly.

Layla chuckled.

"It was fine," she said. "And again. Not a date."

"Yes, I'm sorry," her mother said. "The study NOT-date."

Layla fell into her mother's arms for a hug.

"But it went well!" Layla said, smiling uncontrollably at this point.

Her mother stepped back and jumped up with glee.

"I'm happy about it," Layla said. "But I do need to finish a few things before bed."

Layla started walking upstairs, her mother following close behind. And behind her mother, Bart followed, sensing excitement in the household. It became something of a parade up the stairs.

"Well, come on!" her mother said, leaping onto the foot of the bed. Bart leapt after her onto the mustard yellow fuzzy blanket he loved so well.

"You're not going to stop there, are you?" Layla's mother said excitedly.

Layla beamed in spite of herself. Her mother and Bart both looked up at her expectantly. She wanted to give more details, but the Portland Posted draft was nagging at her brain. She was ready now—eager, in fact—to see what was written there.

"Well, I mean," Layla began. "It was fine, and we got to talk a lot. I just. Mom, I'm tired. And I just don't feel like talking about it right now. Is that okay?"

Layla's mother looked surprised, but she quickly turned

her face into a smile and nodded.

"Hey, that's okay. We'll talk tomorrow," her mother said, standing up from the bed. She motioned for Bart to get down, and the two of them stepped out.

It was just Layla and her laptop now.

To her surprise, when she opened up the laptop, she found not one or two sentences but three paragraphs of words on the screen.

She asked me to hang out on September 26th. The day Mom was killed. The day I will never forget but never remember.

It's so hard, all of this. Putting on a face. I can't keep all the faces straight sometimes. Chris, Jake, and Sam—they didn't say anything today. And it was strange, because I didn't even want them to. I hoped they wouldn't. Because we're just not like that, me and the guys. In fact, the reason I hang out with them so much is because it's so easy to NOT talk to them. They never ask me what I'm thinking or feeling.

Layla is different. She's special. She might ask me. She might want to know. And I wouldn't know what to say. I wouldn't know what to say most days, but especially not today. I hope she doesn't ask. What would I tell her, anyway? Your old pal Caleb's mom died twelve years ago and, oh yeah, he was there when she died, but he has no idea how it happened. Because his brain refuses to think of that day, no matter how hard he tries. No matter how much work he does. No matter how many psychologists, doctors, and other professionals his father hires to pick away at his head—to tear it open and get the details out—he just can't. His brain is a faulty machine, hoping one day to start working again.

No, Layla wouldn't understand that. No one understands that. My mom is gone, and I can't remember anything about it. I can't even properly grieve her because it doesn't make logical sense to me that she isn't here anymore. I can't wrap my head around why the door doesn't open like it always did at 4:15 pm every day to her coming home from the bakery to hug me. I can't figure out why I don't hear her singing first thing in the morning— too early, dark early, but always singing. Still, to this day, I think she might, just once, be the one who comes into my room to say goodnight to me before bed. But it hasn't been her for twelve years. And I am told it will never be her again.

Layla looked down and noticed her hands were shaking. Without realizing what she was doing, Layla rose, and nearly tripped over her desk chair. She slid past Bart down the hallway on the wood floor, and swung her mother's bedroom door open so hard it hit the wall with a thump.

Her mother swung her body up from the bed, tossing a book out of her hands.

"Mom!" Layla stood before her, now realizing what unnecessary theatrics she had just performed. "I…"

"What's wrong?!" Her mother's mouth hung open.

"I just…" Layla started. Her eyes were fixated on her mother's countenance as if she were solving a math problem.

She walked over to her mom and hugged her tightly.

"I just love you so much," she said.

CHAPTER FIFTEEN

"These seats are amazing!" Layla yelled over the crowd to Mia as they took their seats at the concert. Layla and her mom had been to many concerts before, but usually they sat on the lawn on a picnic blanket. She wasn't used to having actual seats, much less being about twenty rows from the front.

"I know!" Mia yelled back, dancing in her seat. "You can practically see his sweat droplets from here!"

Layla was so happy that Mia's mom had finally caved about the concert. Mia had worked hard to make it happen, of course. A few days ago, she created a PowerPoint for her parents in which she graphed her success in all of the core subjects over the past ten years. She then made a composite graph with Harry Styles album release dates, and had somehow proved that her grades were directly proportional to his performance on the Billboard Hot 100. No one could ever claim that Mia wasn't a hard worker.

It was also nice, because Layla was able to meet Mia's parents before the show. They, of course, fully interviewed her about her background and her goals and what her major was going to be (which was a tricky one, because she was only sixteen, after all). But Layla knew it was important for their friendship, and it actually went really well. All things considered, Layla was kind of a catch as far as best friends went.

Layla laughed to herself, realizing how quickly she had

assumed that she was Mia's best friend. Mia had a lot of close friends, so who really knew if Layla was her best friend. But as she watched Mia singing her brains out before her now, Layla kind of wanted Mia to be her best friend. *It doesn't really matter if it's reciprocated or not*, she thought.

After the show, Layla dragged Mia to the JBC for a postshow dessert. They talked for an hour about which songs Harry had performed the best. Layla introduced Mia to Spencer, and Mia practically drooled all over the glass display case. Overall, it was a lovely night. One of Layla's favorite nights to date.

When Layla got home, she sat at her laptop and opened up her Blogiophile dashboard. Over the past few days, she had been thinking hard about what she was going to write on her blog. Up until this point, when she had truth-written on her blog, she'd just saved the writing as a draft and transformed it into her own words before posting. She had done this because the drafts about her mom and Gavin seemed really, really personal. She'd felt like she had to take the names out and rearrange the details so that no one would suspect a thing. The thought of leaving in details had felt cheap, almost like she was plagiarizing or something.

But with Caleb, the details were so rich and compelling to her. It was a novel she hadn't been able to put down for the past few days. And she couldn't wait to see what would happen next.

After seeing an amazing performance by a true artist, Layla remembered that truth-writing was her gift. She was able to channel other people's thoughts into writing because it was the truth. How else had her dad been able to write such universally meaningful poetry? How else could he have made such incredible art for his entire life?

It was her turn to use her gift the way it was meant to be used. She was writing the truth.

And it had to be told. It was ready to be told.

Layla was nearly shaking when she went to click Publish.

Swipe up for secrets.

A New Perspective
October 2

She asked me to hang out on September 26th. The day my mom was killed. The day I will never forget, but never remember.

It's so hard, all of this. Putting on a face. I can't keep all the faces straight sometimes. My friends, they didn't say anything today. And it was strange, because I didn't even want them to. I hoped they wouldn't. Because we're just not like that, me and the guys. In fact, the reason I hang out with them so much is because it's so easy to NOT talk to them. They never ask me what I'm thinking or feeling.

Gwen is different. She's special. She might ask me. She might want to know. And I wouldn't know what to say. I wouldn't know what to say most days, but especially not today. I hope she doesn't ask. What would I tell her, anyway? Your old pal Michael's mom died twelve years ago and, oh yeah, he was there when she died, but he has no idea how it happened. Because his brain refuses to think of the day, no matter how hard he tries. No matter how much work he does. No matter how many psychologists, doctors, and other professionals his father hires to pick away at his head—to tear it open and get the details out—he just can't. His brain is a faulty machine, hoping one day to start working again.

No, Gwen wouldn't understand that. No one understands that. My mom is gone and I can't remember anything about it. I can't even properly grieve her because it doesn't make logical sense to me that she isn't here anymore. I can't wrap my head around why the door doesn't open like it always did at 4:15 pm every day to her coming home from the bakery to hug me. I can't figure out why I don't hear her singing first thing in the morning—too early, dark early, but always singing. Still, to this day, I think she might, just once, be the one who comes into my room to say goodnight to me before bed. But it hasn't been her for twelve years. And I am told it will never be her again.

CHAPTER SIXTEEN

"Slam!" Caleb tossed a crumpled-up piece of paper into the garbage on the opposite wall of Layla's living room. "He does it again! The crowd goes wild."

Caleb circled the room with his arms in the air. His tank top hung low under them so the muscles in his chest were clear as day.

Layla looked down quickly, instinctively, so he wouldn't see her eyes go there. She clapped slowly and rolled her eyes at him.

He took his seat next to her on the couch again and read through his assignments.

"Do you think we're ever going to finish this one last problem, Caleb?" Layla asked.

It was Sunday, and Caleb had come over to study for Friday's exam. They had made lots of progress together the previous Sunday, so Caleb had texted her earlier and suggested they study again this weekend too. Layla had played it cool and tried to sound half as eager as she was to see him. Which, by the way, was a lot.

Layla had suggested Caleb come by her place instead of meeting at Davis Street Café again because she knew they were hosting a book club there tonight. Looking back at her past experiences with truth-writing, it seemed to work better when it was just her and the subject, with no one else coming in and out.

"Yeah, when I have my first interview on ESPN, I'm sure they're going to ask me what the cosine of x is."

"Well, you never know, now do you?" Layla laughed.

"One more round of ghost, and then I am officially back in the game," Caleb said. He raised his eyebrows coyly at her.

"You are SO obnox—"

"Just one more round. I promise!"

"Fiiiine," she conceded.

Caleb got up from his chair, spun it, and sat back down with his legs straddling it. This was his power stance.

"Jennifer Aniston. Got it?"

"Okay, I got it," Layla replied.

"Okay, first one is Adam."

"Oof... Um… Oh! Oh! Sandler!"

"Danggg, nice job. Okay, umm… Ben."

"No way! What? Ben?"

Layla stood up and spun around, thinking hard about a Ben who shared a movie with Jennifer Aniston. She couldn't guess it, and she fell into the golden sofa in defeat. "I got nothing."

"Stiller!" Caleb yelled out, gesturing wildly with his arms. "*Along Came Polly*. You haven't seen it?"

"No, but you're right," Layla admitted.

"Ohhh, you gotta see it," he responded, shaking his head.

Layla's phone vibrated suddenly on the table. It lit up to show a Blogiophile notification. Instinctively, Layla grabbed her phone before Caleb could see what it was. She felt strange doing this, because there's no way snatching your phone up in front of someone isn't at least a little suspect.

The truth was, she didn't really need to hide her phone at all. There was pretty much no way he would ask about her blog. And even if he did, it was unlikely he would ever go search for it, not to mention spend his time reading it. And even if he did read it, there was almost no way he would understand what it was. It could easily just have been artsy short stories, made up lyrics for a song, or poetic musings. How would Caleb know Layla was blogging for other people?

Well, he might know if he read the most recent one, Layla thought, swallowing hard. She decided to just check the notification later on.

"Boyfriend?" Caleb asked, watching Layla fumble with her phone.

"N-n-n-" Layla stammered. She turned to look at her phone again, which she then realized was a very strange thing to do. "Uhh, no. No. I don't…"

Well, this officially could not have gotten more awkward.

"What I mean is, I don't have a boyfriend," Layla said, finally. She could feel Caleb's eyes on her as she shuffled her papers nervously. "At the moment."

Oh god, oh god, what am I saying right now? she thought to herself. *Please be normal, please be normal, please be normal.*

Layla finally got the nerve to look up and meet his eyes again, but when she found them, she froze. Caleb was looking at her more intensely than he ever had before. His deep, blue eyes were holding her gaze so powerfully they stopped time. She was overcome with emotion.

Before she had the chance to overanalyze what she should say next, Caleb's hand fell on hers.

Caleb's eyes continued to look into hers just as intensely. But he had a half-smile, now, as if to ask if what he had done was okay. Layla smiled back and brushed her hair behind her ears. Her stomach was in knots.

Before she knew what was happening, Caleb's face was inches from her own. Layla desperately wanted to hold the universe where it was, but also, just as desperately, wanted to see what was going to happen next. As his lips landed on hers, Layla felt an overwhelming sense of pure bliss envelop her. The kiss was perfect.

When Caleb pulled away, he smiled and held her gaze. Layla's face lit up.

Out of the corner of her eye, Layla saw her phone light up

again, and she pulled away. It was just Blogiophile again. Only, she had to take a second look because it didn't look right to her.

987 likes, 136 comments. *You have 475 new followers!*

Her stomach was in knots again, but now the knots were there for a different reason. She was a little shocked to see the huge uptick in followers on her blog, but she forced her eyes to Caleb instead. Right now, it was all about the fact that she and Caleb had just had their very first kiss.

"Wow," Layla stammered. She fiddled with her sweater sleeves.

"Yeah," Caleb said, looking sheepishly at her. "To be honest, I've wanted to do that for a while now."

Layla's heart was ready to explode inside her chest. She could feel a distinct fullness come upon her again. She had only felt it a handful of times before, all of which occurred when she was texting Caleb. He brought out something in her that made her feel so safe.

Layla's phone lit up again, but this time it was a text. Caleb noticed her shifting in her seat and looked at her suspiciously.

"Oh, I, umm." Layla smiled widely and motioned toward her phone. "My mom. She's texting me from upstairs saying that it's probably time to get to bed soon."

Caleb sighed, rubbing the legs of his jeans awkwardly.

"Totally," he said. "I should take off."

They packed up their things, and Layla walked Caleb to the door.

"I'll see you tomorrow," he said. He nodded at her and turned to go.

She stood in the doorway, watching the legs of his black Levi's move toward the edge of the porch. As he walked, his arms moved through the sleeves of his black coat, his hands hidden in them only to reappear on the other side, strong and beautiful. The motion of his body tousled his hair ever so slightly, and he lifted his hand to tame it. He pushed it behind his ears and looked ahead into the night. She could have watched him until dawn, tracing his outline as it grew smaller in the distance. She knew she would keep this image of him and think about it later. Add it to the collection.

But in this moment, Layla felt the urge to tweak the image a bit. In an instant, she remembered that this was still him. He was right here, right now. He wasn't a fond memory… quite yet.

Feeling a surge in her legs she hadn't felt before, Layla fell into a jog down the porch steps and after him. Her mind was running so fast that she couldn't even feel the cold, damp ground against her bare feet. Reaching Caleb at the sidewalk, Layla grabbed his shoulder before she really knew what she was going to do with it. Just to have a shoulder for a moment was a gift. Caleb spun toward her, his face wrinkled in confusion.

Then, as if she had done it a million times before, Layla lifted herself onto her tippy-toes and pushed her lips into his. Her whole body sunk into him, and everything made sense. Her feet now understood why they were cold, and her hand now understood what it had done. It was an electric instant, the landing. Both of their faces lit up from the shock of it all. It was a passion she had never known before.

"Goodnight," she whispered, her body still against Caleb's. She pulled away and ran off back into her home. And just like that, the scene of him walking across the lawn that she had wanted to save for later—to archive, then watch and re-watch, alone in her room—had a surprise ending. She had written a new scene. And this time, she was in it. She was the main character.

Layla woke up the next morning in a state of unmatched bliss. Everything felt light and hopeful. It was like the first day of spring in October. She couldn't physically stop herself from smiling, which was hilarious and also a little bit obnoxious. Looking at her face in the mirror, she almost grossed herself out, even.

She had already told her mother what had happened, and her mother, too, couldn't wipe the dopey grin off her face if you'd paid her. So now, both of them were just sort of twirling about the house. Layla had to put this to an end.

"Okay, it's getting way too Disney Princess-y in here," she said, spreading cream cheese on two bagels as her mother poured the coffee.

Her mother chuckled. She wrapped her arm around her daughter and sighed gleefully.

"Young love. It's just so beautiful!" she ejected a sentiment that Layla had now heard a total of seven times.

"So, so beautiful," her mother repeated, grabbing Layla's hand and taking her to the table.

Make that eight, Layla thought to herself. She picked up her backpack and took out her laptop to check her email.

Suddenly, Layla lost her breath. She had gotten another update from her Blogiophile page. Apparently, she had amassed 2,078 followers on her blog overnight. She looked at her phone and noticed her Instagram followers had increased substantially as well.

In her DMs, Layla found twenty or so messages from random people. One read:

Wow, PP, this new story you're telling sounds really familiar. Is this that local mystery about the lady who died in the bakery?

Another read:

I thought she died from Carbon monoxide poisoning, what's so hard to remember about that?

Another:

PP, you're tapping into a whole different sphere with your blog lately! I'm loving it.

Layla swallowed hard. She had no idea this was going to happen. Who was reading this? And why was it resonating so much? It was just a random anecdote—a side note, really. It wasn't what she intended the blog to be about.

The blog was lighthearted and fun. It was just a few stories about being a normal teen in Portland. But now she was adding a teen boy's voice. What was the big deal?

I guess his story is unique, isn't it? Layla thought, closing her laptop and shoving some bagel in her mouth.

"Are you okay, love?"

Layla had almost forgotten her mother was still standing—still dancing—right there at this very moment. Portland Posted was, and would remain, a secret. So even though Layla really could have used some advice at this moment, she had to make sure she didn't tell her mother. It took everything in her to grin widely and say "Totally!"

The entire drive to school, Layla had to coach herself to breathe. She reminded herself that, while 2,078 followers was a lot of followers, there was still no way anyone at Burroughs cared about a local blog. And there surely wasn't anyone who would care enough to figure out who wrote it.

"Have you heard about this ridiculous blog situation?"

Layla froze with her face inside her locker. *Of course*, she thought. When she'd considered the curiosities of Burroughs's finest, she neglected to remember the curiosities of one Mia Tanner.

Layla exhaled and spun around to see her best friend gesturing wildly behind her.

"This blogger writes stories about people in Portland. Or, well, she uses fake names, I think. But the stories are weirdly similar to some of the town's history. They apparently go here or, at the very least, *watch* people who go here. They seem to know these crazy details about people's lives! And you're not going to like this part..." Mia continued, making eye contact with Layla.

Layla was pretty sure she knew what Mia was going to say next. But she had to act surprised, nonetheless.

"I mean, they definitely know a lot about Caleb," Mia said, hesitantly. "They never mention Caleb explicitly, but the story of this person's mom dying... It's weirdly similar. The date of her death is even the same. So I'd be worried if I were you. Might be an ex-girlfriend or something."

Layla bit her lip. She had of course screened the blog for names and details that seemed too close to the real thing. But dates. She had forgotten about dates.

Layla watched as Mia grew more and more animated. She should have known that Mia would be the first—and hopefully the only—person she knew in real life to read the blog. Layla realized now that she could probably start organizing her books again, because at this point Mia was just sort of soliloquizing. A response was not required.

Layla dug through her calc notes while Mia paced back and forth behind her.

"Definitely worth looking into, Layla. You never know when ex-girlfriends are going to pop their heads back up again. You never know..."

"Mhmmm, yeah. Absolutely." Layla replied, looking up at Mia again and nodding to show she was very, very interested.

"This person—a girl, I'm assuming, though it's very hard to tell because she sort of writes like a different person in every post—seems to be on a mission to solve the mystery of Caleb's mom's death. There's even an earlier post about the bakery Caleb's mom used to run. It's utterly fascinating."

"Okay, okay," Layla said, nodding some more. "And did sheumm, they—solve it?"

"Well, not yet, Layla!" Mia ejected, shaking her head as if this were a ridiculous question. "I don't know if she will. I don't know if there will be more. I have so many questions!"

"Oh yeah, mmhmmm," Layla said, nodding more enthusiastically now. "Me too, so many questions."

Mia rolled her eyes at Layla's sarcasm.

"Okay, fine. Act like you're not even a little bit curious. I know you pretend not to care about school gossip, but this is about to be huge—"

"What do you mean?" Layla interjected, starting to panic

internally. "It's just some stupid blog."

Mia swallowed a big gulp of her coffee and looked down at her phone.

"Yeah, I mean, maybe. But look at this," Mia said, showing Layla her phone. It was open to the Portland Posted blog, with all the likes at the bottom. Mia then opened up her Twitter and showed Layla a tweet. It was from a senior, Chelsea Richmond, who notoriously created drama where there wasn't any. It read *Someone at Burroughs is majorly stalking the Strauss family. And I'm going to find out who it is.*

Mia then scrolled through a string of retweets from a bunch of Burroughs kids, including Amanda. Layla's stomach dropped.

"Oh... oh my god," she whispered.

"Yeah," Mia replied. "That's what I was saying. The entire school has it."

Layla's heart was pounding as she continued to attempt to casually place her books into her locker. Her mind was racing with thoughts of how many people knew about the blog and who had read it. There was no use going back and changing the date or tweaking the story at all now. It was already out there. She could never have imagined her fellow students reading her blog, much less speculating about its author and retweeting it to the masses. This was all happening so fast.

Of course, this was what she wanted. Ultimately, her goal was for people to read the blog. On top of that, she wanted to be like her dad, speaking for others in a unique way that they didn't think possible. But the truth-writing made it all so much more complicated. It was her writing, but technically she wasn't even really in charge of what she wrote. Technically these were other people's thoughts and feelings, not hers.

Layla started to feel sick. Her stomach rumbled and she immediately felt the need to go to the restroom.

"I—I have to go. I'm sorry. Talk later," Layla muttered, grabbing her English books and taking off down the hall.

When she got to the bathroom, Layla splashed some water

in her face. She breathed deeply, calming herself.

"It's okay, no one knows it's you," she whispered to herself in the mirror. But that didn't change the guilt she felt in sharing words that weren't really hers to share. Secrets that she probably shouldn't have known in the first place. She would think about all this later, but first she needed to find Caleb. He definitely knew about the blog by now, and she was sure he would be feeling at least a little confused about it. She exhaled deeply and set out to find Caleb.

Normally, Caleb's locker (and subsequently Caleb himself) was hardly visible in the large group of basketball player guys that hung out in front of it. The two times Layla had sought him out at his locker, it had taken her several minutes to excuse herself through the crowd and actually reach him.

Today, however, the group of guys wasn't there. They had migrated over to Ben Wheeler's locker, which was on the other end of the hallway. The only person in front of Caleb's locker today was Caleb.

When Layla approached, Caleb was standing completely still, just sort of staring at his books in the locker. He was in no rush to grab anything or go anywhere. He was just sort of... there. Layla gulped, and tapped him on the shoulder.

"Hey..." she said, quietly. He turned around and Layla was taken aback. His face was pale and expressionless. His eyes were empty and cold. It was as if he was completely numb to the moment. He didn't say anything, but just stared at her for what felt like an eternity.

"Umm... are you all right?" Layla asked, inching closer to him. She grabbed his arm, which felt like an appropriate gesture to greet the boy she liked with, especially now that he knew she liked him.

"Uhh, yeah?" Caleb said, as if he were asking rather than answering. "Weird day so far."

Caleb snapped out of his daze for a few seconds to turn around and grab his books. It took him longer than usual to collect the things he needed, as if he had forgotten where he was going next.

Layla wasn't sure what to say, exactly. She wanted to just talk to him like she usually did, but he clearly had other things on his mind. She was furious at her alter ego for throwing a wrench into everything like this.

"I'm sure you heard that there's some mind reader on my trail," Caleb said. He looked into Layla's eyes now, still expressionless. "Portland Promises or something."

Layla felt sick again hearing him say the blog name (albeit a little butchered). She immediately wanted to log in and delete the entire blog and forget this ever happened.

"I did hear…" she whispered.

"I didn't write it, if that's what you're thinking. Everyone thinks I wrote it."

"Oh, I didn't think you did," she replied. Though thinking he did seemed better than knowing *she* did, in that moment. Layla was livid with herself now. What had she thought would happen when the world figured out she could essentially read minds? Did she think she'd become famous and beloved by people who maybe wanted their secrets to remain, well, *secret?*

"Ughh," Layla exclaimed, without thinking. Caleb looked up at her again, perplexed. She caught herself, immediately adding, "This must all be so confusing for you."

Caleb nodded solemnly.

"Do you have any idea who wrote it?" Layla asked, sheepishly looking at her shoes.

"No idea. And it could just be some random story that's similar to mine… It could just be someone messing with me… But the fact that everyone at school knows about it, has read it, and keeps asking me about it is just… a lot right now."

"Absolutely. I can't imagine." Layla inched closer to him and tried to find his eyes again. "I personally think it's nothing. Not worth thinking about."

Caleb nodded again, getting his backpack ready for the day.

Layla wished she could read him a little better. Maybe he

needed to be alone. After last night, she was still hoping they'd be able to talk a bit today. But now this blog thing was throwing everything off. She sighed again.

"I gotta go," said Caleb. He offered her a half-smile and held her gaze for a moment. This made her smile back. She nodded, and they parted ways down opposite sides of the hallway.

Layla sat at her usual table at the JBC, looking over her chemistry notes. Mr. Morrisson had started the new unit, and it was super difficult for her. She read and reread the chapter he had assigned, but she was still struggling to interpret it. It wasn't as mathy as chemistry usually is, which made her feel frustrated.

Her phone vibrated in her pocket. It was a text from Caleb. Or, as she had added him in her phone: C A L E B. She had felt like his name written normally, as every other name in her phone, was just... anticlimactic. How could his name look like the others when he was so uniquely himself? Plus, seeing a message from C A L E B drew her attention in an instant. Layla didn't love texting as it was, and usually she would let texts that weren't from her mother sit in her inbox for hours before even reading them. But she couldn't help but notice messages from C A L E B. They turned her world upside down.

Hey, sorry about today. I've been out of it.

She thought for a minute. It was sweet of him to say something. But she didn't know if this meant he was ready to talk about it or not, and she didn't want to force anything.

Np. I understand. But like I said, I'm here to talk if you need it.

Thanks, Layla. What are you up to?

Layla realized it probably wasn't a good time for her to explain to him that she studied at, and practically lived at, the café his mother used to own and run.

Just walking around.

Why did she say that? Why was she saying this?

Sounds nice. Where?

Oh no, he wanted coordinates. Of course. What did she think, he wouldn't ask any follow-up questions? This was Caleb she was texting. Layla thought for a second. Did it really matter where she was supposedly walking at this moment? She was always bopping around town on foot or by bike, and Caleb knew that about her. She loved to see the town. She could easily be at the library, or another café. She could easily be heading to visit her mom at the university, or walking through the park.

I want to see you. Can I come find you?

Layla's heart stopped. Caleb wasn't like other guys. He wasn't much for texting either, which she loved. She loved that she didn't have to decipher cryptic messages like she had done with Gavin last year. It was nice to know that he wasn't not texting her because he didn't want to talk to her. He just didn't like to do it much.

That's why it was surprising now that he had texted her twice in a row, less than three minutes from one to the next. Layla felt caught in a lie. She scrambled to come up with something.

Just walked into Frog & Toad to do some studying. On Fourth and Tyler. I want to see you back.

Layla began to pack up her things. The book store was only four blocks away. So she could study over there today, no big deal. She liked the smell of old books, anyway. The lighting wasn't as good, but it would work out okay. Layla giggled at how ridiculous it all was.

"You off?" Gavin called from behind the counter. He cocked his head to the side, perplexed. Of course, he probably reasoned that she would be staying until her mom got off work, knowing her as well as he did. She resented how well Gavin knew her.

"I am!" she called back, saluting him as she sashayed through the door.

He saluted back, grinning.

That's right, she thought. *I do what I want. Or, in this case, what I have stumbled into.*

She hit the sidewalk and looked down at her phone.

Okay if I join?

She buzzed down the street in an excited tizzy.

Always.

When she arrived, she waved wildly to Matilda, the eccentric older woman behind the counter, and offered a pat to Baxter and Donnie, the two cats who sat perched on stools in the fiction section most of the time. Then she made a beeline to the restroom to make sure she was looking at least somewhat cute on this, the day Caleb would arrive at a place she had casually just lied about being.

There was something exhilarating about it all, she thought, as she stood at the mirror and attempted to add any semblance of volume to her extremely straight blonde hair. She crunched it and floofed it, but still it straightened back out in real time before her eyes. She removed her glasses and applied the mascara she had conveniently packed in the inside pocket of her backpack for such an occasion. Technically, she had put it in that pocket months ago for an occasion involving Gavin. She smiled to herself, remembering how silly she had felt sneaking into the alley behind the JBC to freshen up just before she entered, saw Gavin, and acted shocked that he would be there, in the place he worked six days a week.

This silliness with Caleb felt elevated somehow. She wasn't sure if it was that she was almost a whole year older now, or that she and Caleb just meshed on a more complex level. Whatever it was, she felt older and wiser in this mirror. It was as if she and the mascara bottle had grown up a good deal since the last time they were together. She couldn't help but laugh at the thought of this journey they had been on.

A few minutes later, Layla took a seat at a table and pulled out her books. She saw Caleb approaching the bookshop door and immediately looked down, pretending to focus on her calc homework. Of course, she continued to monitor his movements through the store in her periphery, but he couldn't know that. If there was anything she knew about love, it was this: the only way to get it was to look like you weren't at all interested in it.

"Hey there," Caleb whispered, sliding a chair up to Layla's table. Layla looked up and saw his big blue eyes staring back at her the way they usually did.

What was somewhat unusual, though, especially given the circumstances surrounding the day, was that Caleb's lips were quivering. They moved quickly, pulling out into a smile intermittently as if out of his control. Layla then noticed that the hand that lay across his backpack on the table was shaking as well. Not so much so that it shook the table underneath, but enough that it stole her attention for a minute.

"How are things?" Layla asked casually, trying not to sound put off by his strange body language.

"Great!" Caleb ejected, then paused and exhaled heavily as if calming himself down. "I mean, fine. You know… weird day."

Layla held his eyes for a moment and nodded empathetically.

"Definitely," she muttered.

Caleb shifted in his seat awkwardly. After a moment, he got out his books and started looking through a notebook. Layla was confused by this, because, as far as she understood it, when boys said they wanted to "study" that didn't usually mean they actually wanted to study. Or maybe it meant that they did want to study, but they also wanted to talk and hang out a bit. And if they indeed wanted to talk and hang out a bit, that usually happened before said studying was underway. Normally, there would be conversation leading up to the studying, even if that conversation was simply about the studying. And although Caleb and Layla had developed something of a disciplined study relationship based on their tutoring sessions, Layla assumed the prospect of conversation hadn't completely disintegrated. Unless, of course, Caleb really did just want to study with her. Which was fine, but also kind of a strange dynamic, and nothing she had ever known before.

Before she knew it, Layla was reconsidering everything she thought she knew about Caleb and spiraling into confusion about all boys that had ever existed. Which was why she was pleased when Caleb interrupted this freight train of thought by saying, "Seth Rogen, remember?"

Layla's eyes squinted up at him instinctively.

"Uhm, excuse me?"

Caleb was shifting again, and he flicked his hair out of his face several times for some reason.

"You know, when we were playing ghost yesterday," he explained.

"Oh, right!" Layla replied. She had no idea why he had come all this way to play a game he had made up during a tutoring session, but if that was really what he wanted then who was she to judge?

"Okay, the name of the game is Seth Rogen," he declared. He leaned back in his chair, looking on at her.

"Okay, umm…" Caleb continued. "Zac."

"Efron," Layla said, cockily. She rolled her eyes, as if the prompt was too easy.

"Correct!" Caleb said. "What about... Joseph?"

Layla locked eyes with him and said, cleverly, "Gordon-Levitt." She made sure to draw out her response so he'd know how easy that one was for her.

"Very good, Miss Whitaker!" Caleb said, chuckling. "I didn't know you were such a Rogen fan."

"Thank you, next," Layla replied, smirking wildly. Layla stood up and stretched her arms up and down jokingly. "Try to actually challenge me this time, Strauss."

Suddenly Layla realized that Caleb wasn't looking at her in his normal way anymore. Instead of wearing his silly grin, he was staring at her intensely from his seat. He was always serious about this game, but today he seemed more serious than usual. Now he was staring so deeply at her, it was as if he were trying to dive into her. She grew nervous, feeling his eyes cover over her like a blanket.

"Will," Caleb said now, so faintly, as if in a whisper.

"What?" she asked, desperately trying to read his face with her eyes. "What did you say?"

"Will," he said again, louder, more confidently.

Layla racked her brain for a Will who was in a movie with Seth Rogen. She ran through the cast of every Rogen movie she'd seen, but no dice.

"Oh... umm... Will Arnett? Was he in *This is the End*?" Layla guessed, stammering now. "Gosh, I can't remember. I feel like that movie had everyone in Hollywood in it."

He continued to stare at her, waiting patiently for her to get the answer. Layla began to pace back and forth, looking at the books on the bookshelves on either side of her as she walked.

"No... umm... It's... Will... Will..." Layla continued. "Bill? Is it Bill Hader? He could be a William, I'm not sure. And he had to be in one of those movies."

Caleb said nothing and looked on at her, as if not hearing anything she said.

"No..." she said, looking around, puzzled. "It's not Bill Hader. It's umm..."

She was growing so nervous, realizing now how long it had been since he'd started staring at her. She was wishing that he would look at something else—anything else.

"Will… Will… Will…" She trailed off, heart racing.

Caleb stood up before her now and moved his chair to the side. She panicked internally and desperately tried not to show that panic externally. In a strange move, Caleb stepped around the table and approached her now.

"Will…?" she continued, stopping in her tracks. She brushed her hair behind her ears nervously.

Caleb reached out to her slowly and grabbed her right hand. She choked. *What is happening?! Internal panic reaching an all-time high!*

"Will..." Caleb said, his voice cracking.

Layla looked around the room nervously.

"Will you go to Homecoming with me, Layla?" Caleb asked, nodding slightly but keeping his eyes lifted up at hers.

"I…" Layla's jaw fell, and she froze. She was completely shocked.

Caleb wiped his hair out of his eyes, looking on at her still, patiently awaiting her response.

"Y…Yes!" she exclaimed, wrapping her arms around him wildly.

"Great," he laughed. He cleared his throat now and swung her around in his arms. "I didn't know you were such a Rogen fan," he said again.

Layla charged through her front door and pirouetted on the creaky wood floors. Bart leapt up into her arms, barking gleefully as if to say *I don't know what we're happy about, but I'm all about it!*

Her mother heard the racket and, without asking any questions at all, jumped into the fray and spun wildly to make three nuts in the entryway. The only thing that could have made that moment better was if her dad had made four.

The next day, Layla and Mia met at their lockers early so Layla could give her the full rundown of yesterday's events.

"You were asked to Homecoming?" Mia said, drawing her words out as if Layla had told her in a different language that needed translating.

"...Yes," Layla said.

"You were asked to Homecoming... by a senior..." Mia continued, just as slowly.

"...Also yes," Layla said.

"And... you made me wait until this morning to find out?!" Mia started screaming. She grabbed both of Layla's hands and the two girls started jumping up and down wildly. Layla was glad they had gotten this dance out of the way before everyone else arrived for school.

"Well, I just really wanted to tell you in person, you know," Layla replied.

"This is so crazy!" Mia said, still processing, as they turned down the hallway to the cafeteria for a coffee.

It wasn't that Layla had wanted to keep her exciting news from anyone. Layla told her mom after their living room dance party, and of course she was thrilled. She let out a scream and then ran off through the house laying out dresses and pairing them with shoes and earrings and headbands. Layla had wanted to call Mia right when it happened, and it had taken everything in her not to.

She played out the conversation in her head over and over again. There would be joy, like her mother had felt, bouncing through the house and humming to herself. There would be squeals on the other end of the phone so loud, the neighbors on both ends might hear.

But there was something so bittersweet about the act of giving people in her life information these days. Her mother's eager eyes would latch onto her like a puppy begging for food.

She would toss something to her, but always just in little morsels. No matter what Layla told her mother, it was never the whole story.

She began to feel a deep disdain for her gift. The ability to know truths no one else did was shrouded with pain and secrecy. She began to understand why her dad had been so cold and standoffish to her mother and to his family and friends. All of it made sense. All of it made her angry.

All she could do was give out the morsels and work to use the truth she learned for the betterment of her family and friends. If she used it selflessly, then nothing at all could go wrong.

It would all be worth it, she thought.

Layla noticed that Mia was concentrating on her phone screen now.

"Still on page two of the Connor and Mia love story? The box office smash we've all been waiting for?" Mia had been talking about her chemistry partner, Connor, for weeks, but she was struggling to move the conversation to the type of chemistry she was hoping for.

"I swear, this isn't going anywhere. All he ever wants to talk about is chemistry. And listen, I love a good acid/base meme as much as the next person, but this is getting a little redundant." Mia showed Layla the Bernie meme on her phone screen that read:

Bases be like: I am once again asking for your protons.

Layla chuckled.

"Give me that," she said.

Layla took a moment to compose a response for Mia.

Ah, the loveable socialist teddy bear that is Bernie Sanders. I feel like our schedule this week is nothing but basic, though. Are you also drowning? Maybe we should catch a lifeboat together in the cafeteria after school this week?

"Seriously, Layla. Can I hire you to be my ghostwriter? This is immaculate. Super casual, but also very much moves the plot forward. I love it!"

Layla grinned. It had been a long time since she felt comfortable offering dating advice to friends. She knew Mia so well now, and being there for her was a no-brainer. Especially with all the support Mia had given her in the Caleb realm.

"Seriously, my dad is hiring writers at his firm. Have you ever thought about marketing? Because this brand voice is on point. It's exactly how I sound. You have a gift."

Layla chuckled a little to herself as they entered the classroom. How right Mia was.

Mrs. Chamberlain passed back the exams at the end of the hour, as was her way. It was kind of her to let the students cry-scream in the comfort of their own lockers, sure. But it was agony to have to sit through an entire class period before you got it back.

She saw the huge 92% on the top of her paper and exhaled deeply. Almost immediately, she looked past the page at where Caleb sat.

His head hung down, stationary. He wasn't smiling, but that didn't mean much.

Was it so terrible that he was crippled by misery? Was it such a good grade that he was frozen in blissful shock?

He was difficult to read at most angles; near impossible to read at this particular one.

Finally he stood up and filed in line with his friends as they left the classroom. Mia was standing before Layla, waiting for their turn to leave as well.

"Yes! Great job, Layla!" Mia flipped her test around to reveal that she, too, had received a 92%. A 92% always felt like a 100% in Mrs. Chamberlain's class, and the two girls grinned at each other in victory.

Layla walked Mia to her art class and then spun back around to see if she could catch Caleb before his language arts class.

She saw him at his locker from afar and realized she was hitting quite the jog to try to get to him. She slowed herself.

"Hey Strauss!" she called coolly as she approached him.

He spun around and gave her an effortless half-smile.

"Anything to write home about?" Layla asked, cleverly.

Caleb bent his head to the side and paused, as if taking her in. He licked his lips and then pursed them.

They stood for a moment, just looking at one another. She knew he was playing coy.

As if he was unable to resist it any longer, Caleb broke into a smile.

"Absolutely something to write home about," he declared, holding up his test for her to see.

He had gotten an 80%.

"A B-, are you kidding me?!" Layla smiled from ear to ear.

"All thanks to you, Whitaker," he replied.

She wanted to hug him, to leap into his arms like they did in the movies. To have him kiss her, and to feel the entire world stop spinning on its axis.

Layla thought for a minute. It was so very like her to watch a moment unfold without really living it. It was par for the course. She knew herself so well that she could predict how the entire scene would play out. Ordinary old Layla would grin and make him feel proud, and then nervously laugh and pretend she was running late and disappear down the hallway. It would all be like clockwork.

For a moment now she was angry at herself. How was it that she could admire beautiful things and just take them home to analyze and pick apart in her journal at her desk? Why couldn't she enjoy the beauty; surround herself with it; take part in it, for crying out loud!

Suddenly, she found herself swinging her arms out as if pushing the ordinary Layla out of the way. She didn't know if it was the confidence from an A- in Mrs. Chamberlain's class or the Homecoming invitation, or both, but something made her surge toward Caleb standing at his locker.

"I'm so happy for you, Caleb," she ejected. Without thinking, she swung her arms up, causing her books to fall, and wrapped them around his neck.

What is this? What am I doing? Thinking started back up again, and Layla noticed that her right foot had popped up the way feet only did when they belonged to movie princesses kissing their princes at their weddings. She almost burst out laughing.

She realized she was so distracted by what she was doing with her limbs in this moment that she hadn't realized what Caleb was doing with his. Almost instantly, his arms wrapped naturally around her and pulled her into him. Nothing seemed funny anymore.

His breath on her neck overwhelmed her at first, making every hair stand at attention. But within a few seconds, she grew used to it there and enjoyed its warmth. He smelled amazing: not too strong, but fresh and pleasant. The scruff on his face rubbed delicately against her ear. Her chin was buried in a wave of his soft hair. She wished she could stay in this moment forever.

As their arms departed and fell to their sides, Layla breathed him in once more.

"Thanks, Layla," he whispered, staring into her.

Layla stumbled, grabbing the books that had fallen out of her bag and casually replacing them.

"It's all you, Caleb," she replied. She stepped backwards, grinned wildly, and turned around down the hallway.

Don't look back, she thought, feeling very cool about the departure she just made. It was cinematic. She knew Mrs. Cooney would be proud.

Layla couldn't help but grin all the way down the hallway and up the stairs. She kept on grinning as she sat down in piano class.

Thankfully, Ms. Krempa was playing Philip Glass on the speakers and moving her thin frame like a blade of grass in the wind at the front of the class. She also had her eyes closed as she moved, which was convenient because Layla had just barely made it in on time. She dug through her backpack to find her piano folder, which she knew would have the name of this song somewhere in it if she just looked hard enough.

But when her hand hit the bottom of the backpack, she felt only one folder, and it was her calc folder. She dug around some more and noticed she didn't have the blue folder at all. She sighed heavily. It must have fallen out during the whole princess-foot-pop scene. Thankfully she had copied her notes into a Google Doc on her...

"Phone! My phone!" Layla jolted in her chair, thankfully not disturbing anyone around her in her tizzy.

Her phone must have fallen out of her bag. *It must be on the ground.*

Layla's hand shot up in the air. "Ba-bathroom!" she ejected, and Ms. Krempa nodded, mid-twirl.

Layla bolted down the stairs and back to the hallway. As she turned the corner, she noticed Caleb at the end of the hall, as if he hadn't moved from where she left him five minutes ago. In fact, he wasn't moving at all. He was frozen, looking down, reading... her phone screen. Which Layla knew was filled with Blogiophile notifications addressed to Portland Posted.

Layla raced up to him, her face pale as a ghost.

When she got to him, Caleb lifted his head, revealing his face. It was cold, and it was stern. This was the furthest his face had ever looked from the bright-eyed boy's in the photo.

CHAPTER SEVENTEEN

"What... What *is* this?" Caleb exclaimed, his voice cracking.

Layla was paralyzed with fear. She felt herself trying to reach out and take the phone from him, but it was too late. All she could do was watch as everything crumbled before her eyes.

Her brain started to go through every possible outcome, trying to come up with some way to explain everything. Could this have been just a coincidence? Could she have been working on a secret project? Could she have hit her head on the pole of that low-hanging pride flag on her porch and just experienced some sort of episode? Nothing sounded like the truth, and the truth was not something she wanted to get into right now.

"How... How... How did you... How could you know?" he stammered, dumbfounded. "How did you know that my mother died? How do you know anything about my mother?"

It was obvious to Layla that Caleb was now tongue-tied and furious. He was breathing heavily.

Layla finally snatched the phone back from him.

"I... I can explain," she said, frantically. "I... It's just... Ummm..." She looked down the hallway and saw other students coming.

"Come with me," she exclaimed, pulling him around the corner into the math center.

As she walked, Layla realized that she really didn't know

what she was going to say. She was trying to buy herself time, knowing she would come up with something eventually. It was rare that she didn't know what to say.

Noticing no one else was there, Layla sat at her usual desk. To her surprise, Caleb did not take the seat across from her as she expected he would.

"Layla…" Caleb began, "I should get to class. I don't know what to…"

"No, just… please. Sit," Layla said, motioning toward the chair.

The room they had sat in so many times over the past few months, just working on math, talking, and getting to know each other, now looked completely different to her. She hated the blues now more than ever.

Caleb sighed deeply and sat down. He looked up at her with a squint, as if he had just woken from a dream and was trying to decipher what was real and what wasn't.

"Please, calm down," she started. "I'm here. I'm here right now."

She wasn't sure exactly why she said that, except that it seemed like something someone who had just woken from a bad dream might want to hear. Though after she thought about it for a minute, she realized it was strange for someone who created confusion to try to be the one to rescue you from it. It didn't make a whole lot of sense. What she wouldn't give to have been someone else in that moment, diving in to save him from herself.

"I don't want to hurt you," Layla said.

"O…kay…" Caleb replied.

"But I have to tell you something," she said.

"Uhh… YEAH. Yeah, you do." Caleb nodded vigorously.

"I just want you to know that I never meant to hurt you and I always want to be there for you," Layla said, shrugging. She tried to catch his eyes with hers as they traced the carpet. She put her hand on his hand, but before it could settle there, he took his away. She felt sick.

"I don't know how to explain it, really, because I've never

really explained it. To anyone. Actually, you're the first person I've ever even tried to explain it to, here presently. Right in this moment."

"Layla!" Caleb declared, stopping her rambling. "*What is going on?!*"

She jolted to a stop and exhaled deeply.

"I have… powers," she said.

She paused, almost wanting to laugh because of the way that statement sounded after it came out. But she thought better of it and just held his gaze instead. Thankfully, he held hers back.

"What powers?" he asked. "I don't understand."

"Well, that's a good question," she replied. "So, I just found out, pretty recently… that I can write… people's thoughts… and worries? Like I can know them and write them down… sort of *for* them, or as if I *am* them. Does that make sense?"

"No." Caleb tilted his head. "Nothing has actually made less sense than what you just said."

"See, it's funny," Layla continued, nervously. "I always thought I was just a mathematician like my mom. But it turns out I can write like my dad! Which, I guess, does kind of make sense, because my dad and I were really close when I was young—"

"What are you saying?!" Caleb interrupted.

"It's just that… I can write the things that you would want to write, or maybe *need* to write… you know, in a journal or something. I write *for* other people."

"I… I don't understand," Caleb said. "Like, you can read my mind?"

"No… no, no, no, no. Well, sort of." Layla was not good at this.

"I can't read your mind. I can maybe… *write* it? Type it, actually. I type it out on my blog."

"Uhhhhh, whaaaaaaat," Caleb stood up from his chair and started pacing back and forth at an extraordinary rate.

"Listen, I… I can't really explain it. Because, well, I'm sort of still figuring it all out right now. But it's true."

She paused for a moment, giving him time to suss it out. After a few moments she continued.

"There are certain circumstances that make it so. The laptop has to be open to a new post already. And I'm starting to think it needs to be only me and the other person in the room. Stuff like that. But when it happens, it just sort of... happens."

She paused again. A few more details here and she would be all done, she thought. Then there would be a few questions here and there. And finally, they could go back to being the perfect teen romance. And go back to class.

"I really am not trying to hurt you. I just found out I had this gift. I blogged about my mom, and your dad once—"

"My dad?!" Caleb interjected, wildly.

"Yes, and then I blogged about you once too, obviously. That's when I learned about your mom and the mystery surrounding her death. And... I don't know, I just thought...."

Caleb stopped pacing suddenly. He looked up at her with that squinty-eyed face again, except redder this time. His lips were pursed. Slowly, his stare turned from confusion to anger. Layla's heart was racing.

"You thought you could find out how my mother died," Caleb declared coldly.

He licked his lips, and held her gaze as his face grew angrier and angrier. She had never seen him so upset.

Suddenly, Caleb leaned over on the desk, full-on scowling at this point. In the next moment, he was so overcome by rage that he threw his arms out and began pacing again at breakneck speed through the study room.

"Listen, Caleb," she started, standing up now herself and reaching out to try to calm him down. "I really didn't mean—"

He stopped walking and stared at her again.

"You honestly thought you could figure it out, didn't you?" he asked, his voice cracking again. "You thought you might be the one to solve the mystery."

"I didn't know if I could, honestly," Layla replied. She took a few steps toward him, her head hung low.

"But I wanted to help. I wanted to be there for you and just… try."

"Layla!" he exclaimed, tossing his arms up in the air again. "Nothing I would have written in a journal—or… you would have written for me, I suppose—would have told you how my mom died."

Layla instinctively reached out to grab his hand, but Caleb turned away and walked toward the back wall. Silently, he stared at the wall for what felt like an eternity.

"My father has hired so many specialists: doctors, psychoanalysts, therapists, police investigators, priests! He has brought more people than I can count over to our house for the sole purpose of talking with me and picking my brain. But you think you're above all of that, huh? You think you can just find the words inside me and write them down? You think the question of my mother's death is something I can answer, but just haven't figured out how to yet? You think it's not a question I have had carved into myself, and feel on my skin every single day?"

"It's no use," he declared. "There's nothing in there to find!"

Layla realized now that what she had done was so much worse than she had thought.

"We are not handed the truth in this life," he said. "I know that better than anyone you'll ever meet."

Layla mustered up the courage to speak.

"I'm so sorry I didn't tell you, Caleb," she said. "It really was just that I didn't know how to explain it to you. But you were the one I really wanted to tell."

Caleb turned around to look at her again. This time he was crying.

"I just thought you were different," Caleb said, swallowing hard. "I guess I was wrong. I have to get to class."

Then, looking down to avoid eye contact with her, Caleb walked out of the math center in silence.

CHAPTER EIGHTEEN

That Saturday evening, Layla leaned back in her chair and stared off out the kitchen window, fidgeting with a pencil. Bart laid at her feet under the table, breathing heavily on her ankle. Layla was in a complete daze, as she had been since the day she and Caleb had had their fight in the math center. She wasn't upset anymore, really. But she wasn't happy with how things ended, either. She just felt numb.

Her mother floated through the room, stopping to check on the roasted vegetables in the oven. She had noticed Layla's moping throughout the week, but every time she asked about it, Layla just shrugged and blamed chemistry. Which was always a fair move, since chemistry was the bane of her existence most days. Every so often, Layla found herself starting to tell her mother about what had happened with Caleb. But before she even let the words out, she would stop them, pausing and remembering that to tell her about Caleb would involve telling her about truth-writing. She knew she wasn't ready to do that. So instead, she had talked about ionic bonds, and eventually her mother had stopped asking.

Her mother had suggested they watch a movie together that night after dinner and eat the Ben & Jerry's that awaited them in the freezer. It would be a quiet night, just the two of them, the way Layla liked it. The only thing that could have made a night of movies with her mom better was if her father had been there too. Layla thought then about how much easier it would be to talk to her father about this, since he'd had this power too. He would understand everything. He would guide her. Maybe, if he had been there, he would have been able to keep her from making the mistake she had made in the first place.

That's it! she thought. *I need to talk to my dad.*

Of course, she couldn't *talk* to her dad the way most other kids her age did. But she had her ways of communicating with him.

After dinner, she headed up the stairs to his study. The room was cold, being as it was at the end of the hallway with a door that was always closed off from the rest of the house. She was greeted by a draft and a painful quiet that surrounded her. You could have heard a pin drop, if pins had any reason to even go into her father's study. It was just walls and walls of books, fully-written, half-written, or read. A beautiful haven for her in a wild world.

Layla approached the desk and opened the bottom drawer, where her mother had decided it was now time to place the truth-writing notebooks they had been looking through before. On top was the one she had begun looking through with her mother. They hadn't gotten far, as within minutes she'd decided against continuing and had gently replaced it in the drawer. There were others like it, equally worn and wrinkled.

She placed the top notebook on the desk and stared down at it. She flipped open the cover and, seeing her father's handwriting filling the first page, breathed a sigh of relief.

"Here he is," she said aloud. "I found him."

What a world, what a wild wonder. Today a man I've seen at Café Du Marquis dozens of times actually took a seat for a moment before picking up his paper and walking out. He is usually in a rush—off to the office, I suppose. But today he is sitting across from me, watching the window as if he's waiting for someone.

I realize now that we are alone, the man and I, because Charlie just went out back for a smoke. It's still early, and the morning rush won't be in for at least an hour. So I suppose I have a minute just to watch him watch the world.

On the next page of her father's notebook, the writing was scattered over the page with no regard for lines or margins. Layla could tell this was the man writing now, and it went on like that for seven whole pages.

She read them quietly to herself.

On the bottom right of each page, her father had placed a piece of blue painter's tape where there weren't words and written on each one a label like *The Newspaper Man, March 1982.*

Layla pulled open two more notebooks from the drawer, and each one was similar in that way. All the pages were labeled with the person he was writing for.

A Girl on the Train, June 1982.
Little Boy Blue, July 1982.
Earnest at the Library, September 1982.
A Woman with Cheese, October 1982.
The Princess of the Bank, June 1982.
The Man Whose Dog Loves Everyone, March 1982.

It went on and on like that in little sections of each notebook. Layla was floored by the sheer volume of writing her father had on these characters.

Real people, she corrected herself mid-thought. These were real, true people. Real people just walking around town.

Layla thought for a second about these *real people.*

The people her father had observed and wrote for were just living their lives without a second thought. They wandered, they read the paper, they called for cabs, they drank lattes. These people were living, breathing humans, with goals and dreams and families at home. These were people who may not have even known they were being written about. They may not have known their writer, and they certainly didn't know him as well as he knew them.

Layla choked on this last thought. Suddenly she could see everything unfolding from Caleb's point of view.

It wasn't as if Layla had been actively pursuing details about his childhood or his family or his inner thoughts. She wasn't trying to pry into his life, not really. All she wanted was to help him find out what happened to his mother. All she thought she was doing was being a friend.

But now she saw what Caleb probably saw: someone who watched him and learned everything about him without his consent; someone who knew too much and just kept on wanting to know more; someone who inserted themselves where they didn't belong.

Layla felt sick to her stomach.

She began now to tear through the pages with a fierce anger. She didn't know exactly who she was angry at. Was it herself? Was it her father? Was it whomever had given them both this super power? This *not-so-super* power?

Layla made her way through, skimming the pages to the very last notebook in the drawer. She opened it up, expecting to see even more chapters on nameless passersby in her father's life. But when she looked at the first page, she was floored to read her own name.

Darling Layla is growing up so much. She's off to the races at a crawl these days, zooming around the house and getting into all kinds of trouble. I just know she'll be walking soon.

A smile instantly formed on her face. As she continued to skim the pages of this notebook, she realized what made it distinct from the others: it was entirely written in her father's own voice.

"I guess that wasn't really you before, Dad," she said out loud. "Now I see you again."

And she continued to read.

CHAPTER NINETEEN

The notebook that Layla had found in her father's study that night was nothing short of a gift in her time of need. She had begun reading it, but it was rather lengthy, so at some point her mother had found her and lured her back downstairs with the prospect of Phish Food and Leo DiCaprio.

The next morning, she took a seat at the desk again. She settled in, unwrapped her Pop-Tart, and opened up this treasure trove once more. Something about the words on the page made her feel at home. Her father had used this particular notebook to collect his observations about truth-writing. It chronicled the tips and tricks he acquired on his own journey, such that it was something of a user's manual for truth-writing. Every page included topics like how to truth-write, the best times of day to truth-write, how to make sure no one knew you were doing it. It was extraordinary.

A word on bystanders.
I learned early on that one can only truth-write for another person if the room is empty save for the two of them. Or, mostly empty. Anyone— passerby, waiter, barista, whoever—can block the powers from working if they come too close. Oftentimes another person will be in the building, but on the other end of the room, and the magic works. When they get too close, it

stops. I have no earthly idea why this is so, but I've had it happen many times. I'll think I'm ready to write for someone, and I'll put all my focus into them. I'll feel my hand starting to move on the page, and I'll know there's going to be a story. But then, suddenly, the bell will ring on the door or the clerk will return to her post and it's all over.

Again, I can't say why.

Layla nodded, pleased that she had already learned this axiom of truth-writing the time she couldn't get any notes on Caleb because the librarian wouldn't stop coming in and out of their study room. She continued on.

The next section of the notebook had notes about settings, times of day, and durations that worked best for him as he progressed through his truth-writing journey. It was painstakingly detailed, the way so many things her father did were.

It struck Layla, as she moved through the pages, that after a while he seemed to write less and less. The specifics that made her father's writing feel like home were few and far between as the pages turned.

It was as if Layla's father had consciously stepped away from truth-writing over time.

Layla paused for a moment, realizing she was reaching the end of the notebook—or at least the end of the writing. The last thirty or so pages were completely blank, so the page that sat before her now was the very last one that had been used at all.

The writing on this page was hurried and sporadic, hanging off the sides of the margins acrobatically and swinging into nothingness.

It has been the longest winter I've known to date. I've been holed up in the attic while Mary Anne is with her parents. I am trying desperately not to believe she has left me for good.

If there is something good that can come from all this, I hope it lands soon, because I can't see it anywhere en route.

I haven't seen or heard from anyone in 87 days, and that's no estimate.

I know I wanted this. I wanted to be a writer, and I wanted to know everything there was to know. I wanted to get to the bottom of everything.

But this knowing everything about everyone makes having friends— and really knowing them—difficult. This is the burden of truth.

And it really does feel like the bottom of everything.

CHAPTER TWENTY

Layla stormed down the stairs to the living room, where her mother lay on the couch with a math textbook in her hands (not an uncommon sight, oddly). Her mother peeked out from behind it at her daughter as she reached the landing panting loudly.

"Darling?" her mother exclaimed.

Layla surged forward but then caught herself, remembering her mother had no idea what she had learned one second prior. Besides that, her mother had no idea what she had learned about herself one month prior. Suffice it to say, Layla had a lot of explaining to do. But she was ready and eager to do it.

"I know about you and Dad!" Layla exclaimed forcefully. Then, hearing what she'd just said, she put her hand over her mouth.

"What do you mean?" her mother questioned.

"Well, just…" Layla began. "Hang on one second."

Layla took a seat on the yellow couch next to her mother's feet and exhaled.

"A few weeks ago, when we were looking through Dad's writing upstairs, you mentioned that Dad had a keen sense of knowing people to their core."

"That's true," her mother conceded.

"It was around that time, roughly, that I began to feel…"

Layla looked down, tracing the pattern in the rug with her eyes. Her mother watched, puzzled.

"I'm not sure how to explain this, but I want you to know. Because it's so important."

"Okay, I'm all ears!" her mother ejected, sitting upright and moving closer to Layla.

"At the time, I experienced a very strange feeling occasionally… when I would be in a room alone with someone else."

"I'm sorry, what?" her mother asked, a concerned look instantly taking over her face.

"Oh, n-n-n-no!" Layla stammered. "Not like that!"

"Phew!" Her mother's face returned to normal again. "Continue."

"I would have my laptop open, and then I'd start having a tingling in my hands. Then later on, I would look at my blog and read words… that I didn't remember writing… And oh yeah, I have a blog."

Layla's mother's eyes filled her whole face now.

"Yep. It's called Portland Posted," Layla continued. "Heh… not sure if you've heard of it."

"What!" her mother couldn't help but blurt out suddenly. "I had no idea! That's you?!"

"And those words were," Layla continued. "Well, they weren't *my* words, necessarily."

Her mother cocked her head to the side.

"They were… somebody else's!" Layla exclaimed.

Her mother nodded slowly as if trying to understand but not really understanding.

"Yeah, so then you told me that Dad had this kind of power to write details about people's lives, and how that made him such a prolific poet, etcetera, etcetera…"

"Yes, I remember…" her mother said.

"And that's when I realized that Dad had a special power called truth-writing. And he did it for a long time. And it must be hereditary. Because I—I have it too."

Layla paused, catching her breath and settling herself. She watched her mother's face as it froze, staring intensely into her daughter's eyes, trying desperately to understand.

"Special powers?!" her mother asked finally.

"Right," Layla replied, matter-of-factly.

Layla's mother rose from the couch, and started to slowly pace through the living room, rubbing her forehead every so often. A few moments went by with the pacing and the rubbing and silence.

"So you can… read minds?" Her mother asked, finally. She stopped pacing and looked at her daughter expectantly.

"Oh, no. Not read them, so much as… *write* them?"

Layla straightened her back nervously on the couch now. She watched as her mother's pacing began again, this time at an accelerated speed.

"And your father…?" she asked. She looked over at Layla again.

Layla nodded. Layla gave her mother a moment with that information, and started to bite her nails nervously. After a few minutes, her mother's pacing started to slow again, and she felt she could continue.

"And so—" Layla started.

"There's more?!" her mother threw her arms wildly in the air.

"A bit," Layla said. "So, I had been… truth-writing… as Dad and I—well, not really Dad anymore, but Dad's writing— call it… for a while at that point. I wrote for the principal, and for Caleb once or twice, and Gavin, and… If I'm alone in a room with someone else and my Blogiophile is ready, the power can come. I never knew for sure that it would, but it did. And that's how I figured out that Principal Strauss's wife died and that she was the one who started the JBC… Also, that's how I figured out that you and Dad used to… fight."

Layla's mother froze. Layla stopped talking and winced a little, realizing what she had just said. She knew this was a lot of information at once.

"I wrote for you once," she continued, cautiously, "and there were details about how you told Dad that if he didn't go to London with you that day or allow you to be a part of the world, you were going to leave. So I knew that you guys had fought, at the end… that there was fighting."

Layla's mother looked down at her hands. She was usually a high-energy lady, but her body was still frozen in time. Layla put her hand on her mother's. She could tell that her mother was starting to cry.

In an instant, Layla went upstairs to grab her laptop, and then returned and opened up the blog on the coffee table for her mother to read. Her mother sat next to her on the couch and exhaled deeply as she followed along on the screen.

After a long while, Layla's mother looked back at her daughter, eyes and face both redder than before. She wiped a tear from one eye and sighed deeply.

"I'm so sorry I didn't tell you, my sweet," her mother muttered. She sighed again. "I just couldn't let you think negatively about your father."

Layla grabbed her mother's hand tightly now.

"I know, Mom. I understand," she said. "I read through all of Dad's notebooks, Mom. He writes a million different stories from a million different points of view, and it's fascinating to read them all. But in his final notebook he says that his powers made life so difficult. He says that he wished he had never had them."

"I had no idea," Layla's mother whispered, still in shock. "I had no idea he had powers, and that you do too. I really, just… had no idea."

Layla's mother stood up from the couch and started pacing back and forth again. Layla could see that her mother had processed everything and was now putting all the pieces together.

"It all makes sense, though, Layla," she declared, gesturing wildly. "The needing to be alone and the writing constantly… He would write these stories that were just so real! It was truly as if he was walking around inside his character's brains. Once he wrote a story about our postman Gerald wanting to propose to his paramour, and the next week they were engaged, I swear it!"

Layla couldn't help but laugh at the thought of her father telling a postman's love story. She leaned back into the couch, getting comfortable now. Her mother was still buzzing around the living room, nearly exploding from the news.

"Mom," Layla said after a while, grabbing her mother's attention again. She looked into her mother's eyes seriously.

"Yes, dear?" Layla's mother responded, pausing a moment.

"Truth-writing for you was an accident, and I didn't want it to happen in the first place. I never meant to write about your life like that without asking. Because I love you so much, Mom, and you and I are best friends forever."

Layla's mother sat down next to her and hugged her almost too tightly.

"I want to know what you'll let me know about you and Dad," Layla continued, voice muffled in her mother's shoulder now. "I want to know whatever you'll tell me. And I'm eager to know it."

Her mother pulled away and smiled wide at her daughter. Layla smiled back.

"But," Layla started again, still grinning. "I don't want to write any of it. I want to hear it from you."

Layla's mother sighed, squeezing Layla again, somehow even tighter than before.

"I can't talk anymore until we've had coffee, at the very least," her mother cried. She grabbed Layla's hand and the two skipped off into the kitchen to make it. They were both laughing, which was something Layla hadn't done in five days. Telling her mother wouldn't solve everything, and it would probably get even more confusing for them both from here on out, but in this moment Layla felt the weight of it all lift from her shoulders. In her home, on this Sunday morning, everything made sense.

"Your father was a brilliant man, Layla. I know you know that." Layla's mother was stirring the cream into her coffee slowly at the kitchen table, while Layla sipped her own mug in the chair across from her.

"Everyone knew him, and everyone loved him. In London at the time, there were a few writers that everyone knew, and your father was one of them. And the others were his best friends. The five of them would hop from dusty café to dusty café, talking for hours and hours. I loved getting out of class and walking into the café to see that the corner table was filled by him and his friends, chairs brought in and gathered round, everyone listening attentively to each other's stories. Without a doubt, students from the university and passersby from the city would be popping over to the table to pick their brains. It was always a lively bunch. You could feel this group in a place from a mile away."

"The Second Inklings," Layla grinned. She already knew this part of the story, but she was happy to let her mother tell it again.

"Precisely! Just like Tolkien and the gang. But more modern, and a little wilder."

"Lots of them were students, too, still getting their PhDs like me. So we would spend our time studying and reading and listening, all of us together. It was a dream. You would have loved it."

"Your dad was the wildest of the lot. He was always fired up about something. So much so that, usually by the time I got there, he would be standing at the table with one foot up on a chair, chanting something, reciting a poem he loved, or just laughing with that boisterous laugh of his that could shake an entire dining room. He was so passionate. Sometimes he would be debating about word choice or which writers were most prolific. Sometimes he would be remarking about philosophy or music or film. Sometimes he would be protesting injustices of the world or yelling about poll taxes."

"The whole gang was a wealth of creative energy, building off each other and helping each other produce their art. Though your dad's friends were mostly also writers, all kinds of people would float in and out throughout the night in those days: artists, musicians, entrepreneurs, chefs, speakers from all over... politicians, even. It was a magical world of people, Layla. Your dad had a way of talking to anyone about anything and making them feel comfortable. I loved him for that. When he spoke, people listened."

"I have a very vivid memory of the day Freddie Mercury died. Your father held an all-day Queen listening event at one of the cafés. It was completely impromptu, but because of the group's influence in our neighborhood, artists from all over just kept coming, bringing their CDs, playing the Queen albums they loved, and chatting about art. More and more people took a seat at the table. Before we knew it, we needed to pull up more tables. And more tables. Layla, your father filled that café in under an hour."

"For so many years it was like that. When I got my PhD, we celebrated with the group. When he won the Kingsley Poetry Prize, we celebrated with the group. When we found out you were coming! We celebrated with the group. And still today, as you know, Uncle Maxwell and Aunt Martha... the whole lot of them will visit on holidays."

"But something happened after your dad published his biggest collection of poems, *The Fun House*. It was like a flip switched for him after that. You were two, and he loved spending time with you and me. But he didn't want to go out as much. He didn't want to see the group so much anymore, and he was always canceling speaking appearances and lectures. He just wanted to be home with us. It was a huge blessing, of course, the three of us being together. But I sensed that something strange was going on with him."

"As time went by, it was like nothing happened for us outside of our little home. By the time you were four, your dad had shut everyone but you and me completely out of his life. He was a complete recluse. And it was fine for a while, but pretty soon it became like he was afraid of human interaction. I had just begun teaching and I needed to give lectures and attend events pretty regularly at the university. He would stay home with you, which was lovely, but I always wished you two would come. He was... so afraid to be around anyone."

"It explains so much, Layla. Him having this power. Because he never wanted to be alone with anyone. He would go to great lengths to avoid one-on-one conversations, even with cab drivers or hallway acquaintances. You helped him with that. He almost never left the house without you."

"I thought when he refused to go stay with Grandma and Grandpa that summer that it was because he didn't care to spend time with my family. But I see now that he probably just couldn't handle knowing so much about others anymore. He always said he was trying to be a New Romantic poet. What Wordsworth says about 'the spontaneous overflow of powerful feelings' and 'emotion recollected in tranquility'— he was doing all of that. But he was doing it all the time for other people and it must have been exhausting. Oh Layla, it must have been so hard for him to hold all of those secrets for so long; to know what people were thinking!"

Layla had heard her mother cry before. When someone was sick or some bad news came on the radio. Normally when her mother cried, she turned her face away from Layla and whimpered softly and quietly, almost as if to herself. She cried in a controlled way, getting it out and over with.

In this moment, however, Layla's mother let out a wail Layla didn't recognize. It was loud and long and carried with it intermittent gasps for breath, one leading into the next. Her whole body shook as it melted onto the table.

"He never told you, Mom." Layla moved her chair next to her mother's and leaned over into her. After what seemed like an hour but must have only been a few minutes, Layla said, "He could have told you about the truth-writing, but he didn't. I'm sure he regrets keeping that secret most out of all of them."

Layla laid her head on her mother's shoulder. She had never seen her mother like this, so she didn't know exactly what to do next. She was terrified.

"I know… I know, Layla. It's just… I just wish he had let me know! We could have gone through it all… together."

Layla's mother spoke so quietly that Layla could barely make out the words. The whispers faded into a silence that hung heavy over the room. Layla looked down at the table, not knowing what to say or feel or if she should move. She went over potential words to say to her mother in her head, but nothing seemed quite right, so she stayed silent.

"I'm so happy you told me about your power, honey," her mother continued. "I'm confused, and I don't know if I understand everything. But I want to be there for you and help you. I'm not letting you go through this alone too."

Layla grinned wildly as her mother wrapped her arm around her.

"Mom…?" Layla whispered to her mother, looking up at her now.

"Yes, sweetie?" her mother replied.

"What happened when you and I came home from Grandma and Grandpa's?"

Layla's mother sighed deeply.

"When you and I got home, your dad had put away his notebooks. He had filled the drawers of his desk with pages and pages of writing. Everything was away. He had chosen to be done writing, then. I just knew it. And we could *live* again."

"Well, then," Layla declared, sitting up straighter now and collecting herself. "I should do that too. I should stop writing and focus on real life."

Layla's mother opened her mouth wide with wonder suddenly, as if she had just realized something. Her eyes lit up and she wrapped her arms around her daughter enthusiastically.

"No, Layla, not at all!"

"What do you mean? You said that this almost tore you

and Dad apart. And everything was better after he stopped writing."

"That's just it, Layla! It only tore us apart because he was going through it alone. I didn't know about it. I couldn't be there for him and help him through it. But I want to be there for you, Layla. I'm here for you now. Tell me absolutely everything about it. This is utterly fascinating!"

Layla's mother jumped up from her chair, as if waking up on Christmas morning. She clapped her hands together and smiled so big and bright that her teeth practically filled her entire face.

Then something quite silly happened. Layla rose from her own chair, and she and her mother began jumping together and laughing uncontrollably. Bart bounded in and jumped up and down along with them. It was as if the weight that had been building up on Layla's shoulders for weeks simply disappeared.

Layla and her mother stayed up late into the night reviewing the details of Layla's truth-writing adventures. Layla told her mom everything: from Principal Strauss, to Caleb, to the time she wrote about the janitor's love affair with the language arts teacher. She felt strange at first, divulging secret after secret, especially since none of them really felt like her secrets to tell in the first place. But she trusted her mother more than anyone, and by the end she felt a sense of clarity she'd never felt before.

Layla's mother was there for her so deeply, just hearing and listening to what she had to say. Layla felt an unmatched comfort just from opening up to her mother with all of it. Her mother didn't have to say anything; she didn't have to offer up any advice or solutions or conclusion. All she had to do was be there, and listen. No tricks, no magic. Just someone being there was all Layla needed.

"I think Caleb might just need me to be there for him, without my powers," Layla whispered to her mother as sun filled the room beside them. Layla looked over at the clock on the far wall of the kitchen. She laughed to herself a little, realizing that, though it felt like they had been talking all day, it was not even noon yet.

"That's funny, my darling. I was just going to suggest the same thing," she responded. Layla rose from the table now, and collected her books from the counter. Her mother approached the sink, getting ready to do the dishes. Layla sighed, heading back up to her room to do a bit of homework.

"Hey," her mother called after her.

"Yeah?" Layla replied.

"I love you, my sweet. You will move mountains someday," her mother declared.

Layla smiled.

As Layla fell into her desk chair upstairs, she was feeling so full of hope and possibility. She got her phone out and, without even thinking, started to type a text message to Caleb.

I'm so sorry about everything. Can we meet? (No "powers" this time).

She wrapped herself in her throw blanket, and stared out the window at the fall foliage outside. After a few minutes, her phone lit up.

Okay. 4 pm tomorrow. Davis Street?

Layla felt a surge of excitement run through her. She was giddy.

I'll be there. :)

CHAPTER TWENTY-ONE

"This is Bart," Layla said cheerfully, as she sat down across from Caleb at the café, holding Bart's leash. "He is my best friend and a black lab and a very excitable creature. He was born here in town and given to us by an old woman who couldn't care for the wild puppies her dog had just had. Anyway, long story short, he became kind of our *three*, me and my mom being *one* and *two*. My dad used to be *three*, but... as you know, we lost him a while back. And actually, I recently found out that Bart was not named after Bartholomew the Apostle, but—fun fact!—he was named with my father's hero in mind, President Josiah Bartlet, the fictional president on his favorite show, *West Wing*."

"Uhh...." Caleb muttered, trying to catch up. "Hi. That was a lot of information at once." He laughed a little bit in spite of himself.

"Sorry, I had coffee before I came."

Layla cleared her throat. Then she motioned for Bart to sit down, and he grumbled a bit as he laid down under the table beside her leg.

"And this, as you know," Layla continued, looking over her shoulder as her mother approached her with two cups of coffee from the counter in her hands. "Is my mother, Mary Anne Whitaker." Layla laughed nervously, realizing how weird she sounded formally introducing her mother to him again.

Caleb sat up in his chair and brushed his hair out of his face immediately.

Layla leaned toward him across the table and whispered, "Don't worry, she's cool."

"H-H-Hullo, Mrs. Whitaker," Caleb stammered, standing up, as he had done the two other times he had seen Layla's mother. "Let me just move all this stuff." Caleb then gathered the books he had strewn across the table.

"Hello, Caleb. Nice to see you again," Layla's mother said. "Oh, don't mind me at all, you two. I'm just here because…" She stopped herself and looked over at Layla.

Layla caught her eye, and then leaned in even closer to Caleb and whispered again, "I told my mom all about the magic. When my mom's here, the magic doesn't work." She smiled at him nervously as he stared, eyes wide, at the two very eccentric Whitaker women before him.

"Well, not *magic*," Layla continued. "I mean, it feels like magic. And maybe it is. But I think of it more as a… gift… kind of a thing?"

Caleb watched Layla's mother bring a chair up and take a seat. She swung her giant canvas tote bag into her lap, took a large binder out of it, and laid the binder on the table.

"O…kay…" Caleb replied.

Layla's mother then opened up the binder and began reading the pages inside it attentively to herself. Layla caught Caleb's eyes and smiled wide at him.

"Right, a gift. So I have this gift. And I got it from my father; he had it too…"

Caleb looked over again at Layla's mother, checking if she was listening to this story.

"Oh, okay," Caleb replied, nodding.

Layla went on to tell Caleb everything about her father's gift and how she had found out she inherited it. Then she told him about how her first time truth-writing happened in Principal Strauss's office, and that's how she learned about the mystery of Caleb's mom's death.

When Layla finished talking, Caleb sat still for a long time, staring down at the turquoise metal tabletop and intermittently rubbing his chin. He hadn't said a thing the whole time, just listened intently to her as if she had been relaying some secret password. Occasionally, he would inhale deeply and put his hands on the back of his head. He would lean back in his chair and absorb Layla's words with wonder. He would look over at her mother, still buried in her notes, on another planet. But through it all, Caleb didn't say a thing.

After a long time, Layla excused herself and brought back three blueberry muffins for them. Then more staring.

When Layla was nearly finished with her muffin—Caleb hadn't touched his—Caleb leaned over and whispered, "So you know… everything… about me?"

Layla swallowed hard.

"No, not everything! Hardly anything at all. There are a few things that I did write for you, but it's all on the blog. I haven't written anything beyond what's already out there. And I should've told you sooner; I know that now. Caleb, I'm so, so sorry!"

Layla reached her hand out and grabbed his. He didn't move at all. He didn't hold her hand back, but he didn't pull his hand away either.

"I really am so, so sorry. I want to be here for you as a real friend and hear what you have to say. I want to hear everything about your life that you're willing to share."

Caleb brought his eyes to meet hers. She noticed that they were warmer than before, and the glimmer behind them was back. Caleb was back.

"I promise you," Layla said, feeling invigorated now by the hope that he might just forgive her. "No more powers. I'm not going to try to know you better than you know yourself. I haven't learned everything about my powers, by any means, but I do know that they are meant to *know*, but not to know *better*."

Layla didn't expect him to say anything now. If it had been her, she would have been upset. Or, at the very least, overwhelmed. In fact, if it had been her, she would have probably walked out the door about twenty minutes ago. To learn that someone has been in touch with your thoughts for a while without you even knowing must be jarring at best—absolute betrayal of trust at worst. She didn't know exactly what he was thinking now, but she did know that he was still here.

She looked on at him as he sat there staring intently out the window. His black hair had curled into the heart shape it so often did on his forehead. It had fallen in whisps onto both sides of his face, draping atop his eyebrows and casting a shadow over his strong cheek bone. His lips were pursed slightly as he thought, making his jawline even more profound. She traced the outline of his leather jacket's collar as it hung open, approaching but never quite touching his neck. In this moment she realized that he hadn't hugged her when she came in, something he had done several times before when he greeted her. Suddenly, she felt the absence of this hug come on her like a gust of wind from an impending storm through a screen door left open. Suddenly it felt like years since her face had rested on that same leather jacket collar. It felt like lifetimes since her lips had brushed against his gorgeous hair as she inhaled his scent and felt his warmth all at once. She felt herself inhaling now, wishing she were closer, wishing he wanted her to be closer.

This was part of her mistake that she hadn't really realized until this moment. Now, she truly saw the way this affected their relationship. Caleb learning about her truth-writing didn't just mean tutoring was going to be awkward for the next few months. It also meant that Homecoming wasn't happening. It meant that he saw her entirely differently. It meant that he wouldn't trust her anymore. It meant that there was a wall between them that might not come down for a long time, if at all.

Layla realized these truths all at once, and her eyes began to well up with tears. Caleb's figure grew blurry before her, and the lights in the room bled into one another. The entire café was shining now, but not in majesty. It shone in sorrow.

Not wanting him to notice that she was crying, she pulled

her feet up onto the chair and quickly bent her head down into her knees. Of course, after doing this she realized just how not subtle this all was. She felt him looking over at her. Before she knew it, she was sniffling audibly. Her mother could obviously hear this. She reached her hand over and laid it on top of her daughter's, while still pretending to be enthralled in her class notes.

"Layla…" Caleb began. He sighed.

Layla lifted her head, her face now wet with tears and wrinkled up with more coming.

"I'm just…" Layla started. "I'm just so, so sorry, Caleb."

Layla wiped her face off with a napkin and quickly shoveled her books into her backpack. Her mother took the hint and closed up her own binder as well. Both Whitaker women rose and walked toward the door, followed closely by Bart. The parade silently, awkwardly walked out the door toward home.

Layla didn't feel like talking for a long while after that. She helped her mother clean up from dinner and lugged her backpack up the stairs for another hour or so of studying before bed. Bart followed her into her room. He turned around in his dog bed until he was ready to lie down on it, which he finally did with a thud.

Layla was staring down at a still-unsolved problem on her calculus homework when she heard a knock on the front door downstairs.

She passed her mother in the hallway, where they shared a confused shrug. She ran to the door and looked through the peephole. It was Caleb.

Layla swung the door open, her face beaming uncontrollably at him.

SWIPE UP FOR SECRETS

"You know," Caleb began, half-smiling and putting his arm up to rest on the side of the doorway. "Customarily, when someone apologizes, they usually give the other person the opportunity to respond. Instead of, I don't know, running away."

Layla's heart nearly exploded at the sight of his smile. Without thinking, she leapt up into his arms. She was a little nervous for an instant, realizing what she had just done. The next, she felt his arms warm against her back, catching her and bringing her closer into him. He was hugging her back. He was hugging her *back*.

"Respond?" Layla whispered. She blinked her eyes into consciousness. She wanted to be present as much as she could in this moment. Layla breathed in his scent, absorbed the feeling of her cheek on his leather jacket, and counted every finger that had the great pleasure of touching his back. Layla fought off the fear that maybe her wild hair was in his eyes, or that her mascara was running, or that, when she pulled away, he might notice she was wearing a particularly unappealing pair of oversized sweatpants. No, Layla wasn't going to let fear make her miss out on this moment. This was the second chance she had been hoping for.

The next moment, Caleb pulled himself out of her arms. But by the look on his face, it wasn't because he hadn't wanted to be there anymore. He gave a relieved grin and looked directly into her eyes. Caleb held her gaze the way he had held her body moments ago, and her heart raced so quickly she wasn't quite sure if she'd ever felt that way before. Then Caleb said something Layla would remember for years to come.

"Forgive."

CHAPTER TWENTY-TWO

Layla and Caleb spent the better part of three hours on the gold velvet couch that night.

That night, the two teens talked about everything there was to talk about. Caleb told Layla that he still liked her, and had wanted to include her in his life. He said he would have eventually given her some of the details she had learned on her own; it just would have taken him a while to let her in. He wanted to get to know her the normal way.

Layla emphatically understood, and poured her heart out to him about how she didn't always know when her powers would come and how she was still learning everything as she went along for the ride.

Eventually Layla told him the whole story: the fact that she had been going to the JBC her whole life almost, and that it had become a second home for her; the details of the truth-writing she had done in the principal's office on the first day; the thoughts she had about mama Strauss even before she met Caleb.

Caleb was surprised, but kind and understanding.

When Layla's mother came down to tell Layla it was time for bed (later than she normally would have), Caleb's arm was hanging over Layla's shoulder and the two were completely silent in togetherness.

"Hold me tighter… in the cold, dark night…" a very loud, airy pop star bellowed through the house as Layla walked up the stairs. She knocked at the door at the top and was greeted by a frantic-looking Mia.

"Why did I think I could do this, Layla? Science Olympiad? Totally. Pilates? Sure! Maybe even throw in a synchronized swimming class if you have to. But Homecoming?! I still can't believe we're really going to Homecoming."

Layla sighed heavily as she entered the room, tossed her bags on the bed, and took a seat on a chair by the door.

"Oh, Mia. Won't you ever learn to just enjoy yourself every once in a while?" She laughed.

Mia was wrapped in a towel, with hair blown wild on one side of her head and tied up high on the other. Her dress was hanging on the door, several pairs of shoes overturned on the floor beneath. She met her reflection in the mirror with a painful, helpless gaze.

Layla rose from the chair and spun Mia around so she was facing her.

"Do you remember Connor?"
Mia nodded.
"Do you remember how you like Connor?"
Mia nodded again.
"Do you remember how you and Connor talk at the lockers every single day and can't get enough of each other?"
Mia shrugged sheepishly.
"Oh, and hey, do you remember how you asked Connor to Homecoming and he said yes?"
Mia's face unfolded into a soft smile now.
"So here we are," Layla continued. "Going to Homecoming with boys we like. It's not some corrupt teen ritual, or a self-sabotage, or a painfully cringey scene from *Saved by the Bell*. It's you and me. Throw in the guys we like, some club music, maybe a little pasta. And that's it. The worst that can happen is

we have to fix our hair in the bathroom or we cut out early because it gets boring."

"You're sure?" Mia bit her lip.

"I'm absolutely sure."

Layla took Mia's hair out of its ponytail and began curling it. The two girls danced around Mia's bedroom as they got dressed and put mascara on and talked about everything under the sun. Layla used her phone to switch the music to Fleetwood Mac, and the girls ended up singing "Dreams" at the top of their lungs.

When it was time to go, they both had one last look in the mirror. Mia looked radiant and happy. Her curly black hair bounced when she turned her head. She wore a mid-length rose dress with a ruched bodice and a tie-belt sash around her waist. It was pretty and girly and fancy: all words Layla didn't usually choose first to describe her best friend. More often she would say "bold" or "wild" or "brilliant." But of course Mia was all of these things at once—tonight especially.

Layla's blonde hair hung down to her shoulders, where, after several failed attempts at getting it to curl, it sat slightly bowed out at the bottom. It was something. Her flowy green high-low dress was perfect. It made her feel tall and powerful. It was long, but not so long that she would trip, and it lifted a little when she twirled. It had a subtle v-neck, with light padding on her otherwise very flat chest. She wore medium-sized gold hoop earrings and a few stacked gold rings to match. Mia had put some blush on her cheeks and some golden-brown eye shadow on her eyelids, so in the light Layla carried a slight glow. It was nice to feel pretty.

As they walked down the stairs, Layla saw Connor on the living room sofa, dressed better than she had ever seen him dress before. He was talking to someone on the other couch that faced him, but she couldn't see who it was.

Slowly, the deep tone of Caleb's voice flowed into the hallway like an organ note gradually filling a sanctuary. Layla hit the bottom stair and, in an instant, grew so nervous she felt like turning right around and running back up. She stood still in a panic.

Mia felt her friend's pause. She spun around with a half-eyeroll on her face, as if she had known Layla would freeze up ahead of time. Mia always seemed to know things ahead of time. It made Layla feel safe.

"No, no, no… that's not what we're doing, Layla. I'm supposed to be the emotional wreck tonight. I got dibs. Don't you remember?"

Layla's lips softened into a smile, and she looked at Mia sheepishly.

"You think tonight could be one of those rare nights where we both just… have a good time?" Layla smirked, hopeful.

Mia grabbed Layla's arm and pulled her into the living room. The boys immediately stopped what they were doing and looked up at their dates.

"Wow, you look…" Caleb exclaimed, rising and taking Layla by the hands.

"Holy cow…" Connor ejected, as he reached out for Mia's hand as well.

"You know," Mia whispered to Layla, as they filed out the door to Connor's Jeep. "I think it just might."

The lights dimmed as Caleb and Layla cheers-ed their chocolate fondue strawberries under the world's (or at least Maine's) largest chandelier. They had danced the night away, done the silly photo booth antics, eaten the salmon-rice situation, and even spent a good portion of time sitting with Caleb's bros and their wildly glamorous dates. Layla was proud of their effort to have fun, and she couldn't have wiped the dopey grin off her face if you'd paid her. Now it was just her and Caleb, ending the night as close as they could possibly be to one another without Mrs. Duchrich trailing close behind, periodically calling out "leave room for Jesus!"

"I'm so happy to be here with you," Layla said, looking into his eyes as if she had just seen them for the very first time.

"You mean, as opposed to being here with Tom Watson?" Caleb chuckled. Tom was an awkward, quiet boy from their calculus class who always worked up the courage to greet Layla. Caleb loved to joke that he'd gotten to Layla just before Tom.

"Yeah, he really almost got to me first." Layla laughed.

A piece of Caleb's black hair fell into his face as he leaned in closer to Layla. His smile widened, and he glanced quickly to the right and then the left. She gave him a coy look, as if to ask what he was up to. Before she knew it, his lips met her own in a strong, powerful kiss. She could feel every millimeter of his lips hit her own, which made the kiss overwhelm her senses. It was as if every part of her body was focused on her lips touching his. Layla wasn't overthinking the motion of her tongue, or where her teeth were, or whether her eyes were open. In fact, she didn't think about anything at all, really. She just let him kiss her. She just felt overcome with him and everything he was. Of course, she had hoped he would kiss her again tonight. But for him to do it here and now, like this, was oddly magical. The music, the hustle and bustle around them, the fake nails on her fingers that intertwined with his on her lap. All these things combined made the moment one she would never forget.

When Caleb pulled away, everything about him lit up. His face glowed. His eyes seemed to shimmer in a whole new way to her now. As Layla looked back at him, she thought about everything that had happened between them so far. She thought about the notes back and forth with Mia about "John Francis." She thought about the math center's too many shades of blue. She thought about trash bin basketball and ghost. She thought about running down her porch after him. And all of this, for some reason, made her laugh out loud, right there on the dance floor.

"I gotta say, I've never had someone laugh after I kissed them." Caleb tilted his head to the side, a little puzzled and suddenly sheepish.

"No! I just…" Layla started. She tightened her grip on his hand to reassure him that she was very happy. She smiled wide to double down. Then she leaned in closer to him. "It was perfect," she whispered.

He smiled back and went in again for another kiss. The world spun madly round them in their peripheries, but they were no longer a part of any of it. Together, Layla and Caleb were alone, truly present, and entirely unfazed by the world around them. It was the warmest, most comfortable feeling Layla had experienced in a long time.

CHAPTER TWENTY-THREE

"Layla!"

Layla turned around to see Mia walking toward her down the hallway from the banquet room. She was grinning from ear to ear and jumped into her friend's arms. The two girls headed into the bathroom together holding hands.

"I have to tell you," both girls said in unison.

"Okay, you first!" they said in unison again, and fell into uproarious laughter.

"He kissed me!" they both yelled at the same time. They then grabbed each other's arms and swung around in a circle wildly. It was a whirlwind of joy.

Mia's kiss had been her first kiss *ever*, so the girls did a total and complete rundown of events before heading back to join their dates on the floor. Mia told Layla she and Connor were heading out soon, and she asked if Layla wanted a ride back with them.

"Let me check with Caleb," Layla answered.

She returned to the table and leaned her body into Caleb's for a hug. The pure bliss of the night was overflowing from her, and she couldn't help but to be in his arms. He looked down at her, surprised but happy. She relayed Mia's message, and he looked off in thought at the crowd on the dance floor.

"Actually," Caleb began. "I thought we could go

somewhere after."

To her surprise, he pulled her in closer to him and smirked.

"What did you have in mind?" she asked, perplexed.

"Well, I feel like you and I always go around my town. School, the café, the Horton theater, places like that. But aside from your house, I really haven't seen your town."

"You want to go to Falmouth?" Layla exclaimed.

"I really do," Caleb replied. He gathered his jacket and her purse from the table and walked next to her out of the banquet room into the hallway. Things were winding down, so the hallway was filled with couples on their way to the parking lot.

Layla agreed that this was a pretty astounding truth. The few times they had gone out on actual "dates," if you could really call them that, were after tutoring, or to the café. It had just made sense to meet up near the school, because that's where they always seemed to be. The two decided to catch an Uber to Layla's place.

They popped into the house to let her mom know they were going to walk around for a bit, and then the two lovebirds were on their way. They wound through the back streets, peeking through windows as Layla showed Caleb the community hardware store where Bart had gotten his nose stuck in a mouse trap one fateful day, and the bakery where she and her mom had birthday cakes made. They walked through the secret forest path behind the library and swung on the swings at her elementary school playground. Layla felt she might have been talking too much, but Caleb was listening to her stories and smiling all the while. It wasn't lost on her that most guys would not be so interested in her history.

"And that's where my cousin sledded into a tree and broke her wrist when we were seven and eight. Boy, was her mother furious. I'd never seen veins in someone's forehead like that before…"

Layla noticed Caleb wasn't walking next to her anymore, and she couldn't hear his feet falling behind her either. She turned around to see him sitting on one of the wooden benches scattered around town. His hands were folded in his lap and his mouth hung open. He looked lost in thought. In front of him was a big window with a wooden sign hanging above it that read *Julia's Bakery and Café.*

Of course, the JBC was right there. Layla walked by it every single day and hardly ever gave it a second thought unless she was in the mood for a muffin. But it was different for her, because her mother hadn't owned the building and come up with the recipes for all its baked goods. Layla hadn't even considered that Caleb might be thrown off walking by this place for the first time in... well, she didn't know how long. While she knew from his journals that Caleb had spent every Sunday at the bakery with his mom, she suspected it might have been a while since he'd gone back to visit as a teenager. He seemed frozen in thought on the bench as she approached him and sat down next to him.

"I'm sorry, I kind of forgot... Well, I didn't *forget*..." Layla trailed off.

Caleb lifted his arm up and put it over her shoulder now, as if to tell her it was all right. She leaned her head on his shoulder. Layla could feel his heart pounding inside his chest, so she squeezed his hand tightly.

What a world of wild thoughts must be going through his head, she thought. For an instant, Layla wondered what would happen if she wrote for him now. Would he want to write about his mother and the time they spent together at the café? Would he recall all sorts of sweet treats and smiles? Would he feel his mother closer, as if she were there with them?

But just as quickly as she had these thoughts, Layla pushed them out of her mind. She remembered the look of betrayal on Caleb's face when he found out she was writing for him, and she couldn't bear to see him like that ever again. She had made a promise that day, that she would never write for him again. And Layla never broke her promises.

They sat in silence on the bench for what seemed like hours. It had been so long that Layla thought she might have the image of the overturned chairs on the front table permanently engraved in her mind.

Layla's neck began to ache a bit from bending into Caleb's shoulder, so she lifted her head and stretched back and forth a bit, exhaling deeply. This movement seemed to stir Caleb back to reality. He turned and looked at her with a content look on his face. His blue eyes were smiling.

"I think I want to go inside," he declared, excitedly.

Layla cocked her head to the side wildly.

"You mean, right now?" she exclaimed.

"Yeah, right now. Why not?" he asked, grabbing both of her hands energetically and pulling her up off the bench.

"Well, I think the 'why not' is that it's not open, and we would therefore be trespassing," she replied, somewhat playful but also very serious.

He didn't say anything; he just pulled her closer to the front door. He peered through the window into the dark café.

"And as far as 'why nots' go, I don't know… I think that's a pretty valid one?" she continued, looking puzzled.

Caleb looked back at her and squinted, as if plotting something.

"My dad owns this place, even though he only goes in early in the morning before anyone else," he said. "And yes, I haven't been here in years, but my name is literally engraved in the back windowsill somewhere, so that's gotta count for something, Whitaker."

Layla said nothing. Caleb leaned in closer.

"And I know the code to the back door—it's always been my birthday backwards," he whispered. "So technically, it's not trespassing at all, but just going into my family's store… but after hours?"

Caleb was elated by the conclusion he had just come to, so much so that he skipped off around the building into the alley behind it.

"Whoa, whoa, whoa!" Layla ran after him, realizing what was about to happen. "Are you sure about this?"

She caught up to him at the back door of the café. Caleb was breathless from running around, and nodded frantically.

Caleb hadn't been inside the café in years. This was where his mother had spent so much of her time and energy. Outside of her family, the café had been her life. Caleb was brave, but was he really prepared for the memories that would come flooding back?

"I'm ready, Layla," he declared seriously, as if reading her mind. He wrapped his arm around her shoulder and the two of them approached the back door together, in a single stride.

"Well, then, let's do it," she whispered back. "But first..."

Something inside Layla woke up then, and before she knew it, her hand was on Caleb's chest. She could faintly feel his ab muscles through his shirt. Gently, but with some force, Layla pushed his body up against the brick wall that met the back door of the café. Caleb's face lit up in surprise. He smirked, and opened his mouth slightly, as if to say something. But before he could, Layla stood on her tiptoes and pushed her lips hard into his. He pushed back and grabbed her hips passionately. The taste of his warm, firm lips struck her and brought her to life. Suddenly, there, under the lamppost she knew so well, she felt a desire she had never known before. His hands pulled her hard into him then, and moved lower down her back, and lower still.

CHAPTER TWENTY-FOUR

The calendar hanging on the door flapped against it as Caleb closed the door behind them. He paused time with a deep inhale as they both took in the JBC kitchen together. Layla had only been in there once before, when Gavin had shown her the recipe book of Julia's. There hadn't been any need for her to go back there besides that.

The room was small and quaint, mostly filled by a long wood counter against the left wall and a massive convection oven. The opposite wall was lined with three sinks, with wood-framed paintings of flowers above each one. Between the counter and the sinks was a wooden rolling cart with cookie sheets on all of its many shelves. Scattered around the room were wooden and silver utensils, stacked bowls, pots and pans. On the wall hung about twenty different-sized rolling pins in a long row underneath the window, whose red and white checkered curtains hung loose and ruffled out at the edges.

Against the wall that held the door leading inside was a yellow desk. It was an old wooden desk with chipped paint here and there and red drawer handles. The top shelf of the desk held a row of recipe books. Layla spotted the one she had seen before. All the books were filled with clippings and overflowing pages of scrawled notes. It was obvious that Grace had tried to preserve them as best she could over the years.

Caleb began moving through the room, reaching his hand out to touch various objects. He appeared to Layla as if he were floating. His eyes seemed to follow every little element of the room, from the tiling on the floor to the edging on the doorway. Layla sensed that he was studying, but she couldn't judge his emotions beyond that in the least.

Caleb paused for a long time at the yellow desk. He pulled the chair out and sat down. He rested his arms on the desk awkwardly and looked down at them, as if trying on the space and seeing how it fit. He slid his finger along the bindings of the recipe books, tracing his mother's handmade labels on each of them. After a long while, he took the light blue one out and opened it up, seeming to know what would be in it. He flipped through the pages and smiled to himself. Layla moved closer to him to look over his shoulder.

Caleb flipped through the pages of the book and landed on a postcard saving a page inside. It had a picture of a beach on the front. Caleb flipped it over to show that, on the backside, his mother had drawn a big cupcake with a note next to it. Layla squinted to read what it said. Just as she got close enough to see it, Caleb turned around, startled.

"Oh, I'm sorry! I was just—"

"Oh, goodness. No, I knew you were there... It's just— you scared me. I was kind of spacing."

"No, I understand," Layla replied. She unfolded a chair nearby and pulled it up next to him. She sat down and placed her hand on his. "Are you okay?"

Caleb looked into her eyes intensely.

"It's funny, Layla," Caleb started. "I was ready for this feeling, sort of. I knew it would hurt to be back here. But this desk, her books, her writing, it's all... It just feels like she's still here."

Layla put herself in the doorway of her father's study so she would be closer to understanding this feeling.

"I'm somewhat familiar," she said softly.

When Caleb had jumped, he'd dropped the postcard on the ground underneath the desk. He bent over now to grab it. As his hand reached the floor, Caleb let out a gasp that shook the room at once.

Caleb got out of his chair, pushed it back, and fell to his knees on the floor now. He reached his hand under the desk again and picked up a box that sat in the leg space against the wall. He lifted it out from under the desk and lay it on top. He stood now, examining the box.

The box appeared to be thin and made of cardboard. It had a flimsy lid that was cracked open, so you could peek inside. Caleb lifted its lid to expose a rather large collection of broken crayons. Layla then realized that it was a cardboard Crayola box, but the outside had been painted white all over so you couldn't quite tell at first glance. Along the lid of the box where normally there would be the Crayola logo, there was instead a long vine with little red flowers painted over the white. Written in calligraphy along the path of the vine were the words *Caleb, you belong among the wildflowers.*

"Tom Petty?" Layla asked sheepishly, getting up from her chair to wrap one arm around Caleb's waist.

Caleb didn't answer. He appeared completely transfixed. He stood a little hunched over, his head falling into his chest. His body seemed to bend entirely into the box of crayons, as if it had become an extension of himself from which he could not look away.

"This box…" Caleb said quietly, trailing off. He lifted his eyes slowly to where Layla stood beside him with a deeply concerned look on her face. She could see now that his eyes were bloodshot and, shockingly, welled up with tears.

"Oh," Layla exclaimed, and wrapped him in her arms almost instinctively. Caleb leaned his head into her and breathed heavily, but his body remained frozen still, holding the box now tightly in his hands.

"My mother gave me this box of crayons—I remember it so well now—when I was little. She would set them out for me on this table…" Caleb shifted out of Layla's arms and scurried a few feet over to the long maple table. He set the crayons down there and stared hard at them, as if he was trying the table on to see how it looked with his crayons on top. "Here, yes. Right here."

Caleb then moved the desk chair over to meet the table, and took a seat there instead.

"I would sit and color next to her while she worked," he continued. "In the mornings. Most mornings."

Layla stood next to him, examining his movements carefully.

"That's so sweet, Caleb. She loved you so much."

Just then, the bell on the front door chimed, jolting Layla into a panic. She ran to the door between the kitchen and the main dining area, and leaned down to peek through the window at who had entered. Whoever it was had turned on the main light in the front entrance but hadn't yet walked under it, or else she had missed them doing so.

"Someone's here," Layla whispered, raising an arm behind her as if to keep Caleb from approaching the window. "Stay down!"

Peeking just over the edge of the window, Layla was able to make out the figure of Gavin, leaned over and rifling through the shelf behind the counter. He didn't seem to have noticed that the light in the kitchen was on. She was thankful for his obliviousness for perhaps the first time ever.

"It's okay, it's just Gavin, the barista. I know him. He must have left something." Layla watched him intensely through the window.

For a few minutes Layla and Caleb sat in complete silence, as if they were trying not even to breathe.

Finally, Gavin ejected a soft "aha!" and pulled out his wallet from the top shelf next to the soup station. Upon grabbing the item he had lost, he quickly slammed it in his pocket and turned the light back off. Layla heard him close the door and lock it behind him.

Relieved, Layla spun around and slid down the door into a seated position on the ground. She exhaled deeply.

Layla searched for Caleb's face, but to her surprise he was now sitting against the wall under the desk, barely fitting with his legs out in front of him. She slid over a bit to get a better view of him, and couldn't help but chuckle. She then reached her hand through the space to touch his leg. His face was completely still, totally unaffected by what had just transpired. His eyes stared forward as if he didn't even notice she had touched him.

"Are you okay?" Layla asked, inching a little closer to him. She felt so small, both of them sitting on the floor of the kitchen with the high walls of pots and pans wrapping around them. There was something so childish about sneaking around and hiding behind doors. It would almost have been exciting, if it weren't for how much trouble she would definitely be in if they got caught.

"Layla!" Caleb said suddenly, as if he had just returned to reality.

Caleb's face looked at hers in disbelief. His eyes were wide in horror, as if he'd seen something devastating. The juxtaposition between their two attitudes was potent. Layla was distraught seeing it.

"Wha—?" Layla stammered. She grabbed his hands between the legs of the desk and looked into his eyes intently. She was shocked to see him so pained.

"Something happened…" Caleb began. He turned to face front again and then rubbed his forehead roughly with his hands. He blinked hard, as if trying to remember. "Something happened *here*. Right here. Just now, what happened with me sitting here and the bell ringing in the front room."

"What do you mean?" Layla asked.

"This, what just happened. The bell rang, and the box of crayons was in my lap like this, and the draft under the desk made me shiver."

"I'm sorry you're cold," Layla muttered, without thinking.

"No, Layla, that's not it." Caleb's face was still in shock,

"It's that this has happened before."

Layla sat up, on the edge of her metaphorical seat, though indeed she was still on the floor.

"What is it? What happened, Caleb?" Layla pulled in closer to him, as if to remind him that she was his friend. She was there for him. Her dress bunched up underneath her crisscrossed legs, but she didn't care.

Caleb moaned softly. He pulled his knees up to his chest and hung his head between them like a child waiting for a verdict on his punishment from his parents.

"I can't... I can't..." Caleb began.

Suddenly, as if in a rage, he crawled out from underneath the desk and stood up again. He threw the crayon box onto the table wildly. The cardboard box wilted from the force, and several crayons fell out and rolled across the kitchen floor.

"I can't REMEMBER!" Caleb yelled, grabbing his hair in his fingers and pacing back and forth in anger.

After a while, Caleb went to the table and picked up the box of crayons. He gathered the loose few and replaced them in the box. Then, he breathed heavily, gathering himself too. Finally, he took Layla by the hand. Silently, Caleb moved them both toward the door, and they left the kitchen as they found it—but down one box of crayons.

Caleb walked Layla home in silence. He held her close to him all the while, as if she had become an extension of his body that rested there naturally. When they got to Layla's door, he kissed her goodnight. He held her gaze in the doorway for a long time, a half-smile on his face.

Layla felt a little helpless but was comforted by his smile. She hugged him again and then watched him walk away down the street.

A few minutes later, Layla managed to get into her pajamas and then fell desperately into her bed. It was a big night, and she would want to write about it. But she was tired now, so she would wait until tomorrow. As she plugged her phone into the charger on her nightstand, she noticed that she had an unread text. She read it before her eyes could blur to a deep slumber.

Will you write for me again?

The question nearly brought her back to life, and she smiled widely underneath her covers. She had promised him she would keep the truth-writing separate from him; that she would get to know him organically, as a friend. She went to respond, but before she could, another text came in.

I know I said I didn't want that, but tonight I felt so strongly that I had been there before. That I was there, under that desk, on the day my mother died. I trust you now, Layla. And I need your help to figure out what happened in that room twelve years ago.

Layla lifted her head up to ensure she got what she wanted to say down all right.

On the one hand, she had promised Caleb she would get to know him the old-fashioned way, without magic. Her father had nearly destroyed his friendships and his marriage with this magic. Was she about to make the very same mistake?

On the other hand, Layla had worked hard to build a foundation with Caleb over the past few weeks—without magic. She had put the friendship first. So, unlike her father, she wasn't letting truth-writing isolate her from others. Additionally, this truth-writing's purpose was different: she would be using her magic to help Caleb, and only with Caleb's consent. Layla could see that she had learned from her father's mistakes and was ready to use her magic for the good of all involved.

The question hit her hard, but in many ways she already knew her answer. Before she drifted off to sleep, Layla read her reply back to herself in a whisper.

It would be my great pleasure.

CHAPTER TWENTY-FIVE

Layla and Caleb agreed to meet at the JBC the next day. They would enter through the front doors this time, with Principal Strauss in tow to greet the staff and let the two into the kitchen. The whole thing would be above reproach this time around, at Layla's request. She hadn't exactly enjoyed the breaking-in part of Homecoming.

Caleb had sat his father down after the dance to tell him what had happened. Well, some of it, anyway—he left out the truth-writing part. And much to Caleb's surprise, his father wasn't at all upset that the two of them had snuck in. Nor was he upset that they had done so at 10:30 pm. Instead, the awkward, quiet man lit up after hearing the story and hugged Caleb tightly. Caleb seemed just as confused by this response as Layla was when he told her.

To save herself from her own discomfort, Layla had texted Gavin about their visit ahead of time. She didn't go into unnecessary detail, just mentioned that Caleb was a friend from school. *What a small world*, she'd typed. *His only reply was I'm happy for you, Lay. But don't you think dating the owner's son is a little far to go to get your hands on some free muffins?* Layla chose not to get into it and responded only with a laughing emoji. This didn't stop Gavin from winking playfully at her from behind the counter upon their arrival.

Layla casually followed Caleb and Principal Strauss through the door into the kitchen. Principal Strauss showed them around the room, pointing out every nook and cranny as if it were a museum instead of a 400 square foot room he was presenting. He stopped every few minutes to talk in depth about one of his wife's baking tricks or a painting of hers on the wall. He'd laugh nervously, and then start in on the next anecdote, seemingly unable to stop one from flowing into the next.

Layla had never seen Principal Strauss like this before. He was positively giddy about his wife, even after all these years. At one point he even bragged about the way Mrs. Strauss folded the dish towels way back when. Layla thought that if she were to end up with someone who bragged about the way she folded dish towels one day, she would count herself very lucky.

While his father spoke, Caleb was right on his tail, taking in everything intently. He was always respectful of his father, but today he seemed especially reverent toward the man. The depth of this occasion was not lost on him. Nor was it lost on Layla.

When Principal Strauss was finished giving the tour, he stood smiling at the back door, taking it all in.

"Thank you so much, father," Caleb said.

"Yes, thank you. This has been so fascinating," Layla added.

"Well, you're both very welcome," Principal Strauss said. He looked at the room longingly and exhaled. The next minute, he checked his watch. He was still giddy, but seemed to sense that the teens wanted to be alone at this point.

"I should be going, but feel free to stay here and do your studying. I've spoken to Grace and Gavin about you both already. They're lovely people. They said you can feel free to eat and drink anything you'd like while you're here. On the house."

Caleb walked his father out through the café while Layla stood alone in the kitchen, feeling the full weight of all that had happened between its walls.

Layla pulled a chair up to the long yellow desk and took her calculus book out of her backpack. She had two notebooks in her backpack as well. She went to grab them, but stopped halfway there and left them instead. She wasn't really sure what was going to happen today, but she knew it was a big day for her and Caleb. Officially meeting Principal Strauss—well, as her Homecoming date's dad, anyway—went really well. It was quick and painless, actually. But on top of that, spending time with both Strauss men in Julia's old bakery kitchen was profoundly moving and emotional for everyone. Layla had felt the significance of the day like a wave washing over her again and again with every exchange of eye contact between her and Caleb.

Caleb had invited her here today to try to figure out what had happened in that room. His asking her to truth-write for him for the first time *on purpose*, and now above reproach (this phrase was getting a lot of use in her brain today, she realized), was a huge step. For this reason, everything she did today was done with proper care.

Suddenly, Layla felt Caleb's arms wrap around her waist from behind. She turned her face to meet his and smiled, breathing him in deeply.

"Mmmm," Caleb moaned, as his lips pressed against hers.

Layla spun around and grabbed the back of his head with her hands, feeling his thick hair wrapped between her fingers. She kissed him harder now, and felt his tongue push into hers. She began to breathe heavily as she moved closer into him. Caleb felt the passion in her and responded by pulling her hips closer to him ever so slightly.

Caleb moved his hands up her back and pulled away from her lips now, as if knowing they were headed somewhere they maybe shouldn't have been. They breathed each other in simultaneously.

"Okay," Layla pulled away and straightened her sweater out with a huge grin on her face.

"Yes," Caleb began in a low, stern voice. "We must get back to work!" He laughed and grabbed his backpack off the side of the chair.

After about an hour or so of the pair looking over the

math pretests next to each other, hand in hand under the desk, Caleb yawned loudly.

"I'm gonna go grab a muffin, because I've heard such good things," he said, smirking at her. He inched closer to her and moved her hair out over her shoulder. He put his lips up to her ear, as if he was going to say something extremely seductive, and said, "Would you like one, darling?"

Her spine tingled. For most girls, this would not have come off as a seductive phrase necessarily, but for Layla this was practically foreplay.

"Mmmm...." she moaned, feigning erotic longing. "You really know how to please a woman, Caleb."

Caleb returned a few minutes later and placed a plated muffin in front of her.

"I was thinking about the other night," he said, thoughtfully, as if he had been thinking of it while he was in the other room. "There's obviously some very strong energy coming from that Crayon box Mom painted for me."

He motioned toward the top drawer of the desk, where he had put the box for safekeeping. Caleb pulled his seat up closer to Layla and fixed his eyes on her. Layla felt her heart beating a little faster in her chest. Then he pulled the drawer open and they both stared down at the box intensely.

"I think there might be something here... something to uncover..." Caleb continued.

"I think, if you're willing... I would like you to write for me now."

Layla swallowed hard. She had of course seen this coming, but for some reason it still made her heart pound.

"If it's what you want," Layla began, seriously. "Of course, I will write for you."

Caleb grinned widely and then squeezed Layla's hand tightly.

Layla quietly and solemnly took out her laptop, plugged in the charger, and booted it up. It was the very same laptop she had used to write about Julia just one month ago. But together, she and the laptop had been through quite a lot. She felt older and wiser, knowing all she knew now about her gift. Layla felt a profound purpose in this moment, and inhaled deeply to prepare herself for the task ahead. She ran her fingers across the keyboard, taking it all in. She opened up her Blogiophile dashboard and clicked New Post.

"I'll start now, and when I'm done, I won't post. For me, as a writer, I normally do post. Even if I don't think anyone is going to read it. Kind of an homage to my father's legacy. But before I post I always remove names, personal information, or anything that I feel is beyond the scope of my purpose. That's broad, I know." Layla laughed nervously. "But I know what my purpose is here today. Anyway, I'll pass the laptop to you, and you can read it over."

Caleb nodded in agreement. His face was serious as she spoke, and he was listening to every word she said attentively.

Then, as if they had been eagerly awaiting this chance to write again, her hands wrapped around the keyboard, ready for takeoff.

Moments went by, and nothing happened.

Layla relaxed into the chair and smiled at Caleb, as if to assure him that this was normal, which it was.

Caleb relaxed into his chair as well.

"Just act like I'm not even here," Layla whispered softly to him.

"What if I don't want to do that?" he replied, showing her his traffic-stopping smile again.

She smirked at him. Suddenly, Layla had a thought.

"Wait," Layla said, staring at him while she went over the details of Caleb's remembering on the night of the dance in her head. "That spot, there. Underneath the desk. That seems to be where you were."

"Where I was—?" Caleb spoke quickly, trying to catch up with her thought process. "Where I was yesterday?"

"No…" Layla said softly, realizing that she needed to be careful about how she spoke now. "Where you were on a

Friday… in 2009."

Caleb's face turned pale and solemn. He exhaled deeply, nodding. "Ohh…"

"I just wonder…" Layla started again, moving closer to him and grabbing his hand now. Her eyes met his, and she smiled softly to show him that she was there for him. They were there together today. "I wonder what would happen if I wrote for you… while you were underneath the desk again. Like you were then, holding the crayons."

Caleb crawled underneath the desk. He barely fit, but somehow he looked perfectly placed there. He looked comfortable and safe.

A few seconds later, Caleb breathed deeply again. Then he looked up at the bottom of the desk and closed his eyes gently.

In that moment, Layla could feel the familiar tingling surge through her. She smiled as her hands began to type effortlessly on the page. Out of respect for Caleb, she averted her eyes from the screen, looking instead at the yellow desk.

This went on for quite a while—what felt like an hour to Layla, but was probably more like twenty minutes. Time never seemed to exist when she was writing for someone else.

Her fingers eventually stopped dancing across the keyboard. The tingling sensation exited back through her arms to her chest, and then disappeared completely. Layla watched as her hands fell, tired and wilted, into the keys.

Caleb stirred and looked over at her, sensing that was the end of it. He then crawled out from under the desk and stood up. He reached out his hand and caught hers before it slid onto the desktop, as if to thank her for what she had just done. Layla stood as well, and leaned into him. They both stayed in that hug for longer than they needed to, as if knowing how important that moment was for them.

Layla slid the laptop across the desk and motioned to her empty coffee mug to let Caleb know she was going to the front to have it filled back up. She closed the door behind her as she entered the dining room.

"What are you two up to back there, eh?" Gavin laughed, as Layla approached the counter.

"Heh…" Layla started. Her voice cracked, as if she had just woken up and needed to get used to speaking again. Only she had just woken up from something that wasn't at all sleep. She cleared her throat awkwardly. "Just studying. We have an exam on Friday for our most difficult unit, and our teacher had the gall to put the midterm less than a week after that!" Layla smiled nervously at Gavin. "Thanksgiving break seems so far off still. I'll take another coffee, please."

"That's cold-blooded!" Gavin replied, pouring her a cup.

Layla took the cup from him and moved down the counter to the self-serve coffee station. She poured cream into her cup.

"I was going to tell you that the band is playing a show next weekend," Gavin said. "It's at Port Emory. We're opening for Blue Cheetah."

"That's great! I love that place."

"Yeah, you should come out."

"You think?"

"I do think," Gavin said. He waved her off as she tried to pay for the coffee. "And hey, bring the boy, too. Unless he doesn't like funk."

Layla smiled, putting her cash back in her pocket.

"That would be fun. Maybe we'll be in need of the study break. I'll let you—"

"That's it!" Caleb's yell from the kitchen shook Layla, and she nearly spilled coffee down her blouse. She hurried back in to find Caleb standing upright, leaning over the yellow desk with the laptop on it. The box of crayons had fallen to the ground such that all the crayons were now scattered across the floor. Caleb seemed not to have noticed this, and was staring intensely at the screen.

"Wha-what happened?" Layla exclaimed, setting the coffee on the table and running to his side.

Caleb lifted the laptop up and began pacing back and

forth.

"The entry. It says that I would draw back here when Mom was baking on her Friday morning shifts. At this table, just like I showed you the other day." Caleb cleared his throat as he began to read from the screen.

"Usually the other baker would serve visitors in the front. But sometimes, Mom would have to go in the front to help customers too. People always wanted to know what was in the fruit tarts or which bread options were gluten-free. She would go up there for ten minutes or so at a time sometimes, but she would leave the door open so I could see her from my spot. I miss those days so much. Being close to her was the only place I wanted to be."

"A few times," Caleb continued reading, pacing faster now back and forth across the kitchen floor. He cleared his throat again. "A few times, I remember, my mom would come back here and tell me it was time to play a game."

Now, as he read, Caleb went back to the yellow desk and moved the chairs out of the way.

"She would say that a customer was here, just like always. But this one was different. This man was one of the bad guys."

Caleb paused. He started to choke up a little, holding back tears. He kneeled on the floor now, inexplicably.

"She'd say that the object of the game was for me to hide," he continued, softly now. "To hide under the desk until she got back."

Caleb sat under the desk now, with his legs sticking out awkwardly. He put the laptop on his lap as he read. Layla crouched down to meet his eyes again.

"The object of the game was to make sure the bad guy didn't see me. Because if he did, that meant I had lost."

Caleb looked up at Layla now, his eyes welling up with tears. He stared at her intensely for what felt like half an hour, and then put his finger up to his lips.

Layla's mouth hung open. She was frozen in space and time.

"Can you pass me the box of crayons, please?" Caleb ejected, in a whisper. Layla grabbed the box. It was now mostly empty, but a few crayons still shook inside as she passed it off to him.

"She would give me my box of crayons, kiss my forehead, and disappear," Caleb continued to read, taking the box and holding it to his chest. He then opened it up again and looked at the crayons that remained inside. He picked them up gently.

"Oh my god, Caleb. This was your hiding spot. The draft made you shiver in your hiding spot."

Caleb continued to stare down at the crayons as if they were relics he had just uncovered. Layla crawled under the desk as far as she could, but it was a tight fit. It was a perfect hiding spot for one little boy, but not so much for two teenagers.

Caleb met her shoulder and fell into it, wetting it with his tears. Layla could feel him shaking against her. He must have been so emotionally drained by reading his thoughts like that, much less aloud, in front of her.

"That's the end of the entry," Caleb whispered. He sighed deeply into her.

Layla could tell there was more to this story, and Caleb obviously wanted to know what it was. She had truth-written quite a lot over the past month, but never on purpose, and never with a specific intent. For this reason, she hadn't thought about what would happen if she didn't find what she was hoping for. She hadn't considered what would happen if she wrote for Caleb and the answer to the mystery didn't come.

Layla felt his face on her now and imagined how devastated and empty it would look if he had to read more words on the screen that didn't give him that answer. She started to feel a sense of regret for starting this whole thing in the first place.

"Maybe this... maybe it's too much," Layla exclaimed, wrapping her arms around him now.

Caleb loosened himself from her grasp and looked up at her. His eyes were red and worn out from crying, but they were also wider and fuller than she remembered. They were peculiarly full in a way she hadn't ever seen before. *Correction*, she thought to herself now. She stared deeply into his face, and realized that it looked familiar to her after all. Caleb's eyes were full of hope, the way they had been one other time she had seen before, at a ribbon cutting ceremony in 2008.

"No, no—" Caleb began, eagerly now. He reached out and held her face in his hands. "This is the closest I've felt to my mother in twelve years, Layla. I know we might not solve the mystery, and I understand that. I don't care if we don't. But to know even a little bit more about that time in my life… it means the world."

"Really?" Layla asked, struck into a slight shivering by his words.

"Really, really," Caleb returned, kissing her firmly under the desk.

"Well, okay, then," Layla muttered, confused and happy and confused some more. Layla and Caleb's foreheads met, and held one another there in that moment. Time ticked by on the clock on the wall, an espresso machine sizzled and vibrated in the next room, the bell on the front door of the café rang as patrons entered and left. But under the desk was just Caleb and Layla. Under the desk was then and now at once. Under the desk was their world together.

After a long while, Layla pulled herself up off the floor and brushed her jeans off. She sat down at the desk and began editing the Blogiophile post. She was sure to edit it as if Caleb were sharing it instead of her. Knowing now how many readers she had at their school, she wanted to make sure Caleb retained his privacy. When she was done, she left it for Caleb to read once more. Then she posted it. Without thinking, Layla grabbed one of the still-fresh muffins she had gotten from the dining room, crumbs falling onto the napkin that lay underneath it. She captioned the photo, *So much life in this little town. You never know what crumbs there are to find.* She added a link to her story:

Swipe up for some of those crumbs.

Collecting Crumbs to Make a Muffin in Reverse
October 24

Being a baker's son was great, because I always got first dibs on sweet treats. Fridays were our days. I sat in the back, and my mom would pull cookies, cupcakes, and muffins out of the oven. I was her special helper on those days, mixing the batters and spreading the frostings. Every so often, I got to taste.

Usually the other baker would serve visitors in the front. But sometimes, my mom would have to go in the front to help customers too. People always wanted to know what was in the fruit tarts or which bread options were gluten-free. She would go up there for ten minutes or so at a time sometimes, but she would leave the door open so I could see her from my spot. I miss those days so much. Being close to her was the only place I wanted to be. And all the hustle and bustle of bakery life was exciting.

A few times, my mom would come back here and tell me it was time to play a game. She would say that a customer was here, just like always. But this one was different. This man was one of the bad guys. She'd say that the object of the game was for me to hide. So I would hide under the desk until she got back.

The object of the game was to make sure the bad guy didn't see me. Because if he did, that meant I had lost.

She would give me my box of crayons, kiss my forehead, and disappear. A while later she would return to the kitchen and "find" me. "You won!" she'd say, and hand me a batter spoon to lick. What I wouldn't give to be back there with her, her special helper forever. I always won.

The next morning, Layla woke up to find that Portland Posted had 7,887 followers. Layla checked her Instagram throughout the day, to see the followers go up, nearly ten every hour. Almost everyone in her year at Burroughs was now following the account. Not only that, but people were liking and commenting en masse. She scrolled through the Portland Posted DMs, which were full of congrats on "going Burroughs viral," which was a silly sort of feeling. On top of that, people were talking at school again. This was not surprising, but it was still hard for Layla to get used to.

Two kids in the hallway had stopped Caleb and asked if he thought maybe the blogger was the one who killed his mom. Layla heard Grace telling Lindsay she couldn't believe Caleb had never told her any of this while they were dating, when some rando had discovered all of it in mere weeks. In psych, one kid raised his hand and asked Ms. Glass if she knew about the "stalker" who was "trying to solve a case about the principal's dead wife," to which Ms. Glass quickly shh-ed the class and changed the subject. To say that Layla didn't know what she was doing at this point was the understatement of the century.

But what shocked her most happened later, when she stepped off the bus that afternoon and saw a text from Caleb.

Fumbling with her books, she stopped on the sidewalk to read it.

My dad knows about the blog. He wants to talk tonight. I think it's time to really meet the parents.

Yes. I agree.

Come over at 7?

I'll be there.

CHAPTER TWENTY-SIX

That night, Principal Strauss sat across from the two teens in a blue leather chair that was so big it almost made him look small. Caleb told his father about the blog, the café, and Layla's gift. He explained it all very simply, as Layla certainly would not have been able to. There was so much to tell, and it didn't help that when she was nervous, she began to ramble. Principal Strauss had a habit of making her ramble more than any other member of the Burroughs faculty. So, Layla mostly just sat there quietly, periodically tapping her fingers on her lap and interjecting a word or two.

When Caleb got to the part about Layla's blog uncovering the details of a hide-and-seek game, Principal Strauss stood up from his chair abruptly. Layla looked over at Caleb as if to ask what was happening, but Caleb looked just as confused as she was.

Principal Strauss began pacing very quickly back and forth through the living room as Caleb told him more about coloring with the crayons and hiding under the desk. When Caleb mentioned the bad guy who he was supposed to be hiding from, Principal Strauss swung his entire body around and grabbed his son's hands. Caleb then rose up out of his own chair to meet his father, whose face was frozen in complete amazement.

"You remember!" Principal Strauss exclaimed, eyes wide

and mouth agape. Layla had never seen her principal this wild-eyed before, and the scene startled her. Instinctively, Layla stood up next to them, but almost as quickly as she did this, she felt very strange for having done it.

"And you!" Principal Strauss pivoted to Layla now and grabbed *her* hands, which were, at this point, sweating profusely. "You got him to remember! Oh, thank you, thank you, thank—"

"Yes!" Caleb interrupted, grinning widely as if he just realized that his father was happy instead of a little bit off his rocker. "Yes, Layla's writing helped tell us more about what happened that day. It was…. well, it was extraordinary."

Principal Strauss grabbed the hair on his head and his entire face filled with a ridiculous grin. Layla smiled politely, still unsure how to respond to it all.

"We don't know anything more than that at the moment, but Layla and I are going to try this again tomorrow and see what else we can find out," Caleb continued.

Principal Strauss was absolutely glowing. He nodded with bright eyes at them. It was silent for a while, and Layla and Caleb, somewhat awkwardly, took a seat on the couch. Principal Strauss seemed to notice that the teens were ready to have their alone time for studying and other things, because he made himself scarce. Mostly scarce, anyway.

For much of the night, Principal Strauss just kept appearing with desserts. First there were two pints of ice cream, then a grocery-store package of cookies, and finally some cinnamon rolls that looked as if they had just come out of the oven.

Layla looked up over her chemistry book at Caleb and mouthed "What is happening?" To which Caleb shrugged animatedly like the shrug emoji incarnate, and they both laughed.

The next day was Tuesday, and aside from having a ton of chemistry homework to finish, Layla was free most of the evening. She and Caleb planned to meet up and try some truth-writing around 8 at the JBC.

"Can't get enough of me these days, huh, Layla?" Gavin joked, as Layla and Caleb entered. He was mopping up spilled milk behind the counter.

"You know it." Layla laughed, and followed Caleb into the back room.

"I hate that guy," Caleb whispered to her, as she took her seat in a chair by the desk.

"He can be a little obnoxious, I get it," Layla replied.

"I'm fine with him being obnoxious, actually," Caleb replied, moving the desk chair out of the way and kneeling underneath the desk to look around. "What I don't like is that he has a crush on you."

Layla laughed nervously, not wanting to get into the Gavin history at the moment. She opened her laptop and put it on the maple table.

"Do you think you're ready to get started?" Layla asked him, partly wanting to be helpful but mostly wanting to change the subject.

"Ready as I'll ever be," Caleb replied. He crawled underneath the desk and got himself situated for another round of truth-writing. He held the box of crayons on his lap. Then he stared ahead, as if ready to be transported to a different world. Layla looked on at him, proud of him for coming back again and wanting to know more, and knowing how hard it must be for him to do it again.

Layla took her seat at the maple table and set up her laptop. Quietly, to herself, she took a moment to set an intention for them. She had never really done this before, but since she felt now they were getting closer every day to figuring out what happened with Caleb's mom, she thought it couldn't hurt to try.

"What does he look like?" she whispered to herself as she opened up the new post tab.

When the tingling came to her, Layla wanted so desperately to watch the words appear on the screen. She reminded herself that Caleb deserved to read it first, but it was hard not to peek. So instead, she averted her eyes from the screen once more, settling them on the crayon box in Caleb's hands as she typed. With her eyes, she traced the flowers his mother had painted, one at a time—pink, blue, purple, and gold. She stared so hard at them that, when the tingling stopped and she looked back at the screen, her eyes brought their silhouette with them.

When her hands were finished, Layla snapped herself out of it and started heading to the front, as was now her system, to get a fresh cup of coffee. Before she could reach the door, though, Caleb slid in front of her and reached out for her hand. She smiled and put her hand in his, and he then took her in his arms and held her tight. For a few minutes he swayed back and forth with her there, neither of them in any rush to move on to what came next.

Layla finally went to grab her coffee. When she returned, Caleb smiled up at her.

"I was so bored hiding down there. Once I stole Mom's lipstick and drew it all over my face," Caleb began to read from the screen. He stood up and began to walk through the room. "This is good, Layla. It's pretty funny."

Caleb stopped reading to take a swig of his coffee. Layla could tell he was enjoying these memories. Of course, she also knew that part of writing about childhood memories was that they always came in glimpses. Children hardly remembered things as scenes, but more as images pieced together, one after another. As Caleb paced, Layla replayed her own childhood memories of the big white balloon, and the smell of macaroni and cheese.

"So when she came back," Caleb continued reading. "And called 'Olley olley oxen-free,' I popped out with a whole new face. She thought that was very clever. She would smile at me and scoop me up and tell me how good I'd done. 'He didn't see you,' she'd say, over and over again. 'That's a good boy. He can't ever see you.' And she would hug me real tight. But the silly thing is that grownups always think that if they can't see you, you can't see th—"

"Oh my god!" Caleb shouted suddenly. His hand immediately shot up to his mouth as he gasped, sending chills down Layla's spine.

"What is it?" Layla cried, slamming her muffin down and running to him.

"The mirror!" Caleb declared, bolting over to the yellow desk. He knelt down again, but instead of crawling underneath the desk this time, he opened up the bottom drawer of the desk. Layla heard him shuffle some papers around. Then, Caleb removed a small cylindrical object, mauve with a silver ring around the middle. This must have been the lipstick to which he was referring. A moment later, Caleb pulled something small and rectangular from the drawer and then shut the drawer behind him.

Caleb turned to face Layla and held out the object. Layla saw that it was shaped like a billfold. As she leaned in closer, she noticed that there was a familiar picture amidst the pale blue color. It was a print of Van Gogh's *Bedroom in Arles*, the famous painting of a bed next to a window with wooden chairs and a table nearby. Layla thought to herself that not many people have a Van Gogh wallet, so clearly Caleb's mom had been a real fan of art. Her eyes ran along the edge of the object, and she noticed that it had a gold latch on the side.

As if reading Layla's mind, Caleb slid his fingers down the side and opened the latch. Almost instantly, the inside of the wallet lit up with a bright light, dizzying Layla for a moment. She realized that the object was reflecting the light from the ceiling, and that it wasn't a billfold at all.

As the two teens leaned in closer, Layla realized they were looking at a compact mirror, the kind adult women kept in their purses. Layla had seen her mother use a compact mirror several hundred times before, but she always thought it a sort of useless item to carry around with you. If you were at home and you wanted to check your hair and makeup, you could just go to your restroom. If you were in a public place and you wanted to check your hair and makeup, you could just go to the public restroom. And if you happened to be out walking around and you wanted to check your hair and makeup in that moment, you could just turn on your phone and put the camera in selfie mode. She supposed adult women hadn't had smart phones as teens, and therefore this whole carrying a compact mirror was something of a lingering comfort from the past for them.

But because compact mirrors were now something of a vestigial structure for women (and men) in 2021, Layla really hadn't thought too much about them. What she did notice about this one very quickly was that, unlike her mother's single-mirror compact, when you opened this one up it had mirrors on both sides.

"Two mirrors?" Layla questioned, leaning even closer to the open compact in Caleb's hands now to further investigate. Suddenly, the zit on her chin that she had been desperately trying to hide from Caleb all evening was all that she could see.

"Oh jeez," she muttered, and jolted back, swinging her hand up to cover the spot, startled and embarrassed all at once. "Wait, why is everything so big in that one?"

"That's it!" Caleb declared, lifting the mirror up to his face and tilting it back and forth slightly. "The second one magnifies."

Layla's heart started to race at these words, knowing now what he had likely known for a long, long time but didn't really remember until just this moment.

Caleb peered down at the open compact mirror again, and Layla saw inside it that his face was suddenly frozen in horror. His eyes looked hardened and penetrating. Yet his gaze lingered on the mirror as if he were watching the story of that day long ago unfold right in front of him.

Then, without explanation, Caleb hurriedly crawled back under the desk. He leaned against the wall there and held the box of crayons on his lap. Then he cracked open the mirror, looking at himself in it. Carefully, as if every movement meant the world to him in that moment, Caleb tilted the mirror ever so slightly. He moved it further and further to his left, and then, suddenly, he flipped it upwards and held it completely still.

Caleb's eyes grew so wide they looked as if they had been magnified, even from where Layla stood.

"Oh my god, Caleb," she ejected, gasping.

Caleb looked up at her from behind the mirror now, eyes glowing. Layla and Caleb both opened their mouths, as if coming to the same conclusion at the same time. Layla rushed to his side on the floor and grabbed his free hand, squeezing it tightly.

"You could see him, couldn't you?" she asked.

"I could see him," Caleb replied, nodding wildly. He swallowed hard. In a whisper, he muttered, "I could see him very well."

Caleb looked exhausted after their session, and frankly, so was she. Instead of trying to truth-write more that night, they made plans to meet again the next day. Then they walked back to Layla's place, hand-in-hand, mirror in Caleb's pocket, and a gentle rain on their faces.

"Got me on my knees, Layla," Caleb sang playfully, as he took his post under the yellow desk in the JBC kitchen after school the following day.

Layla laughed audibly as she took her usual seat at the wood table and opened up a clean new post tab. Layla had saved the draft from the day before, knowing how important it was that she take her time with this one. They had gotten into a nice rhythm with this truth-writing adventure, and Layla really enjoyed this time they were able to spend together. Still, in the pit of her stomach she felt a fullness, knowing that they might not actually glean more information about Caleb's mom—or at least not more pertinent information. She had only been truth-writing so long, and she barely knew how to make it start, much less how to use it for a specific purpose.

This time around it went really quickly, which made the pit in her stomach a little fuller. When she was done typing, Layla went for a quick walk outside. The birds sang in the trees, and it was a beautiful Falmouth afternoon, all things considered.

When she returned, Caleb was sitting in the desk chair with his feet up on the yellow desk, studying the laptop in his hands. Unlike last time, Caleb read the screen in sort of a daze. It was obvious from his expression that there wasn't anything truly profound or earth-shattering on the page. The fullness grew in Layla's stomach even more. She imagined that Caleb had put even more stock in this process now that he had gone so far as to tell his father about everything. Layla felt a little disappointed but tried to keep a soft, sweet smile on her face so as not to show it.

"Any more information?" she asked him, timidly. She pulled her chair up next to him and showed him that smile she was still forcing.

Caleb sighed and ran his fingers through his hair. He cleared his throat and started to read.

"My mom let me try everything in the case: the cannoli, the muffins, the croissants, the rolls. Just a taste of each so I didn't get sick, she said. Except the roles—I loved the rolls because I could eat a whole one of those and they tasted like honey."

Caleb stopped reading and sighed deeply again.

"Well, you're not wrong, they do taste like honey," Layla quipped, attempting to break the tension.

"Valid," Caleb replied. He smiled, which made her smile genuine. "There's a lot of bakery info in here, Layla. And not a lot of anything else."

"Well, that makes sense," Layla said softly. She moved her eyes across the room and gestured with her hands. "I mean we are *in* a bakery."

Caleb nodded. He put the laptop on the desk and leaned forward so his arms fell onto his thighs. He looked closely at the screen as if searching for more.

"Well, the man is mentioned here," he said, pointing at the screen. "But it's not much, and I doubt it will help."

Layla leaned closer to him and looked at the spot he was pointing to.

Caleb read again.

"The women came and went, asking for samples of the new quiche. They wanted to take one home for their kids. They were dressed in bright red, turquoise, yellow green, and tickle me pink. The men came in wearing brown and mahogany."

"Is it just me or did you have a very good vocabulary as a child?" Layla interjected.

"The bad man came to the counter all in beige, and I hated beige," Caleb continued.

"Beige?" Layla asked. "These colors are so randomly specific."

Caleb turned his head to face hers, and his eyes looked wide and bright. His look was so intense that Layla could tell the gears were moving. She tried to follow the color breadcrumbs but was having a lot of difficulty.

After a while, Caleb reached down and took the box of crayons out from under the desk. He opened the box and dug around. Then he pulled out seven crayons and laid them across the desk. Layla watched him closely as he put them in order. When he was finished, he read them off, one after the next.

"Red, Turquoise, Yellow Green, Tickle Me Pink, Brown, Mahogany, and Beige," he declared.

"Oh my god," Layla mouthed, reading the names through to herself as he spoke. Caleb had been comparing the colors he saw in the mirror to those in his box of crayons.

"My rather colorful—pun absolutely intended—vocabulary came from these guys," Caleb explained. He ran his fingers across the row of crayons. "I don't think there's anything here except that I liked my crayons a lot. And that the bad guy was wearing all beige, for some reason. Doesn't tell us much except that he was a weirdo."

Layla thought hard about what he said. She began to pace back and forth in the room, studying everything they knew and trying desperately to piece something together. Suddenly, she was struck by an idea.

"Wait a minute!" she exclaimed, jolting to the desk chair to get a better view of the laptop. She moved the draft to the side of the screen and went to her Blogiophile inbox. She remembered that users had been leaving comments and messages for her. She thought maybe something in these words might be a clue to what all of this meant. Layla was suddenly in a research mindset, and reading every little comment with intensity.

Caleb walked behind her, checking what she was up to. He read over her shoulder as she scrolled.

After a while, the cursor landed on a comment from a user called @june-bug1980.

Layla read the message aloud.

I wish I could help more, but for what it's worth, I used to run Mick's Pharmacy (that's how I started following you, I heard you shared a post about us a while back). I remember Julia and her bakery opening very well.

Layla thought. Her fingers hovered over the keyboard. After a few moments, Layla took her phone out and searched @june-bug1980 on Instagram. She found the account, clicked New Message, and started typing.

Hi June Bug, I saw your comment on my recent blog post regarding running Mick's Pharmacy in the early 2000's. I appreciate your note.

June Bug entered the chat. She started typing, and Layla sat up in her seat. Caleb was reading the exchange from behind her.

Hello Portland Posted! Great to hear from you. I have been following your blog posts for months, and I'm eager to see what comes next.

I'm so happy to hear you're enjoying the posts. Listen, I was going to ask you, what can you tell me about being a business owner in the area at that time? Did you interact with Julia Strauss much? For my research. It would be very helpful.

I'm glad you asked.

June Bug was typing.

You probably know this, but prior to all of our little shops going in, there was a big department store on that block. With the parking lot, it took up the whole space, and all of Falmouth did their shopping there. I don't know the details, but the entire chain went out of business, and they tore the place down. But it was still a legacy, and hard to replace with a bunch of smaller shops so quickly. Sales were low at first for this reason. It felt like we were all new to town, fighting for attention from everyone who walked down the street. Lots of big signs in the windows. Coupons in the newspapers every week just to get people in the door.

But in a way, struggling together made all of us owners feel closer. We got into a routine together. Silly little things, like I'd pop over with some new cola delivery for everyone to try. Julia would bake cookies and deliver them in little tins. On sunny days, and especially weekends, Dalton at the record store would pop open his doors and play these punk records loud enough for us all to hear. It was kind of a crew. We waved to each other rolling out our trash cans on Monday evenings. We passed by one another on the way to the market for more of this or that. Wednesdays and Thursdays were especially slow in town, so we would linger in the doorways and chat about what was happening that week. Never deep conversations or anything, just in passing. We opened earlier on Fridays together, because that's when the city workers came to clean the streets and water the planters in front of each shop. Of course, Julia was always the first one there anyway, baking up a storm. Her husband and son would always stop in my store on Fridays too, I remember. They got the paper in the morning, and a coloring book for the little guy from time to time. Anyway, we were never that close, Julia and I. But those little moments felt so big at the time. And those months of trying to make it in this town together meant the world to me.

 I hope you find out the truth, Portland Posted. It would be nice to know what really happened to such a beautiful individual as Julia Strauss.

Layla stopped reading, sighed, and leaned back in her chair. Caleb slid his chair next to hers and took a seat. Layla, noticing this motion, thought Caleb might want a better look at the message. She handed the phone off to him, and Caleb read it again to himself, intently.

Layla thought about the kind message as she moseyed to the counter and ordered a cookie for herself. When she returned, she was surprised to see that Caleb had gotten out his laptop and set it up next to her own on the yellow desk. Next to that was the phone, leaning up against a Calculus textbook and still open to the Instagram message. Layla took in the array of technological devices as she approached.

"This kitchen is looking more and more like an office every time I walk into it," Layla joked, taking her seat again and biting into her cookie.

She noticed that, while her own laptop was still open to the Blogiophile dashboard, and the phone was still open to the Instagram message from @june-bug1980, Caleb's laptop was open to something she hadn't seen before: the City of Falmouth website. Layla continued eating her cookie, wondering what he was up to.

Caleb scrolled and clicked through the site, checking out the public works and recreation pages. On almost every page, he scrolled slowly through paragraphs of city information next to images of city workers and projects. These men and women could be seen smiling while digging and lifting, standing in front of city hall, planting trees in the park, and doing other odd jobs around town. Of these many people, almost all of them were wearing either collared shirts or coveralls. And all those collared shirts and coveralls were the same color. Beige.

At this point Layla felt herself lunge forward in her chair and lean over Caleb.

"Do you see what I see?" Caleb asked in a whisper, as if reading her mind.

"The beige outfits," Layla replied, pointing at each one on the screen now.

Caleb watched her finger move across the people on the screen. He reached his own hand up to cover hers and hold it still, stopping on the figure of a man holding lumber in the beige coveralls.

"This one," Caleb declared. "He was wearing this exactly."

CHAPTER TWENTY-SEVEN

Layla generally considered herself pretty well-rounded as far as life experiences went. She had lived for a few years in England with her parents, and she had traveled from there to Paris one summer. She had camped up north with her mother two summers ago, and there was the time they had gone to New York City to see *Wicked* on Broadway. She had been around, as they say. But she had to admit: she had never, ever been inside of a police station conference room with three uniformed officers on a Wednesday evening before. That is, until today.

"It said *City of Falmouth* on his uniform pocket. I remember it, clear as day!"

Caleb was leaning over the table, across from Cadet Francis, the officer who had heard this entire story five minutes ago at the front desk in the main lobby. Cadet Francis was quiet and unassuming. He was jotting down notes, trying to keep up with the story as Caleb let it out. Caleb was speaking in wild torrents, and Layla tried to squeeze his hand to calm him down.

About an hour before, back at the JBC, Caleb had remembered what the man at the café looked like, all of a sudden and in great detail. Layla had helped him jot down the details, and the two had raced to the police station to explain the situation. Now it was just a matter of getting the officers to care about a case that hadn't been solved twelve years ago.

"Well, unfortunately, we can't let you look through confidential files just because you remember someone's uniform, Mr. Strauss. You'll need to present the evidence and have an adult with you to officially file the report. There are more steps than just... remembering," an officer with long brown hair and an emotionless look on her face said from the place where she stood against the wall in the back of the room. Layla read the tag on her uniform. *Officer Craig.* She was serious and intense, and the way Cadet Francis and the other officer—whose name Layla couldn't quite make out at this angle—responded to her movements showed that she was obviously in a higher position than them. After a few minutes, Officer Craig addressed Layla. She made a joke about how, in her dark blue collared blouse, Layla "fit in well around here." Then she smiled at her. Officer Craig was quickly becoming Layla's favorite.

"My dad will be here in a minute." Caleb sighed. He and Layla took a seat in the chairs on the opposite side of the room, as Cadet Francis suggested.

Cadet Francis and the other officer left shortly thereafter, and returned about a minute later with Principal Strauss in tow.

"Oh, Caleb!" Principal Strauss exclaimed, running to hug his son.

Someone had clearly caught him up, though Layla couldn't quite pinpoint who, as they had now told their story to four separate people in the building.

"Hello, Layla," Principal Strauss said, greeting her with a handshake. He had wild eyes, and his smile to her now was one of joy and gratitude.

"Principal Strauss, hi," she declared, nodding knowingly at him.

Principal Strauss went on to open up one of several binders he had brought with him, showing the officer the details of the case. Together he, Caleb, and Officer Craig moved into a smaller conference room to the side. Layla was permitted entry, at Caleb's request, as she had been the one to get the physical description of the man on paper.

Layla obliged, and took a seat in the room while the three of them poured over the detailed files for a long time.

"My son, Caleb, here," Principal Strauss motioned to his son. "He was the only witness, and he was only five at the time. We didn't want him to... we were afraid he would... he was so young. He was unable to provide testimony because he had repressed the memory."

Caleb leaned into his father now.

"Until today," Caleb added, confidently.

Beaming with pride, Principal Strauss looked over at his son. He wrapped his arm around him, and Caleb leaned further into his father.

"Until today," Principal Strauss declared boisterously, kissing his son's hair as they separated again.

At this, Officer Craig rose from the desk, not taking her eyes off of Principal Strauss and Caleb. Slowly, solemnly, she walked through the door behind them. She returned to the room a few minutes later with a thick file in her hands.

Officer Craig stood and looked through the file on her own, in silence.

After a moment, Officer Craig closed the file and took her seat again. Her face was serious and focused. She asked Caleb to describe the man once more, with as much detail as possible.

"He was big, like, tall and stocky. Just big, you know, like his arm and leg muscles were really big, and he took up a lot of space. He had dark, longish hair visible under his city cap. But not to his shoulders or anything. He was white, but very tan, with reddish coloring in his cheeks and forehead. But not in a Santa Claus kind of way—not jolly at all. More like he was about to get upset every time I ever saw him. Oddly, though, he wore a smile all the time. I remember at first I thought he might be just happy all the time, but then I saw the way my mom acted when he was around. She would start to move faster, getting his coffee and food in record time. She was always looking past him, around the room, almost frantically. He would talk to her, watching her intensely as she worked. Mom would respond, as she always did, but with quick answers, and never looking directly at him. She always got caught up in something else, and tried not to engage him. I knew pretty quickly that this was not a good guy. I can't say enough that this guy was involved in what happened to my mother."

Officer Craig stood up again and left the conference room. When she returned a minute later, she brought Cadet Francis and the other guy with her. The officers looked at one another and nodded.

Principal Strauss held Caleb closer, unsure what exactly was happening.

Cadet Francis opened up a folder he had brought in with him and began to lay several photographs out on the long, thin table that stood against the far wall on the other end of the room. Then he returned to the group and asked Caleb and Principal Strauss to come with him to look them over.

"These are our city workers," Cadet Francis began. "All of them. From the time of one year prior to the incident up until one year after the incident. Our vetting process is quite strict, so it's hard to imagine any of these individuals being criminals, but we can't rule it out. Take a look at these images and see if anything is familiar. Once we find out who this person is, we will go from there."

Caleb and Principal Strauss approached the table slowly. From where Layla sat, she couldn't quite see the looks on their faces. Something about the slowness of it all made her think that they were each mentally preparing in their own way as they walked. It was as if they knew that they were going to find something, but were both unsure if they were ready to see it. After so many years, she couldn't imagine how hard this must be for them both.

Before she could fully consider the weight of everything for them, though, Caleb let out an unfamiliar, pained noise, and slammed his hand into the table. Next to him, Principal Strauss ejected, "This man!" in a yell that completely shook the room.

Principal Strauss lifted the paper and brought it closer to his face, as Officer Craig approached at a run. Both Strausses were now surrounded by the officers, so Layla could no longer see them clearly. But over the top of the group, she heard Principal Strauss say something else. Words she had never heard before, but that would echo in her mind for years to come.

"Alan Rigby."

CHAPTER TWENTY-EIGHT

Alan Rigby—as Layla would learn over the next forty-eight hours, between the conference room at the police station (from which she would finally be kicked out when the images of him would be blown up and hung from ceiling to floor throughout the space) and the edge of her bed (where she'd sit for hours getting updates from an audibly shaken Caleb)—was a man from Julia Strauss's past. But not an old friend.

According to Principal Strauss, in his own senior year at NYU he would officially meet Julia Reynard, a junior at the time. Strauss (then an awkward, comic-book-reading young man called Johnny) would pull her aside and compliment her writing at a poetry reading. The two would spend three hours after the reading on the bench outside in a blizzard, talking about Robert Frost and Bob Dylan. Seasonal depression and French film. Breakfast cereal preferences.

Of course, before that, there were lives apart.

Principal Strauss recalled seeing Julia around campus the three years prior, always hoping to meet her but never getting the chance to talk. She was, from his description, a force of a woman. She was passionate about so many causes. She was always hosting events on the NYU campus, from rallies and protests to fundraiser concerts to, of course, charity bake sales. Halfway through Julia's freshman year, she started hanging out with Alan

Rigby, another freshman, who was known for heading a group of hippie kids around campus. Strauss was a sophomore at the time and didn't know either of them, but they were the sort of couple who made themselves known.

"They were almost never apart," Caleb told Layla over the phone.

Apparently, Alan and Julia were kind of the quintessential hippie couple on campus, leading protests on the quad and hosting poetry readings together in the library. Stories swirled about the two sneaking into the tunnel between the classroom buildings and making a fire out of a final exam study guide. Tales circled of them breaking into the athletic center's pool late at night. It was also well known that Alan was selling acid out of his off-campus apartment. Strauss said that he saw the two of them at parties, but that they only ever talked to their close friends and each other. Over time, it seemed they only talked to each other.

As Strauss got to know his new paramour senior year, he learned that Julia and Alan had not had the picture-perfect love story that outsiders saw in the years prior. It was a very toxic, co-dependent relationship, as Alan quickly requested to be involved in every aspect of Julia's life. He was taking over as a louder voice at the protests, owning the room at the concerts, and stealing the mic at their poetry readings to drunkenly lead the crowd in some old Irish drinking song. He was everywhere she was, and she loved it at the time. But she realized later it was too much for her. She was technically still living in the dorms—Rubin Hall, at that time—but he would come up with a reason for her to sleep at his off-campus apartment in East Village almost every single night. Then, as she began experimenting with drugs, he was her dealer and she got a great discount. So she was using more than she probably should have been. After that, things got blurry. Those stories that had circulated around campus weren't the full truth. In reality, she had been in the middle of pulling an all-nighter to study for her English final when Alan danced away with the study guide and dragged her to the tunnels with his cronies. And the pool thing was not her idea; the truth was she hadn't even liked swimming at all. Alan was wild beyond anything she had imagined, and she knew she had to end it with him if she wanted to keep her life on the path she knew it should be on.

Caleb explained to Layla that he had had no idea about this Alan guy. After all, Alan had dated his mom twenty-five years ago. His mother never mentioned Alan, and why would she? According to Principal Strauss, however, the relationship with Alan wasn't exactly over when Julia ended it. When Julia tried to explain to Alan that the relationship wasn't working, Alan had told her he was going to kill himself. Principal Strauss started to get choked up telling the story to the room of officers and his son. Caleb hadn't seen this happen in many, many years.

Alan would call Julia from his off-campus apartment in East Village at all hours of the night, saying he needed her and if he didn't get her back, he would take pills or slit his wrist. He told her there was no one else who cared about him, and he didn't deserve to live if he lost the only one left. Julia was deeply troubled by this. She didn't know what to do, and she felt completely alone in the burden of caring for him. She found herself going over to his place in the middle of the night to plead with him not to do it, calling his therapist and explaining the situation, and even calling the police and sending them to his house. She would talk to friends and family about it to ask for their support, but mostly people couldn't help. It was too big for them to understand.

Eventually, Julia agreed to stay with Alan, because she felt she couldn't leave him.

Julia was unhappy, but felt safer knowing where he was and how he was doing at all times than she did being separated from him. So, against her better judgment, Julia moved in with him the following year. And again, they were hanging around campus, looking happy as ever together. Julia stayed on campus that Christmas— Principal Strauss remembered, because he saw her in the science lab while he was there finishing up a project. Strauss had wondered why she was still there. Years later, he would learn that Julia didn't go home to her family in Maine for

Christmas that year, and instead claimed that she was behind on studying for finals and that her entire study group would be on campus as well. It would behoove her to stick around and cram with them. It turned out that, actually, Julia didn't feel she could leave Alan alone.

Julia felt so bad missing her family's Christmas that she decided to visit her aunt in Newark for the weekend of New Year's celebrations. This way she got some family time before returning to school. While she was with her aunt, she got a call in the middle of the night from Alan, saying that he couldn't be without her. He said that he missed her so much that he was going to fight his neighbor if she didn't come back. Alan was already starting fights just for fun. But something in the way he said it made her feel like she needed to get the next train home. There was, Julia explained to Strauss later, a familiar feeling of a fire starting that only she could put out. She told Alan that she would be there soon.

Julia left a note for her aunt that she had a lovely visit, but had to catch up on laundry before her roommates got back and took over the washer and dryer.

When Julia arrived back in East Village, it was around 2 am. The front door of their house was open. She called through the house, but no one answered. Alan was nowhere to be found. A surge of dread pulsed through her as she imagined the worst. She ran to the backyard, hoping he would be there smoking a cigarette, but he wasn't. She went to the basement, hoping he would be there sleeping in front of the TV, but he wasn't. She ran up to the bedroom, thinking he might be asleep there, but he wasn't. Julia searched for something, anything in the room that might give her a clue as to where he was. Nothing.

She fell on the floor, crying. She described this moment years later to Strauss as an epiphany moment. Not because she saw her own potential to thrive without Alan. She didn't. As far as she could see, she was stuck with Alan forever. It also wasn't because she could clearly see a way out. There was nothing clear to her now at all.

As she told Strauss, what Julia saw that day in the room she shared with Alan, as she laid her body against the rough carpeting on the floor, was bottles. So many of them. Bottle after bottle of Jim Beam under the bed. They lay there, looking back at her, clear as day. She stared at them for a while and then removed them to get a better look. Each bottle was completely empty. And as she pulled them out from under the bed, she noticed that there were more just like them packed neatly behind the others. She pulled those out only to find even more behind them. She was frozen in time and space. Suddenly, the last year and a half of time spent with Alan played back in her head all over, but it looked completely different now.

Julia was back in the moment when Alan told her he loved her at the garden party last September, only this time she couldn't keep her eyes off the outline of the flask he had hidden in his coat pocket. She was back at her family's home upstate, when Alan came with her for Easter and met her parents, but she could only see herself pulling him aside to ask how many drinks he had had beforehand. She was back at the bonfire their friends threw last summer, only all she could see was Alan bringing out stacks of folded up beer cases, one after another, to add to the torch.

In the next ten minutes, Julia ran through the house she had lived in for four months or so now, digging through drawers, cabinets, and closets. She moved furniture and opened luggage bags.

"I remember her telling me that, in the end, she found about thirty empty bottles of booze in her home. All under her nose the whole time, but she had no idea," Principal Strauss told the room. When Caleb relayed this story to Layla, she could hear that he was holding back tears at this part, because his voice cracked here and there.

Strauss went on to tell the room that Julia did find Alan that night. He was a few streets behind the house, lying against the curb, knocked out and bleeding from his head. She called an ambulance and he was taken to the hospital, where he was later diagnosed with a hematoma and admitted for the weekend.

"Julia visited him often while he was in the hospital, and remained supportive of him, but also wasn't quite sure she recognized him anymore. She told me that she was terrified to leave him and upset with herself for not knowing he had a problem."

"I remember vividly something she said back then," Principal Strauss continued to tell the group, his voice growing more solemn by the second. "She said 'It's not fair that someone who said "I can't live without you" could mean "I'll kill myself if you leave me." Pouring out what remained in those bottles was all I could do at that point. This made me feel like at least I wasn't the only thing in the house manipulated and empty.'"

Eventually, Julia did finally break it off with Alan, of course. Strauss explained that, a month or so after the incident, she worked up the courage to tell Alan she needed to move out. She was met with her body being slammed against the dining room wall and a lip the size of Long Island. He caught himself before he hit her a second time, and let her go. And she ran to a friend's house faster than she had ever run before.

But Alan's torture didn't end there, Caleb continued to relay. He would go on to spend the next year or so calling her in the middle of the night. She never answered. Her friends were there for her more at this point, thank goodness. They told her not to respond to any of his attempts to reach out, because if she gave him an inch he'd take a mile. But it didn't change the fact that he still knew her class schedule, and her work schedule at the library. Not to mention where she lived.

"My dad said that avoiding contact with someone who knows all that is very difficult," Caleb continued. "I guess Mom was doing everything right to protect herself, but Alan still seemed to know details about her life that would chill her to the bone. Once, Alan beat up a guy at a party because he thought the guy might be pursuing Mom. Another time, Alan sent a Christmas card to her family's home saying that he missed them. It was really creepy stuff like that. At that time, though, no one seemed to believe he was anything but a hung-up old boyfriend.

Dad said he remembers she was terrified that Alan would come to her dorm, so she reached out to campus security and told them about the issue, hoping they'd offer some extra security measures for her. They never responded."

"We don't know much more than that about their relationship. As Dad described it, my mom was a force of a woman, and by the time she and Dad were together, Mom had almost completely rebuilt herself."

"But Dad did say that he likely only knew a fraction of the damage Alan had caused her. He did say that he suspected that Alan had something to do with Julia's decision to graduate early and move in with Dad in their little apartment in Portland. In Maine, Mom was visibly more relaxed. Early on in their engagement, she mentioned Alan once, saying that she'd heard from an old classmate that Alan had moved to Chicago. Dad said that Mom was elated to tell him the news, and it looked as if a massive weight had finally been taken off her shoulders."

Apparently, all of this new information about an old boyfriend made the officers want to look into things more. Layla could hear over the phone how excited Caleb was by this new development.

"You'll never guess what happened next, though, Layla," Caleb said. "The other officer in the room... The tall and skinny one... Why can't I remember his name? Anyway, he identified the guy in the photo right away as one of the city water meter readers. He said his name was David Cruze. This guy David Cruze worked as a water meter reader for about four years, starting in 2005. He left his post to move out to Montana with his wife, Jillian, in 2009."

"All of a sudden, in a frantic tizzy, Officer Craig stood up and waved a separate file in the air. She came up to the group and opened up this other file, which, as it turned out, had what's called a Protection from Abuse Order mom had filed against Alan Rigby in 1997."

"Oh my god!" Layla exclaimed loudly. "Your poor mom!"

"I know!" Caleb roared, impassioned. "Then we all

gathered around this file, and they showed me and Dad the photo of Alan Rigby that was attached to this protection order. And Layla…aside from the beard and some much longer, hippie-dude hair, Alan looked super similar to David Cruze. Officer Craig just stared for a long time and said 'Could it be?' over and over again."

"After that, Officer Craig grabbed all of the paperwork and the three binders my dad had brought in, and took her guys to some room in the back. Dad and I were a little confused, so we waited a bit to see what was going to happen. But Dad decided we needed to go home and get something to eat and some rest. So, we left. We're going back first thing in the morning."

Layla told him she agreed with this decision. She could hear the exhaustion in his voice. So much had happened over the past three days; it seemed impossible to digest it all. She told him she wanted to be there for him in whatever way he needed. She knew she couldn't be present for the meetings anymore, for confidentiality's sake, but she wanted to talk as often or as little as Caleb needed to. There was silence on the other line, and Caleb's breathing grew slower. She lingered on the line to hear it for a few minutes, thinking about the weight of it all.

She couldn't get one thought out of her head: the thought of young Julia, just a few years older than Layla was now, falling in love with someone. There was no way Julia could have known that this someone would cause such devastating pain. That he would haunt her for years to come. That he would ultimately end her life.

Layla couldn't help but feel lucky to be talking to a man who was good, who would never do those things to her. A moment after that, this feeling turned to survivor's guilt. Layla hadn't done anything differently than Julia. Women everywhere would experience young love like theirs. It just so happened that Julia's would be the young love that, instead of building her up, would drag her down again and again.

Layla felt sick, wishing that she could do something to give Julia those years of fear and running back. But she couldn't.

Layla kept listening to the sound of Caleb's heavy,

rhythmic breathing on the other end of the line, thanking her lucky stars for his good heart. Before she knew it, she was asleep too.

CHAPTER TWENTY-NINE

Layla's mother's long, beaded skirt rattled gently along the floor as they walked through the heavy metal doors into the conference room the next morning. Something about her eternally bright-eyed mother being in the room, adorned with a purple knit sweater, her yellow-rimmed glasses, and a leather backpack—in effortless hippy-mom fashion—made Layla feel way less nervous to be there. Truly, there was no better way to make an intimidating environment feel benign than to put your mother in it. Having a mother to bring with her into this room, especially, made her feel so lucky.

Caleb had convinced Officer Craig that Layla and her mother be permitted to attend the presentation of evidence, since Layla had played such a big role in what Caleb kept referring to as "talking through repressed memories." He said this because truth-writing wasn't his power to reveal to the world, and Layla appreciated him keeping her secret. He also said this because, even if he *had* said she magically extracted the truth from his mind and onto a page, the officers wouldn't exactly have believed it. Grownups were silly like that.

Caleb turned around from his seat at the front of the conference room to see her. His hair was disheveled, flopping loosely in his face and draping over the bags under his eyes. Seeing Layla enter gave him a distracted smile. Layla couldn't help but notice that this wasn't the usual smile that unfolded on Caleb's face when he saw her. Normally, his lips extended the full length of his face effortlessly, reminding her of the perfect dimples on either side of them. His cheeks would rise, and his eyes would round, soaking the room in a cool, clear blue.

Today Caleb smiled with just his mouth, as if on edge. His eyes remained empty and intense.

Layla was shocked to see that there were six officers at the front of the room: Officer Craig and her team of two cadets from yesterday, and three new officers from the fleet. One small-statured, bald officer with a tough look on his face sat to the right of the podium. Next to him was an awkward-looking fellow with glasses and a pleasant look on his face. On the far end was potentially the biggest man Layla had ever seen in her life, tall and handsome with a kind face.

When Officer Craig rose to take the podium, the rest of the team behind her hushed immediately. It was an interesting dynamic; nothing about Officer Craig was threatening, really, but she must have been something of the "boss" from the way the room responded to her. She was a badass lady.

"Today we are here to present the findings of my investigative team," Craig said. She then introduced every member of the team, who stood in turn and waved coolly to the group. "My team has worked overnight to compile evidence for case 58974239-BD, the death of Julia Serene Strauss on the date September 26, 2009 in Heron County, Maine."

Officer Craig then took a seat, and Officer Ron replaced her at the podium. Layla shifted in her seat, eager to hear what would be said next.

"We have located David Cruze in Stillwater County, Montana, where he now resides. After extensive investigation of fingerprints, health histories, and court records, it has been determined that Alan Rigby used the help of a friend in the judicial system to perform a name change for himself through Chicago's First Municipal District Court in the year 2001. Though records of this were limited, they were sufficient to make the change and eliminate Alan Rigby from any records thereafter. It has been confirmed that Alan Rigby and David Cruze are the same person," Officer Ron declared.

At this, Principal Strauss gasped and rose from his seat. Almost instantaneously, Caleb rose after him and grabbed him around the shoulder. Layla couldn't help but gasp too. Layla's mother looked at her and mouthed "Oh my god." She grabbed her daughter's hand, which had begun to shake.

"Therefore," Officer Ron continued. "We have the liberty to treat both sets of records—those of Alan Rigby and David Cruze, respectively—as records of the same person."

The officer with glasses rose and took the stand.

"My name is Detective Ryan McDermott. I am here to present the relevant information regarding Alan Rigby's records as they relate to case number 58974239-BD, the death of Julia Serene Strauss. It has been discovered that Julia Serene Strauss registered an Order of Protection, also called a restraining order, against Alan Rigby in the year 1997 in New York County. This restraining order was extended to her living situation at 35 5th Ave, New York, NY 10003. Protection against Alan Rigby was continued further in Maine through a Protection from Abuse Order registered at 365 Frank Street in Portland, ME in Cumberland County. This particular Protection from Abuse Order was finally extended to Cumberland County address 475 Carroll Street in Portland, ME."

Layla shook in her seat, recognizing that address. The charming light blue mansion in West End where Caleb would sit on the porch and give her their third kiss.

"She had a restraining order against him for all those years?! He couldn't come to our house?!" Caleb exclaimed, gesturing wildly.

Principal Strauss was shaking his head rapidly now, as if in a complete daze.

"No," he ejected, at a volume Layla hadn't known Principal Strauss could actually reach. "Alan couldn't come to our house. But Alan wasn't Alan anymore."

Before anyone could say anything else, the man with the glasses left the podium and was quickly replaced by the large, handsome officer at the end of the line of chairs. The man looked very serious, and solemn.

"Hello. I am Officer Ryan Connor. I am here to present the relevant information regarding David Cruze's records as they relate to case number 58974239-BD, the death of Julia Serene Strauss. David Cruze began working as a meter reader for the city in 2005. Cruze was in charge of the meter reading for the Eastern district of Falmouth, extending from Coolidge Rd to Casco Bay."

"No!" Principal Strauss exclaimed, falling to his knees in front of the podium. "He was right here all the time? He was after her for *years*?!"

Layla could see that Caleb's face was frozen in shock from hearing this news and watching his father nearly fallen on the floor in front of him. Everything was unfolding for everyone in the room at once.

"He was on her trail the entire time. He must have read about the JBC's opening online and found her again." Caleb spoke in a cold, empty voice now. "This man moved here to watch her, and got a job essentially checking in on her place of work?"

Caleb had approached the podium now. And his voice was no longer empty. It was full of rage.

"AND NO ONE DID ANYTHING?!" Caleb demanded in a scream that filled the entire room instantly. Layla's heart sank for him. She scanned each officer's face as each one turned from a serious straight face to a look of desperation and sadness. Each set of eyes grew wide with pain and hopelessness, and it felt as if they were apologizing.

Principal Strauss stood up now. He paced back and forth quietly as everyone watched. The entire room seemed to be waiting on him to speak.

"She didn't want to be in the papers, but I never knew why. Her team pushed her to get more and more press, and she was always so torn up about it. Eventually, she gave in. A few big pushes on the opening, press from the fall festival that year, the big restaurant week events… she did it for her team, and for her business… and for us. She did it for us. He must have come to visit her every month, and she put on a brave face. For us."

He stopped, and looked at his son now. He wrapped his arms around him desperately. When he pulled away, he held Caleb's face and locked eyes with him. He spoke quieter now, as if this message was only for his son. "I can't believe it, Caleb. The bakery has always done so well because of the choices she made. We didn't know that these were the kinds of choices she faced. She didn't want us to know."

Caleb's face was flooded with tears, and he gasped for breath. "She did everything right," Caleb whispered only to his father.

"She did everything right," his father repeated back to him solemnly. The room was frozen in time as the two Strauss men held one another tightly.

"She must have been so scared," Caleb whispered to his father.

"She must have been so scared!" his father repeated back to him in a yell.

"But this man killed her!" Caleb screamed suddenly, infuriated.

Principal Strauss instantly folded into his son's arms, sobbing wildly.

Officer Craig's team of men stood up from their row of chairs and solemnly lingered around the father and son.

"I'm so, so sorry," Officer Craig declared.

She cleared her throat now, and began to read from her files.

"We have reason to believe that David Cruze was at the scene when Julia Strauss died. We have taken David Cruze into custody."

Both Strausses looked shocked to hear this. They straightened up and listened attentively.

Officer Craig paused, visibly fighting back tears.

"David Cruze has been questioned extensively. We have reason to believe that he brought his own coffee mug to use at the establishment. Inside the mug he had a heavy object, potentially a rock, which he then used to apply a firm blow to Julia's forehead. The intensity of this blow knocked her unconscious. It is suspected that Cruze proceeded to lock the front door and prop open the swinging door between the dining room and the kitchen with the door stop. He then turned on the gas stove, using the apron hanging nearby to remove his prints. He took the weapon and the mug with him."

Everyone in the room was looking at Caleb and his father. No one moved, no one spoke. It felt almost like everyone was holding their breath at once; like everyone was holding off on continuing to live in a world where all of this was true.

But they had to breathe again.

Principal Strauss went first, letting out a huge breath as he folded into his son's arms again, sobbing wildly. Layla had never imagined Principal Strauss like this; his vulnerability was so potent and unrecognizable. For a moment, she thought about how he must have lived for the past twelve years, not knowing who had taken his wife from him. Caleb had told her once that his father created an environment of order and expectation. Almost obsessively, his father ensured that everything was as it should be at home and at school. This was hard for Caleb growing up, because he always suspected there were things outside of his father's control, but he never saw them. It was as if his father had bottled up all of the disorder, all of the unknowns of their world inside him, bubbling up. Now, in real time, Principal Strauss was letting all of the chaos out. Thankfully, Caleb was there, ready to catch it.

Officer Craig began again.

"It was at this point that David Cruze heard sirens coming and realized Julia had pressed a panic button before his attack. He then left through the back door and fled the scene."

Suddenly Caleb, still cradling his father in his arms, turned to look at Layla. His eyes filled his entire face, as if he was frozen by this particular aspect of the report. It looked like he was shaking. Layla reached out as if holding him from across the room, and mouthed "I'm here." Caleb remained frozen.

"He—He was there with me," Caleb ejected, his voice cracking and bending back into sound. "I remember now."

Principal Strauss stood up straight and stared at his son, mouth hanging open. Strauss's head moved from his son to the officers, then back to his son again. He appeared dumbfounded.

"But he didn't see me," Caleb whispered. "He didn't ever see me, because I was still hiding. I knew I had to keep on hiding."

Overjoyed at this, Principal Strauss opened his mouth wide.

"He must not have known anyone else was in there, then!" Principal Strauss took his seat again, grabbing his son's arms with pride. "I can't believe it!"

"No," said Caleb. "He didn't know I was there. I watched him walk out the door from where I sat. I remember it now." Caleb was poised and contemplative. He spoke from his heart, which finally seemed to open up completely in this moment. He didn't need a truth-writer to reveal his truth anymore; he was ready to do it all on his own.

"And I must have opened the door after him, because—"

"Because," Principal Strauss interrupted, "Because you're alive today!" Principal Strauss grabbed his son, squeezing tightly.

The Strauss men were both in tears and holding each other. Respectfully, the officers lingered in silence. After a few minutes, Officer Craig looked at Layla and her mother in the back. She nodded and tilted her head to the side, inviting them to join the group. Layla couldn't remember a time when she had run faster to meet someone than she did to meet Caleb and his father that day. The group wrapped around the Strauss men, feeling as much as they could of their loss. They held Caleb and his father, in a way, carrying them into the future with what they had gained.

CHAPTER THIRTY

Soon after the group huddle ended, it was time to head to Burroughs for classes. All the officers congratulated Caleb on his way out, shaking his hand and thanking him for his help with the case.

As the teens and their parents walked to their cars, Layla's mother pulled back and talked to Caleb alone. Layla couldn't hear what was being said to her boyfriend, but she knew it must be something he needed to hear. Her mother was good at that.

"Layla!" Principal Strauss called, jogging through the parking lot to catch up to her. As he got closer, Layla could tell that he'd been crying so hard his face had grown red and worn. Somehow, though, a smile had formed, and had pushed through the haze of tears and pain.

"Please know that we owe you an immeasurable gratitude," Principal Strauss said, returning to his usual formal mannerisms. "I don't know how you did it, Layla. But thank you."

Then Principal Strauss reached out to shake her hand. Layla was taken aback by this for a second. It felt like no time at all had passed since the first time Principal Strauss had shaken her hand, that September morning on her first day at Burroughs Academy. At the same time, so much had unfolded since then. So much friendship between her and Caleb. So much trust between her and her mother. So much shared joy between Caleb and his father. Really, she felt that the entire world had been held inside those two handshakes.

"No, I—" Layla started, stammering. "I just—"

She realized then that she didn't need to say anything at all.

To honor all that the past few months had meant to all of them, all she had to do was reach out and shake his hand. And she did.

Layla couldn't help but lean into her mother on the car ride over to Burroughs. They had both watched the emotional scene in the police station with such intensity that they felt the pains and joys of it deeply. It felt as if time hadn't existed between those four walls, so Layla was shocked to see it was only 8:00 am. She'd be just in time for first period. Both mother and daughter were exhausted, mentally and emotionally. At the same time, however, they felt empowered by the justice that had just been won before their very eyes.

"That was... a lot," Layla declared, somehow conveying all of it at once.

"Yes. Yes it was," her mother responded, rubbing her daughter's shoulder as she drove. "Wow..."

The Whittaker women pulled into the Burroughs parking lot, with the Strausses coming in right behind them. Layla watched as Caleb leapt out of the car, pulled his backpack over his shoulder, and then approached her car window with a huge grin on his face.

Something was so different and new about Caleb's expression. His hair hung over his thick eyebrows, as it so often did. His chiseled cheekbones tugged at his lips as they danced into a coy smile across a few days' scruff. He was more handsome than ever, somehow.

But the major change was the light in his eyes. Suddenly, his eyes appeared to swell with something altogether new behind them. The icy blue wasn't icy at all anymore. His eyes were full and warm, stunning to look at.

"Mom?" Layla said to her mother, not taking her eyes off of the boy waiting for her outside.

"Yes, darling," her mother replied.

"Do you think I should tell the police about my… special gift?"

Layla turned to look at her mother, and then instantly felt awkward because she could feel her own face turning red. Sheepishly, she stared up at her mom, and held her gaze in silence. Layla was shocked to find that her mother's eyes appeared fuller than before, just like Caleb's. It was as if something had grown within everyone today, enough to make them feel safe and whole again.

"Hope," Layla whispered to herself.

"Oh, my darling," Layla's mother exhaled sharply. She grabbed her daughter's face in her hands suddenly, and looked at her sternly now. "Please don't tell me you think truth-writing is what brought you all this way. It was you, Layla. You did this all on your own."

Layla's eyes welled up with tears as she opened the car door and stepped out to meet Caleb's outstretched arm.

"Will you let me walk you to class, Layla Whitaker?" Caleb asked, with a soft, sweet smile on his face.

"It would be my great pleasure," Layla replied.

For Amy B, and all the other women who didn't make it out.

ABOUT THE AUTHOR

Brigitta Burguess is a Detroit-based YAF writer, marketer, content creator, web developer, and storyteller. Her passion is, in the words of Sylvia Plath, to "live, love, and say it well in good sentences." More than anything, she loves writing Layla's journey, Ritter Sport chocolate bars, and making her little boys laugh.

Photo by Mark Clancy Linehan

Made in the USA
Columbia, SC
19 October 2023

24675633R00148